TEEN SEX TRAGEDY

Teen Sex Tragedy

Brett Yates

Marygreen Press

Published by Marygreen Press

Cover art by Quinn Wang

ISBN 978-1-949948-00-4

Chapter One

During preadolescence I began to suffer from a recurring daydream—or diurnal nightmare—in which, upon my return home from some social activity or excursion, my parents would fail to recognize me, reacting as though a stranger had wandered into their house. In the imagined scene, my mother and father wouldn't meet me with hostility, but they would look up from a sink full of sudsy dishes or a half-eaten plate of leftovers—always some mundane task—with puzzlement and slowly building alarm to find an unknown boy suddenly inside their home. In my own panic-tightened chest, I would register instantly what was going on, sometimes comprehending instinctually even before coming inside—from the interior glow that radiated through the windows into the dimmer evening light, that peculiarly intense, exclusionary coziness that emits from strangers' houses when you're feeling lost and lonely—that the home to which I thought I belonged was in fact not my own.

Yet I would pretend otherwise at first, willing myself back into the household routine through aggressively homey, casual behavior, tossing my coat haphazardly onto the nearest chair, slumping onto the couch in an exaggeration of my usual careless comfort, as though ready to turn on my favorite TV show. But my surroundings, though unchanged in appearance, now bore only the uncanny familiarity of déjà vu, as if my sole prior acquaintance with the room had come during a dream.

My mom and dad would continue to stare at me from the kitchen in a confused silence, increasingly difficult to ignore. Eventually my dad would awkwardly step in as manly protector—defending his family, which did not include me.

"Excuse me," he'd say, in a tone of both firmness and concern. "Who are you?"

Hesitantly I would stand up and face him, yet I would have no answer. I couldn't tell him that I was his son, that I lived here, that I'd always lived here. I couldn't even tell him my name, because I was no longer sure of that, either. The look on his face, emptied of recognition, told me all: I did not really exist. Whatever I was, I had entered the opposite of the "parallel universe" of science-fiction cinema—where we're typically meant to assume that the protagonist's standard universe is the sovereign reality, and that any deviant timeline or substitute world into which he may stumble belongs to some shadowy, illegitimate corner of the cosmos. This was not the cautionary vision of *It's a Wonderful Life*, designed to reassure me that the well-being of my family and town hinged upon my presence. With rapid, heartsick intuition, I would understand that this new version of things, the version without me, was the correct and superior iteration of my family's existence: the replacement children would remain off-stage, but I would sense their habitation as I illicitly inhaled the happiness-scented domestic air that belonged to them, and I would know that they were better than I was—that they were the children with whom life at 24 Caswell Road, that two-story house at the end of the cul-de-sac, truly made sense.

My school guidance counselor once told me that I suffered from low self-esteem, which was true. But my low self-esteem was not a neurotic problem brought on by bullying or parental neglect; it was, I believed, really nothing more than a clear-sighted, fair-minded evaluation of my character by the person who knew it best. I didn't feel that it ought to be corrected. I esteemed myself fairly: I was not handsome, creative, or generous, nor was I especially ugly, stupid, or cruel. I was a "regular Joe" without any of the bonhomie or earthy masculinity that the phase connoted—an "average kid" who, if presented as the protagonist of a realistic young-adult novel, would nevertheless somehow fail to be relatable.

In every school, there are a few children unlucky enough to be born to servicemen, missionaries, professional athletes, or some other type of parent whose career requires that they move frequently. These kids show up midway through the school year, when everyone else has already made friends, and—either for self-protection or because their rootless circumstances have stunted their social skills—they tend to draw little attention to themselves, and it hardly seems worthwhile for their peers to learn their names. By the following school year, they've disappeared to some other town, like reassigned spies, and nobody notices that they're gone. I spent my entire academic career within the same school system, but my role there even as a senior was roughly equivalent to that of these benign gypsy children.

And—odd to say—at home it was sort of the same way: my parents always loved me, of course, but they did so to so little purpose and with such little justification that their love seemed unreal. I felt even as a kid that children didn't receive care and adoration for nothing; they reimbursed their parents with beauty, lightheartedness, innocence, spontaneity, a belief in magic—they were intended to imbue the lives of their mothers and fathers with a renewed sense of meaning, purpose, and wonder. I felt confident that I never possessed these qualities or abilities, and that my parents' love for me consequently came from a place not of joy but of habit and obligation, as surely much of the love in the world does. I wasn't the sort of child who inspired jaded adults to see the world with fresh eyes and a feeling of infinite possibility; experientially, I was more like a meal at a casual-dining chain restaurant or a visit to the dry cleaner's —the sort of thing that subtly makes the world seem smaller and flatter.

Yet while you're eating your mozzarella sticks at T.G.I. Friday's or, later, dropping off your marinara-stained dress shirt, you may perceive at some unfathomable distance a side of the universe where the food tastes better, the whites are crisper, the stars shine brighter, and people's hearts are fuller. This was the place where my family existed without me.

In the conclusion of my nightmare—which, though I regularly experienced it while a conscious and active participant in daytime affairs, had the enveloping vividness of a REM-sleep dream—I would turn and slink out of the house the way I'd come in, without protest, never to return.

At age twelve, I naturally couldn't imagine a life that didn't take place inside my family's home, under the steady and competent administration of my mother and father, so it was clear to me that, after my expulsion, I'd simply dissolve fart-like into the ether.

During that period, every time I visited a friend's house after school, the terror would set in a half hour before dinnertime: would my parents still know me when I bicycled home? A nauseous poison would seep from my tiny overheated brain into my guts: I once vomited a neon puddle of liquefied Fruit Roll-Ups onto Travis Burkhart's trampoline for no reason except my irrational fear of being cast out from the analgesic comfort of my watery and insufficient familial womb later that evening. Even after my parents had greeted me normally and we were all sitting together at the kitchen table, I often felt too sick to eat.

I should note that this sickness never overcame me in the classroom: I never doubted that my mom would recognize me as I disembarked from the school bus. Nor did I suffer any anxiety at soccer practice or during the parentally scheduled, tightly monitored play-dates of my elementary school years. It came with the initial approach of maturity, when the broader world began, in its mild, necessary way, to stake its claim to me —it came with the loosening of the filial tether, the shapeless pubescent group hangouts and their obligation to misbehavior, which, in my suburban community, amounted to very little: a shoplifted Snickers bar; the sharing of pornography; the occasional carving of the word FUCK into a park bench. All in the normal course of things—yet my fear of parental rejection increased in proportion to what I perceived to be the severity of my peer-pressured transgressions. The problem was solved only when my peers stopped inviting me out—I'd become too nervous and weird for them.

I didn't know why I was, as boys said, such a pussy. But I felt it deep inside me, not as an identity imposed from without: I contained the heart of a worm; blood the greyish color of sterile, elderly semen; a soul the consistency of diarrhea.

At the age of seventeen, I was working to fix all of this, somehow.

In August, however, on the night of Victor Bogdan's end-of-summer party, I felt like I was in middle school again.

I'd woken up with the intention of having breakfast at McDonald's—strictly for something to do, a manufactured excursion to start the day—but a preliminary visit to the McDonald's corporate website, spent examining the nutritional information for items both breakfast and (ultimately) not, waylaid me for more than three hours, and by the time I was able to pull myself away from the computer screen and drive to the newly renovated fast-food fortress on Route 18, I had already thought too much about the contents of my planned order—a meatless Egg McMuffin, a hash brown, an orange juice—to want to consume them. I felt ill as I approached the front of the line, and when the gainfully employed brown-skinned teenager behind the counter, seeking in his polite uniformed attitude of service to make possible distant collegiate dreams that would soon be given to me for free and without labor, finally asked me how he might help me, I processed the question as a more general inquiry than had been intended. I had no answer. Overwhelmed by the uncontrollable and chaotic nature of "real life" even within a strictly regulated corporate environment, I apologized to the cashier and went back to my car, drove home, dozed off to the gentle hum of my laptop, and slept until just after sunset. That was my day.

The evening didn't go all that well for me, either. It was my own fault. I'd been getting weirder lately, the weirdness growing unbidden inside me like an infection: an internal gravitation not so much toward strange habits as toward strange states of mind. And while I sensed that the correct course of action might be to cultivate this weirdness into a stylized eccentricity by channeling it into an assortment of off-center but nonetheless recognizable hobbies and interests, like obsessively researching celebrity suicides or writing erotic internet fan fiction based on Japanese children's television shows—and that, given its due, this weirdness could even become a controllable and useful asset within an "interesting" personality, not an assault upon it—I nevertheless felt unable to alter my solidly boring daily self, its practices and projections. The countercurrent contained no guiding principle; I was still stuck being me, yet now with this strangeness that beset me as a bewilderment of random directionless surges, not as an investigable mania for anything in particular—and so I had no recourse but repression. I acted normal as best I could. It was like holding in a cough: doable when the cough announced its imminence ahead of time, but occasionally it just burst out without warning.

I'm not blaming alcohol, but it's a fact that I usually didn't drink at parties. Normally I just walked around sipping from a Solo cup full of watered-down cranberry juice. Yet I "partied" frequently, attending as many backyard bashes and keggers as was possible given that no one ever asked me to come. I learned of forthcoming social events from whispers in the grass and changes in the atmospheric pressure, and I turned up of my own accord. Nobody deliberately made me feel unwelcome at these parties—I was, by then, no outcast, having attained a degree of social standing where, at any gathering, I *might* plausibly have been invited. Still, I could tell that no one ever especially wanted me there. On a fundamental level, I failed to grasp "parties," much as I tried: a bunch of people in the same space ... for what? To do what? Conceptually, they seemed flawed, as though the inventor of partying had never gotten around to figuring out what the fourth step of the constitutive process— after "people," "music," and "alcohol"—should be.

Thus I was amazed by kids who functioned skillfully within large gatherings. It obviously required an astounding quantity of social deftness and in-the-moment imagination: an ability to navigate creatively and confidently an indefinable set of parameters. High school parties weren't for conversation; they weren't for dancing; our concerned parents thought they were for sex, but much of the time no actual sex seemed to happen, at least at the ones I went to. Very few people appeared to know what they were supposed to do there, apart from drink—which was pre- sented as a means to an end, but what was the end? I just stood with my back to the wall, hoping—as most everyone else did—that "something" would happen, possessing none of the ingenuity or vision necessary to conjure a sense of excitement or communion out of thin air and cheap beer.

I went to parties uncertain what my endgame was, certain only that I would never achieve it. In my stupid boy's heart, I wanted the same thing as all the other lame people—all those who could never fully enmesh themselves in the evening's intended wild energy, those who didn't really enjoy it and were only faking it like I was: I wanted to meet someone of the opposite sex; forge a powerful and instantaneous connection that would suddenly render the rest of the party irrelevant, a screaming horde whom the two of us could no longer hear; and, after leaving the repulsive orgy behind, talk quietly beneath the stars with my newfound soulmate until the first blush of daylight struck us at the very moment during which we shared our first tender kiss. Yet I knew that this was the wrong thing to want—I knew that those who attended parties even though their greatest wish was to *escape* them were doomed to be miserable at every party they would ever attend, barring the miraculous appearance of the abovementioned soulmate, and even that could happen only once in a lifetime, whereas those who partied for the gratification of partying itself, rather than as a means to find someone who would allow them to leave all the confusing social madness behind, had fun at every party they went to. If they sought sex, they sought it not as a reprieve from the general revelry but as its culmination; their sex took place within the continuity of the event, which was what made it possible—it drew from the vitality of the night at large instead of fighting against it. It didn't ask for a miracle.

I drove to Victor's house with my friend Matt Spruell, who was not only better at parties than I was but also enjoyed them more: never at any social event—in the midst of the terrifying thing itself—had it occurred to me that my own pursuit of pleasure might be as relevant as my anxious doubt as to whether others took pleasure in me. Matt had mentioned Victor's party in passing a few days earlier, during one of our preseason soccer workouts, and I pretended that I already had plans to go and offered him a ride, hoping that his companionship would legitimize my own entrance.

Matt, who didn't have a car of his own, was from the "poor" section of town—still upper-middle-class by the national standard, probably—and shared a bedroom with his younger brother. I had noticed that kids whose parents earned less than $80,000 a year possessed a special ability to extract some kind of comparative enjoyment from literally any outing. As a consequence, Matt was a good, low-pressure person to hang out with—when we were together, he never appeared to be yearning too strongly to be hanging out with someone cooler, though he had cooler friends. With strong effort over the years, I had managed, by my mid-teens, to reduce the minor-key unpleasantness of my company to something like an odd smell, untraceable to any particular source: a mild rottenness that took most people a few minutes to pick up on and yet still, after a while, often became unbearable. Girls always sniffed it first; the duller male species occasionally failed to detect it at all.

When we pulled onto Clearwater Drive, I asked Matt which house was Victor's.

"It's down toward the end, the white one on the left," he said.

I drove a little farther and then parked on the street when the house came more clearly into view. We got out and walked. It was half-past ten. I was wearing dark, straight-leg jeans, a beige polo shirt, and inconspicuous designer sneakers. I looked like a normal person.

"There are a lot of people here already," I said. I was silently counting the cars.

The patchy ribbon of parallel-parked Acuras and Infinitis that lined both sides of the two-way street pointed unilaterally in the direction of Victor's. The remaining blacktop narrowed and widened like a partially occluded artery according to the carelessness of the vehicles' happily entitled teenage operators, some of whom had parked as many as five feet from the curb: it didn't matter. Matt and I walked in the middle of the street instead of using the sidewalk.

The houses we passed were enormous, silent, black-windowed boxes, varyingly adorned with gables, brick glazes, and false balconies, yet shabbily identical in a pathetic obvious way underneath their decorative façades, like any row of lower-tier McMansions, as insufficiently differentiated as public housing units, and I felt a small shudder of giddiness as we approached the lit-up cardboard castle where Victor lived. I didn't actually want a party; all I really wanted was an open door, the private material of human life unhidden—the family photos, dirty dishes, and medicine cabinets, open for public viewing.

"You know, I can drive us home later if you want to drink a lot tonight," Matt said.

"You're not going to drink?" I said.

"No, I'm just exceptionally good at driving drunk. Safer than when I'm sober. It's a gift."

I had played soccer with Matt since the age of eight, and he was probably the only guy now on the varsity team who had a "sense of humor" of any kind. By now I knew all of my teammates well enough to regard them as discrete individuals with specific and varied character traits, but I could also see how their broader contours hewed to the thickheaded jock stereotype, albeit within some vaguely neutered, upscale style: this was soccer, not football.

In fact, our forward-thinking public school district had discontinued its football program two years earlier, citing safety hazards endemic to the sport, but since no obvious inciting incident—no tackle-induced coma or paralysis to stir up the panicky moms—had occurred on our local gridiron, the cancellation registered more as a municipal rejection of "football culture" than as a strictly medical concern: part of an attempt to remake the town within some lame suburban interpretation of the progressive ideology, with tougher, more confusing recycling laws and unusable bike lanes alongside our high-speed thoroughfares. The football team had held publicly visible, player-led yet dubiously inclusive team prayers before every game, and the various offensive linemen and running backs seemed to feel some historical obligation to attempt, feebly, to uphold a traditional standard of bullying and homophobia on campus—posing no real threat, however, without the backing of the institutional power structure that presumably enabled the lettermen at Midwestern high schools to sustain their reigns of terror and abuse. The football players here were terrible at their sport and scholastically mediocre in a place where academics mattered; computer nerds and band geeks openly mocked them. Getting rid of the team, in our town, was like getting rid of a pothole. Administrators encouraged students who had already accustomed themselves to wearing helmets to take up lacrosse instead, and a year later, coincidentally or not, Weybridge High elected its first openly gay class president: Adrian Benson, then a junior like me, the pride of our school.

Yet the happy decision to forgo football had some strange, minor effect on the school's soccer program. Although every Weybridge dad spent Sundays captive to televised NFL games, soccer had always been the favorite sport of our town from a participatory perspective; our identically well-meaning mothers viewed it as safe, teamwork-oriented, confidence-building, and (as a consequence of its international popularity) "diversity-friendly" even as virtually everyone who played it locally was white. And like volleyball, its springtime counterpart, it was a game whose presence within urban school districts was negligible enough to allow a gutless, affluent town like Weybridge to flourish in athletic competition. Team tryouts were exponentially more cutthroat than they were for football, and we'd won five NJSIAA group championships over the past two decades. Still, as long as football had existed, we soccer players had not been "the jocks"—we were only hale, well-rounded, attractive American teens: everything our mothers, teachers, and friends wanted us to be.

But with football gone, we became unmistakably the premier fall athletes and the recipients of whatever jock-resentment nevertheless simmered within a town where every child's specific talents were valued and nurtured and nobody had any real reason to be resentful of anything. We became "the popular kids," not in the sense of being actually popular (although some of my teammates were) but within the terms of those broadly sketched, underdog-oriented high school movies featuring tyrannically bitchy cheerleaders, conscienceless prom kings, and righteous misfits—we became symbols of "popularity" as the opposite of individuality or integrity.

For me, being hated for my popularity was ironic, since no one had actually liked me in the first place, but the shift in our collective public image compelled me to reevaluate my own perspective on my teammates: they kind of *were* "dumb jocks"—not significantly dumber than I was, maybe, but somehow more purely physical, mentally uncluttered in a dull, healthy way, responsive only to life's clearer and less complicated currents. They were reasonably well-behaved and fairly studious and had unanimously voted for a gay boy for class president—and still sometimes I wondered whether they might actually be worse than their unreconstructed, shoulder-padded counterparts from the 20th century, in the way that the low-calorie version of a fatty junk food was always somehow more pernicious than the original. Yet without them I did not exist—they allowed me to be a "normal kid with plenty of friends" and granted me whatever small degree of identifiability I possessed at our high school.

Matt and I were on the doorstep now. I was thinking about my clothes.

Should I have worn a T-shirt instead of a polo shirt? Matt was wearing a T-shirt—simpler, cleaner, less reminiscent of a French tennis player or a Best Buy employee. I looked back at my car down the street, perfectly parked, the wheels an inch from the curb. It and the polo shirt— which I'd ironed—both seemed part of a particular rigidity, antithetical to summer fun: it was the end of vacation, and I hadn't done it right—I'd gone to the parties, but I had never located the season's deeper rhythm of lazy pleasure. I could sense that for some of my peers—kids like me, with endless time and a forever-full tank of gas, but also not like me— summer was an unbroken current of hangouts and shore trips, luxurious boredom, pot smoke and beer pong, concerts and hookups, toes in the grass, and peer-assisted orgasms that flowed so naturally as to be virtually unnoticeable within the general bliss of life without responsibility, risk, or thought, as one house party seamlessly transitioned into the next. I could participate in the activities—some of them—but could not penetrate the current, could not live my life lyrically. Even in the summer, the rhythm of my life was the rhythm of a toothache.

I was on the verge of asking Matt, as if whimsically, whether he wanted to switch shirts with me. We were about the same size, and I had a strong preference for other people's clothing over mine. I borrowed from my brother's and even my dad's wardrobes regularly and had secretly adopted each stray shirt and sock accidentally left behind at my house during childhood sleepovers, those few I'd had. Every garment I'd ever bought at a store bore that off-putting visible trace of its own procurement, the deliberateness of the process. Only by stealing the clothes of others— with which I imagined a higher authority, knowing in every case what was right, had supplied them at birth, as it bestowed stripes upon a zebra —could I liberate myself from the particular try-hard aura that clung to every media-influenced, insecurity-driven purchase that I made at our local mall: the leather jacket, the Che Guevara T-shirt, the boat shoes, the panama hat. What the fuck had I been thinking?

But there wasn't any time—Matt was ready to go. He came in through the front door without knocking, and I followed. I always tried to arrive at parties when they'd reached a pitch sufficient to obliterate exclusivity: the noise welcomed us in—it was no longer the private home of an individual but the stage for a large public event. I was nobody's guest, but I was an unobjectionable and familiar-looking variant of the public. Ideally, I wouldn't even have to say hello to the host—although, in this case, we ran into Victor almost as soon as we entered the house. His handsome features were relaxed and sort of ambiguously smiley: drunk.

"Hey, Victor," Matt said.

Victor looked at Matt, then at me, and squinted slightly, trying to figure out who I was.

"What's up, guys?" Victor said.

"Pretty good," Matt said. "How's it going?"

"Nothing much," Victor said.

That was all. I had failed to register as a distinct entity but had passed some lower-level test all the same. Victor headed off to some more important task, and in the kitchen Matt poured himself a cup of vodka and orange juice from the room-temperature bottles on the countertop. I poured a quarter of a cup of plain orange juice for myself when he'd turned away. It was the ubiquitous red Solo cup, which held a sort of totemic thrall over me and apparently everyone else: I knew they sold other plastic cups in other colors at the supermarket, but the red ones made us all feel like we were teenagers having a party in a movie, which was half the point of having a party, or maybe the whole point.

Usually, the imitation didn't work all that well, for all the obvious reasons, but as I made my way through the sliding glass door to the deck overlooking the pool, this particular party struck me as an uncommonly accurate facsimile of its cinematic antecedents. The deck stood roughly five feet above the rest of the yard, and for a brief, out-of-character moment, I processed the oddly dazzling panorama before me as an aesthetic experience: the pool's subaqueous lighting system lent the liquid an Instagram-filter indigo, creating from the rectangle of still water an extraterrestrial vortex whose magnetic neon glow was framed, just beyond the backyard fence, by trees dark as spider legs—and within this tableau frolicked the Platonic ideal of youth, vibrant, swift, unpimpled, moving between bright spaces and dark ones. Like a party in a movie, it felt paradoxically sweeping and curated: the enormous guest list was a triumph of self-policing, hewing naturally to the prototype of Victor himself, whose skin was not only acne-free but somehow the very opposite of acne; whose car, parked always near the front of the school lot, retained a perpetual airbrushed quality like the female bodies in lingerie catalogues. There were a lot of good-looking, charismatic rich kids at my school, but Victor exerted a particular hold on the student body's collective imagination in large part because of parties like the one I was now attending. His parents were always going out of town, apparently, and his house had become the closest local approximation of the *Less Than Zero* teenage fast lane, with Victor, in his somewhat sanitized fashion, embodying a necessary element of casually glamorous irresponsibility within our unglamorously responsible universe—good grades and strong extracurriculars with a dash of cocaine, a right-side-of-the-tracks bad boy.

Some people had gotten into the pool, some in swimsuits, a few guys in their boxer shorts, one girl topless, which I pretended wasn't a big deal to me. All of our school's "elite" personages—by some traditional metric—were here; it seemed extremely comprehensive. Settling into a solitary corner, I tried to feel grateful to be at this party. I was aware that there were a hundred kids at my school for whom the idea of sharing social space—even as unnoticed bystanders—with the homecoming queens and preppie drug addicts of our town belonged to the realm of dreams. I could sense them all across Weybridge, alone in their bedrooms, consuming corporate media products with an inappropriate level of emotional investment, or masturbating furiously, or dreaming of a Columbine-style school massacre in which the soccer players would be the first to get brutally and justly executed now that the football team was gone. And I knew that I was the only one at Victor's house thinking of them, these sad losers—that in some sense I was their representative, whether they liked me or not. And I wanted to do right by them, even if it would only make them dislike me more: if I succeeded here—if I had fun, or made friends, or convinced some girl to touch my dick, or whatever the criterion for success was—it would in some sense be their triumph, too.

But after a few minutes of staring tactfully at the half-submerged breasts of the shirtless girl and doing nothing about it (what could be done?), I began to feel annoyed that the masturbators and aspiring school shooters were not sending any reciprocal prayers in my direction—as I stood upon the battlefield in their stead—and it occurred to me that maybe one was better off with no popularity at all and no hope of achieving it than to labor at the fringes of it, where it was so close and yet, on account of some nebulous defect of character or physiognomy, unreachable. This was the worst of all—I might have fared so much better in some other milieu entirely.

What I wouldn't have given, in truth, to start high school over as a "nonconformist," with skateboarding instead of soccer, art instead of academics, aloof sarcasm instead of social anxiety, and a tightly knit group of three or four like-minded friends united by mutual rebellion and shared humor instead of a squad of eighteen blockheads united by a truncated icosahedron of stitched polyester. I had classmates like this, who played in bands and wrote poetry and found some way to feel bohemian even though they lived in the same subdivisions and shopped at the same malls as the rest of us. They were aware of Victor Bogdan and his parties only abstractly, as embodiments of a mainstream culture at which they smirked with confident irony—and when they finally went off to Oberlin or Bard, they would talk about how *unpopular* they were in high school, not as a genuine regret but as a show of virtue, and would sleep with various nose-ringed, pink-haired girls whose liberated sexual practices were more advanced, more generous, and more exciting than those of any of the jocks' girlfriends. And of course I had no girlfriend at all.

....

The night began to pass somehow. I meandered for a while and then went back to my corner; I did laps. Reentering the kitchen, mired in my own thoughts, I came very close to bumping into a conspicuously pretty green-eyed girl whom I didn't recognize, but at the last moment we managed to avoid each other by an inch or two: her wavy and copious black hair—casually flung beyond the margins of her own body like a long scarf or a cape, resting comfortably on the dividing line between sloppiness and glamor as certain undulations curled into small knots and translucent frizz—touched my shoulder as I passed, too lightly for her to notice. Almost instantly I realized that this utterly insignificant moment of near-contact would, by the end of the night, in the feverish imagination of my lonesomeness, strike me as the evening's great misfortune—if only I had been just a little clumsier, I might not have accidentally averted the meet-cute from which was meant to unfurl my high-school rom-com, my anachronistically tender tale of first love, my teen sex comedy, my modernized *Romeo and Juliet* tragedy, my young-adult paranormal romance novel, anything to replace the unnatural nothingness in which I stood stranded night after night: moping later, I would imagine my life as a long series of moments in which the source of a potential plotline was ignored, the inciting incident missed due to shyness or inattention or staying home to jerk off—a movie somehow stuck on its mundane opening scene. With relative happiness I would have accepted any kind of interaction between myself and the unknown female human in Victor Bogdan's kitchen, good or bad: a minor collision of non-erogenous body parts followed by an apology by me and an indifferent nod of acknowledgement by her—it didn't matter, all my interactions went equally nowhere—but the absence of any interaction whatsoever would torment me, and of course I consented to be tormented, not turning around to catch up with her (to say what?) but instead pausing to ruminate and allowing the girl's face, eyes, and hair to continue to accumulate imaginary detail—physical features not observed in our half-second encounter but invented by me—to the point where, if I saw her again that night, I likely wouldn't recognize her.

I did have some conversations with girls. I talked to Jillian Heller, from last year's Spanish class, about the upcoming school year, and we were both "sad that summer's over" but "actually kind of looking forward to school starting again" as well, since senior year was "gonna be awesome"—that sort of thing. I talked to Gail Aselton, a player from the girls' soccer team, about the prospects of our respective squads: we each believed that our teams had both problems and potential. I conversed like a Martian who had recently perused a beginner's manual on casual human discourse, and I performed near-imperceptible what's-up head-nods with those of my teammates who showed up over the course of the evening.

Most of the guys at the party were wearing shorts and flip-flops, not jeans: Matt too had gotten this wrong. It was a pool party—not the kind where *everyone* went swimming, but the kind where the pool was nonetheless the evening's nexus, and prankish dudes occasionally shoved each other unexpected into the water, or pushed a girl in as last-resort measure to get her attention when every milder flirtation had failed, a hand grazing her butt during the playful altercation. A month or two earlier, I had tried wearing flip-flops a few times in non-beach situations, as I had attempted to do every year in hot weather, but once more it hadn't worked—they looked dorky on me, the way they looked dorky on guys over forty. Again, I couldn't do summer right: in the middle of July, I had found there was, within me, an invincible February.

To take my mind off the green-eyed girl, who seemed to have disappeared quickly from the premises, I became somewhat focused during the night on Victor and his generically hot, long-legged girlfriend, Alice Brubaker. She'd been wearing a bathing suit when I'd arrived, splashing around in the pool, and then had disappeared casually upstairs, with no overnight bag or oversized purse in hand, to change into shorts and a tank top, which possibly meant that she had clothes that she kept at Victor's house, a drawer of her own—a degree of boy-girl intimacy I could hardly imagine. I'd had a few classes with Alice but had no idea what she was like, despite a few short conversations that I could sort of recall: I was the kind of guy for whom all girls existed on a faraway plane, equally mysterious, their real selves never quite emerging from the fog of my dreams, which were so much more extensive and powerful than any actual interaction I'd ever had with them, even at age seventeen. Of all the people whom I envied, I envied most those boys for whom girls were tangible, differentiated human beings, not a homogenous supernatural entity—that was half the loneliness of my loneliness, the absence of particularity. Sometimes I couldn't see them properly even in the physical sense: I had no idea, for example, what hair color Alice had, even as I looked at her—I could only know that her hair was perfect, whatever the shade. (And yet her hair might *not* be perfect—it might be her least attractive feature, the one she fretted over daily, trying and failing to get it to behave the way she wanted; I would never know.)

Victor ignored Alice for most of the evening. It was my impression that he had a girlfriend for the sole purpose of creating the tantalizing possibility that he might cheat on her—a complex and seemingly effective tactic. I never saw him making out with anyone else that night, but he drank a lot and chatted with other girls, touching them playfully, and always appeared to be on the verge of sticking his tongue into one of their mouths. I could see his tongue as he talked, weirdly protuberant and pink as bubble-gum, reaching out toward Chelsea Caldwell and Rachel Bransdorfer—a slimy little ectotherm, seeking a warm space. He checked on Alice occasionally.

Alice: an old-fashioned name, wasn't it? An old-fashioned girl, maybe —helplessly drawn to the "alpha male" of her pack, capable of pursuing her attraction only within the terms of a monogamy in which Victor manifestly had no genuine interest. I kept looking at her.

....

The first strange event of the evening—which would be followed by two more at Victor's house—was not of my own doing (the next two were). It happened past midnight: I noticed that my cell phone had stopped working. It had plenty of battery life, but I wasn't getting any service—no reception, zero bars. I waited a while for it to relocate its connection to the omnipresent intangible web of data—the invisible ones and zeros that encircled us like ultrafine dust particles in the air, sustaining our 21st-century lives—but it just didn't happen, and when I tried, as a test, to send myself a text message, it failed to go through. Yet this was not *so* strange; my iPhone had given me problems before, and I already was dreading going to the Apple Store the next day to get it checked out, too lazy to Google the problem myself.

But then Matt approached me. "Hey Jeff," he said, "can you look up the word *YOLO* on Wikipedia for me? I was having a debate with Brad about whether Drake really invented it back in like 2011 or whether it had already existed, but for some reason our phones aren't working."

"Mine's not working either," I said.

"Oh," he said. "What's your carrier?"

"Verizon," I said.

"That's weird. I'm on T-Mobile."

We both kind of shrugged, but I felt a little uneasy, and I thought he did too. I noticed a few other people pulling out their phones, looking puzzled at first and then quickly desperate, smacking and shaking them like early primates. We looked up at the sky, searching for some strange weather event, but we saw nothing: just an indifferent, starry cosmos, suddenly a lot vaster than it had been.

None of us knew whether the disturbance was limited to Victor Bogdan's backyard, or whether it was town-wide, or nationwide, or global, because we couldn't text our friends elsewhere to ask whether their cell phones still worked. None of us could speculate in any useful sense about what might have happened to cause the problem—which seemed to affect everyone at the party—because none of us really knew by what means cell phones were supposed to operate, and we couldn't use our cell phones to look up the information. I listened to Gavin Strauss's and Cole Edmonton's conflicting interpretations: Gavin believed that our cell phones received their data from outer-space satellites (one of which must have "gone down"), while Cole insisted that they communicated with local radio towers (one of which, again, must have "gone down"), but neither professed to have a clue as to why the solitary orbiting satellite with which all our phones supposedly communicated should suddenly have tumbled from the sky like a cast-out angel, or why, if a local radio tower had tipped over in the summer breeze, our phones couldn't reach out to some slightly farther one.

So it had become a party without Instagram, Twitter, or Snapchat: we all looked at each other, determined not to panic. It all felt too much like a humanistic gag concocted by our well-intentioned, technophobic English teacher, with the goal first of revealing to us our unhealthy reliance upon digital additives, and then of helping us discover a purer, more rewarding social experience within a traditional, unadulterated reality. This was not a totally unattractive proposition: in our newfound isolation, we might initially freak out and then, in our healing, come together in a closeness we'd never known before. Removed from the pressures of the outside world—the hierarchies perpetually reinforced by social media—we might shed our artificial layers and "open up" to one another. It could be a large-scale *Breakfast Club*—or *Lord of the Flies*. I'd have welcomed either one.

But instead everyone seemed committed to the pretense that losing access to our phones was "no big deal," so determined were we to deny our addictions and learn no sentimental lesson. It wasn't so hard, after all. The only real loss was that, when I had nothing to do, I couldn't pretend to be texting my friends while actually reading Wikipedia articles. I just had to stand there, unambiguously alone and unoccupied.

Victor kept drinking—alternating between beer and liquor, contrary to some rhyming adage that a lot of my peers seemed to take very seriously—but seemed to be doing fine, his energy level high, his patter intact. Then, at about two in the morning, I noticed that he'd fallen asleep on a deck chair. He somehow looked confident even in unconscious repose, like a boy-king who had drifted off secure in the knowledge that his heedful, vigilant servants would watch over him through the night. Alice was still awake, chatting unenthusiastically with her girlfriends and, without seeming to recognize the beauty of Victor's slumber, glancing over at her boyfriend with visible exasperation, as though her glare might agitate him from his drunken coma. If my life had been a movie, she and I would have made eye contact during this period, as she realized that Victor was a hopeless jerk, and we would have run off together. We didn't, but even so, I felt liberated by his sleepiness. The party was still going strong, but having exhausted my limited conversational possibilities, I hadn't talked to anyone in the past twenty or thirty minutes, and without any visible activity on my side of the deck, it was getting harder not to come across as a voyeur, so I left the backyard and started to wander around alone inside the unprotected house.

The kitchen had a new-looking gas stove and dishwasher but no granite-counter island, which the more deluxe McMansion kitchens all had. The living room, meanwhile, was full of framed family photos but, endearingly, contained no professional portraits. I inspected various frozen iterations of Victor and his older sister, now presumably in college. She was almost annoyingly gorgeous at every age. Why had these parents—ordinary, frumpy adults, based on the photographic evidence—had such attractive children? I imagined that they'd actually birthed five or six kids and had strategically given up all but the best-looking two for adoption.

And why were they always going out of town? Where did they go?

Was it possible that they took weekend getaways not to rekindle the romance within their middle-aged marriage of sagging flesh but for the specific purpose of advancing their son's social career by providing him with an unsupervised venue at which to throw enormous parties? Did they buy the booze themselves—all those bottles, for which none us of had been asked to chip in—and give it to Victor on the grounds that, if someone called the cops, he'd claim that the college-aged boy next door had purchased it for him?

I went upstairs, which may have been off-limits for pure snooping purposes, but who knew—I could have been looking for an extra bathroom while the one downstairs was occupied by some extensive vomiting session, or a spare bedroom in which to have sex with another drunk-but-not-too-drunk-for-consent person: there were legitimate reasons for straying beyond the central partying area. The first door I opened was that of the linen closet; the second was that of the master bedroom. Then I found Victor's room: a queen-sized bed, a desk with a MacBook, an acoustic guitar, a dresser, a book shelf that oddly still held some childhood soccer trophies amid other memorabilia: he hadn't made it as far in the sport as I had—I was better than he was at something.

I opened the drawers of the dresser: all boys' clothes, none of Alice's. I looked down at my own outfit—I'd spilled a drop of orange juice on my shirt, the stain just barely visible on the beige cotton. Why had I worn beige? I looked like oatmeal, like an old man's coffee-stained teeth.

I took the shirt off and picked up a folded T-shirt from the drawer. It was soft, with thick horizontal blue stripes. I tried it on; the hemline was a little low, but it hugged my reasonably muscular chest in a more flattering way than the polo shirt had. It somehow felt several pounds lighter.

Still, I didn't look right. I took off my sneakers and socks, and then I removed my jeans and dropped them onto the floor. I picked up a pair of red and gray board shorts from the dresser and put them on, transferring my wallet, car keys, and nonfunctioning phone to its thigh-level zip pockets. I looked a lot better: flip-flops didn't make sense for me, but my bare feet seemed natural. I was a surfer, kicking back after an epic day on the waves.

Occupying that odd state where, having been ignored by everyone all evening, I felt like I could do anything and nobody would notice or care, I padded downstairs in my new outfit. For a moment I considered my behavior: could the theft (and donning) of clothing conceivably be a "prank" at the expense of the passed-out guy, in the classic tradition, like drawing a dick in Sharpie ink on his face? Well, no, probably not. But it was easier just to keep going than to acknowledge the weirdness of what I'd done, so I decided to stop thinking about it.

To that end, I went to the kitchen and filled two-thirds of a Solo cup with vodka. I drank it in two gulps.

Then I remembered that I hadn't eaten in the past 36 hours. This happened to me sometimes. I had some kind of medical condition or something—I'd never told anyone about it, so I wasn't sure what it was —wherein I never experienced actual hunger under any circumstances, and although I tried, mostly successfully, to maintain a healthy, nour-ishing diet for athletic reasons, I sometimes forgot to eat for a day or two, especially now that, with my brother away at college, my mom had more or less relinquished her 1950s kitchen duties in anticipation of my own imminent departure, regularly ordering pizza or Chinese takeout that she and my dad ate, leaving leftovers behind, instead of staging formal family dinners. My empty stomach seemed to welcome the vodka as though it were actual nourishment, absorbing it with palpable glee and then sending it forth, like good news, to the rest of my body: the alcohol flooded my limbs, my chest, my head—those, too, had been empty, and now suddenly they'd been filled. I felt good, spiritually more substantial and yet light on my feet. I stood silently, alone, in the kitchen for an unknown amount of time, paralyzed by positive energy, before deciding to rejoin the party.

I threw open the sliding glass door—*whoosh*—and reentered the outdoor space. Victor was still knocked out. Nobody paid any attention to me—except, maybe, Alice? She was looking at me now, I thought. Not at my clothes specifically: not with narrow-eyed suspicion, just looking at me. There was an empty chair next to her; some girl had gone inside to throw up, probably. It was getting to be that time of the night when the popular kids were readying themselves to eject their fluids—vomit or semen or both.

I sat down in the chair and looked at Alice. *She was saying something to me.* I couldn't truly hear it or make sense of it. I was just staring at her. I believed I could finally see her (her hair was *brown*), and I was trying to figure out whether she was "beautiful," a cheesy term that only guys who never got laid used, and it struck me that it was possible that she wasn't— and that, someday, standard white girls like Alice, whose attractiveness was almost certainly a boringly straightforward product of youthful skin, slimness of figure, and some kind of general low-grade conformity to popular Western beauty standards with whose dictates I'd been helplessly inculcated from birth, would strike me not as miracles of creation but as average humans: she had no soul-piercing eyes, no particular Helen-of-Troy facial structure. What was the difference between her and me?

I blinked, and then I was kissing her. I wondered at first whether she had initiated it. I had never kissed a girl on purpose, nor had I ever had a girl truly determinedly kiss me; the few kisses I'd experienced had been more like accidental facial collisions, never fully intended by either sad party. I wasn't capable of kissing anyone, even if a girl signaled that I should. The kiss might nevertheless *happen*, but for me it was like waiting for a butterfly to land on my nose—I had no control over the event, and anything I might do to compel it to happen would only scare it away. Yet as I found my mouth engulfing Alice's, I quickly realized that, in this case, I *had* initiated, violently. I had kissed her so badly that the word *kiss* didn't fit at all: it was a sort of tongue-cudgeling.

Her lips breaking free, she was shouting now—at me, maybe, or at others, for help. I was committing a sexual assault, I thought, and even in my fucked-up state the import of this registered dramatically upon me. Nearly stumbling out of my seat, I kept pressing my face forward, help-lessly, making contact at various points with her face and neck and lips and shoulder—my eyes fully open, yet somehow I could see the whole event more vividly from Alice's point of view than from my own, the horror and terror of it. I was right there with her, hating me, fearing me, feeling violated and furious on her behalf. Eventually I stopped.

Victor had awoken, his expression disoriented but already animated. He stood up. There were other people around me, but his was the face I saw. I saw it seeing me: wearing the stolen clothes from his dresser, attacking his girlfriend.

I stood up and literally ran away.

It happened very fast. I wondered whether they'd even seen me go.

Running while drunk, I felt more keenly the impact of each step, the weight transference from side to side, how it jostled my vision. I did not see very well where I was going. I knew the backyard was fenced, but somehow I made it over or past the fence without identifying where it was or noticeably climbing anything, and I emerged back onto the street. I saw my car and wanted to unlock it, but I kept touching the area where my pockets would have been if I had still been wearing the jeans that I'd taken off at Victor's house, missing the lower pockets on the board shorts, and after a while I recognized that if I was too drunk to find my keys, I was also too drunk to drive, so I kept running until I tripped and fell onto the sidewalk, and the street I was on, by then, didn't look familiar.

I opened Google Maps on my phone and waited a few seconds before remembering that my phone didn't work. I'd owned an iPhone since the age of twelve and had never had to make my way around town without GPS assistance: I had no idea where anything was in the physical world —I had no idea where I lived in relation to anything. I knew how to get from the high school to my house without computerized guidance, and that was all, the only route I had inadvertently memorized. My phone had long ago replaced my brain as memory bank and source of all information, freeing my mind to nestle fully, without the distraction of the real world or any of its data, into my undiagnosed anxiety disorder. My phone knew more of my life than I did—the gods of 4G had been right to take it away.

I started walking—I didn't live that far from Victor: an eight-minute drive, maybe. My house would turn up eventually, wouldn't it? There were 50,000 people in Weybridge, and if the average house contained four people, that meant there were only 12,500 homes. I'd already ruled out the five houses I could see from my seated position on the sidewalk, next to the tree whose overgrown root had elevated the up-tilted square of sidewalk that had tripped me: only 11,495 to go.

I needed some time to think things out, anyway. I had never before in my life done anything like what I'd just done and couldn't seem now to internalize the reality of it. What, exactly, *had* I done? What would be the consequences? And if I returned home, would my parents recognize me?

I was wearing someone else's clothes and reeked of alcohol and unsuccessful rape: I was not myself. I couldn't figure out why I hadn't vomited yet. I would've preferred to. The liquor was coursing through my brain like battery acid now, actually painful, yet I felt no unease in my stomach; my body, it seemed, was working rapidly to expel the poison through the skin, as a viscous, vodka-perfumed sweat now oozed liberally from my pores. Encased in cold, stinky goo like some kind of disgusting newborn animal, I began to shiver in the warm night.

I remembered that I had once smoked a cigarette with my older cousin Kyle, and afterward, when I'd realized that its acrid mustiness had permeated my clothes and perhaps even my hair and skin, I gradually became convinced that smell, not sight, was in fact the mechanism by which my parents recognized me, as though I belonged to a family of blind dogs, and that the wicked olfactory stain of the tobacco would thenceforth estrange me from them. I found myself drifting back into this moment as the reprobate sting of the alcohol continued to fill my nostrils.

I got up and started to walk, periodically checking my phone to see whether reception had returned. It hadn't. I was trying to retrace my steps back to Victor's street, but after about fifteen minutes, I found myself crossing Route 18, which definitely was not correct. Some more time passed, and then I looked around and saw nothing.

I lived in one of those New Jersey towns that were not really towns —on the hinterlands of Manhattan's commuter territory, south of the denser ethnic agglomerations of Essex and Union counties, east of the Waspy pseudo-countryside of Somerset and Hunterdon counties: a non-oceanfront flatland whose characterless, cultureless subdivisions overlay land that, until the construction of the New Jersey Turnpike in the 1950s, had been solely agricultural. The northern, eastern, and western edges of Weybridge blended seamlessly into the other non-towns of Central Jersey, but on the southern end of our bedroom community lay one of the minor interstices of the Northeast megalopolis, just beyond the immediate grasp of New York City, not yet far enough down to belong to the suburban territory of Philadelphia. Sprawl had begun to consume this land, too, but not in the form of single-family homes or strip malls. With an odd semblance of harmony, a newly assembled fleet of enormous, flat-roofed warehouses shared space with a few still-functioning farms whose vast, soothing, rectilinear dimensions they seemed to mimic.

Somehow I was headed thitherward, regardless of which direction I pointed myself: I had reoriented several times to no discernible effect. Earlier, I had made a left turn onto familiar-sounding Erwin Road with the hope that it might guide me toward the grammar school building with which I associated it—I'd attended Joyce Kilmer Elementary on Erwin from age five to age eleven, and although I no longer possessed in my conscious mind the route from the school to my house, I had some sense that it might secretly be hardwired into my deeper circuitry and that, if I cleared my head and walked with a sort of mental blindfold from such a point, I would wind up at home. Yet the road seemed to lead out of town in both directions, and before long, raucous eighteen-wheelers replaced the sedans and minivans that had sporadically crawled the nighttime streets of the civilized section of Weybridge. Eventually, the sidewalk disappeared, and as I made my way tremblingly along the shoulder, shrinking into myself, I realized that I needed only a rain cloud and a black eye to complete the delectably vulnerable image I now embodied for whichever sexually predatory trucker was surely about to pull over and offer me a ride.

The only pre-1950s housing stock within the town limits existed in this area: mildly decrepit farmhouses whose occupancy status was, to me, not readily identifiable. Stranded within their darkened half-industrial landscape, they did not emanate rustic warmth, nor were they sufficiently ornate or decayed to warrant a gothic fascination, but I was completely panicked by now and felt that I needed help, and when I spotted from a distance one such home with its lights on, I hurried toward it. It would have a phone, a landline. I couldn't imagine what I would possibly say to my mom when she picked up, but I believed in her general ability to save me from serious harm—to guide me back into the slower, safer misery where I belonged.

As I came closer, it struck me that the light inside the house had a strange quality, a sort of orange hue suggestive of certain streetlamps. I attributed it at first to my own muddled perception but grew more certain as I approached—yet I kept approaching, with every passing Mack Truck spurring me faster, a metal monster in pursuit. Then I'd arrived, and up close the orange light in the window looked still strange but now more organic, as though, trapped as the farmhouse's residents surely were in some prior century, they might be burning oil lamps or utilizing some other system of pre-electricity whose visual effect was unfamiliar to me but nevertheless wholesome. The house had a covered front porch that I expected to creak like the bones of a reanimated corpse when I stepped onto it, but in fact it didn't make a sound. I lingered there for a moment, and the porch felt good, somehow, cozy despite its emptiness. Covered front porches were an unknown architectural feature in my subdivision —we had only rear-facing decks, like Victor's, so that neighbors never had to see one another.

There was a peaceful silence now. The trucks, for a moment, had vanished, and I realized that the front door of the house was open. I stood in front of it, more curious than unnerved, peering into the strange light, my skin still exhaling vodka but my brain swaying more gently now in its skull, like the wooden rocking chair that had, in some earlier rural decade, when this house's presence on earth had still made sense, probably occupied the porch upon which I now stood.

I don't remember anything else from that night.

Chapter Two

In the tenth grade, my older brother Luke packed an additional outfit to school every day in his backpack, changing at lunchtime—not because he had some glandular disorder that caused him to sweat through his clothes or any particular habit of otherwise ruining them but simply because, for whatever reason, he liked to wear a different outfit for the second half of the day. He wasn't otherwise fashion-obsessed and never fully explained this practice to me, but I sort of imagined that the change of clothes served, for him, the same psychological function of renewal as a shower or a short nap—a personal recharging or reloading—so that he could greet his afternoon classes with the fresh clear-headedness with which he'd faced the morning session.

About my immediate family members, that was the only eccentric detail I ever observed. I was weird, but my family, by and large, wasn't. My family was happy. I say this not in order to be able later to contradict myself, subtly, with an increasingly nuanced portrait of the internal vicissitudes and complex private histories of people whose lives only *seem* secure and untroubled; I say it so as to explain why I have so little else to say about my parents and brother.

Where I lived, *everyone* was happy. People may or may not have experienced it this way: they may occasionally—or frequently, even—have had emotions that told them that they were unhappy, but these emotions simply didn't represent an accurate assessment of the situation. These people were happy, whether they knew it or not.

What were my parents like? They were two college-educated, financially secure American white people who imagined that they weren't defined by any of these characteristics. They had a stable marriage and a large home in a neighborhood where they didn't have to worry about locking the front door. They were two people who, on a dying planet, elected to have children together for no purpose except to raise those children to be the same as everyone else in the world, like two pieces of IKEA furniture that for some reason take eighteen years to assemble but are no more beautiful or useful for all the extra effort. If happiness—pure happiness—was not the catalyst for this decision, I can't imagine what was.

Happiness presents a peculiar challenge to the imagination: it might be easier, conceptually, to believe that, under her normal-mom guise, my mother was as desperately unfulfilled by her wifely chores and maternal duties as the brittle suburban housewives of all those acid satirical depictions of the bourgeois despair that's concealed by immaculate white picket fences, or that my father was so bored by his well-paying job that he'd initiated a secret love affair with a fifteen-year-old transgender boy. But to cast my parents as "human beings" of any kind—with gifts and foibles, distinguishing marks and smells—would probably be less true, within my own reality, than to say that they were simply parents. If there was anything more, I just was not interested; at some point, I'd begun to see the truth in the broader outlines—to see people within their larger demographics, as advertisers and economists did, and to see only obfuscation in the smaller details that, for them, comprised the substance and meaning of their lives. This shift didn't emerge from misanthropy or anger, but it did seem to indicate something unpleasant inside me.

This was when I realized, also, that I was going to write a very bad college admissions essay—that all-important document which, in its goal to reveal what the raw data of grades and SATs could not, was necessarily humanistic, locating within some personally significant narrative a proof of the soul. But I had none, no soul, or at least none of substance —I knew my own particularities, but I didn't believe that they were of any consequence. I dwelled on myself not out of fascination but out of compulsion: to me, my brain was just a hangnail.

Yet I accepted the reality of my happiness. I wouldn't have changed anything about the circumstances of my life even if I could have. I would choose the same parents, the same house, the same school, the same town.

Never in my childhood did I, for example, experience Weybridge—a stereotypically "boring" suburb on the surface of things (and beneath the surface of things)—as a dystopian wasteland of garishly bland corporate architecture and robotic citizenry. It never struck me as an artificial human habitat. The quietly prosperous cul-de-sac where my family lived—several pedestrian-impassable miles removed from the nearest commercial activity, thanks to draconian municipal zoning laws—possessed for its child inhabitants the serenity of the country, its soothing negation of the complexities of human society. My brother Luke and I experienced the pruned shrubbery, fertilized grass, and geometrically arranged trees of our subdivision as true nature, or something even truer and more natural. We felt as much luxurious detachment from civilization as if we inhabited a desert island with unlimited food and TV. It was not merely that we lived far from town; it was that we did not even understand the idea of "town," with its competing protocols and uneasy borders—we had only our own well-fed, unworried lives, guarded by a system of privilege so vast as to be itself as invisible to us as the unknown perils from which we were protected. Our private lives did not by necessity contain anyone except ourselves. Even as a senior in high school, I had no idea who my neighbors were unless they had kids near my age; the families surrounding mine were self-sufficient and comfortably asocial—they made no demands upon one another, not even the demand of friendliness.

To believe, as some people seem to, that the environmental and aesthetic apocalypse of far-flung urban sprawl is the opposite of "nature" is to believe that, for human beings, nature is a physical reality of plants and rocks and bodies of water, not an abstraction or a metaphor. As far as I can tell, what we experience, truly, is not nature but naturalness, of which the nature that we visit on hiking trips is only a symbol, its real essence being the absence of external forces of pressure or constraint. To my family, in its peaceful bliss, the opposite of naturalness, then, was commerce, industry, law, the strange desires and expectations of other people: naturalness was ourselves, our desires and their satisfactions. Sometimes, when I took late-night walks past my neighbors' houses in my early teens, I felt that I was inhabiting not a space in the real world but purely my own mind, so unchallenging was the threatless landscape that surrounded me.

And ultimately I wondered: would any of those so thoroughly socialized as to be capable of experiencing the densely coded public spaces of cities and town centers as stimulations rather than intrusions ever know a serenity as untainted as that which I enjoyed within a bedroom community so distant from its urban wellspring that, for those who stayed within its boundaries, it seemed to serve no purpose at all, as though life on earth were actually gift? In reality, Weybridge existed solely to serve Manhattan's labor mills, like most towns in the northern half of New Jersey, yet New York City hardly ever crossed my mind. It was an unfathomable and irrelevant place. The purpose of suburbia, I eventually realized, was to make everything outside your own home seem unreal: that was its healing power for stressed-out commuter-dads and stay-at-home moms who'd given up on their professional dreams.

I understood that the phrase "bedroom community" was semi-derogatory, a reduction of a simple but nevertheless multipart organism to its most basic and essential function and thus a criticism that it didn't contain more. Still, I embraced the term when I first heard it in high school, since, to me, Weybridge *was* more or less a bedroom—a hermetic, unshared place where no one would ever interrupt your dreaming. The adults who had chosen to live here were ones who, in a wholesomely American rather than sociopathic sense, cared only about themselves. My dad had his work life and his family life, at any given time occupying wholly one or the other; he had no social life or apparent need of one. The town didn't have a single bar, for instance: there was nowhere he could have gone to escape us if he'd wanted to—which he didn't, because he was happy.

....

When I was ten and Luke was twelve, we were kicking the soccer ball around on the far left end of the front lawn. We'd used duct tape to mark a twelve-foot stretch of the side wall of the garage as the goal; Luke was playing goalie, and I was taking shots at him from a patch of grass that technically belonged to our next-door neighbor's property. It was very important that I get at least a couple past him, but I hadn't yet learned to kick with both force and accuracy at once. I began with careful aim, but after a few shots that hopped and skidded awkwardly toward the corners of the imaginary net like fumbled footballs, more embarrassing though they required actual saves than any wildly off-kilter fastball would have been, I switched gears, sending three relatively forceful blasts directly to Luke's chest—which he caught easily—and then, finally, winding up and knocking a ball high over his head and onto the garage roof.

We waited for it to come down. It didn't, which didn't seem to make sense given the pitch of the garage roof, but it occurred to us that it must have gotten trapped up there within the junction between the garage and the house proper. We owned other soccer balls and normally thought very little of losing one—we had, with careless cheer, left at least a dozen behind at practices and tournaments, our parents scolding us in a way that simply did not register, so completely had they failed at some crucial early juncture to instill in us any respect whatsoever for our eternally replaceable possessions—but the idea of retrieving the one that had sailed onto the roof started to look like an appealing adventure. Neither of us had ever been up there. There was a ladder in the garage, which we'd seen our dad use for clearing the gutters, but this, as a yardwork tool within roughly the same category as the forbidden leaf-blower, struck us as off-limits in some way that devising a "natural route" to the summit perhaps was not: if, for example, one of us could access the roof first by snaking through the open window of my bedroom onto the small overhang that topped the kitchen alcove and then, with five white-knuckled toes clinging to the sloped perch, by swinging his right leg outward as far as it could go, rounding the corner to solid ground, and, while clutching the frail hollow downspout of the tinny gutter for moral rather than physical support, simply shifting his weight, with a little hop, from the left foot to right, and landing, like a man who had jumped from a slow-moving vehicle, onto a surface broad enough to accept his imperfect dismount, was he not entitled?

There was no need for both of us to go, but we both did. It wasn't all that hard; however, once we got up there we quickly realized that the ball couldn't have lodged itself anywhere on the roof. If we had bothered to think about its semi-celestial landscape for a moment or even to glance at it from any angle except that which had immediately presented itself before our ascent, we would have understood this. What had struck us from the leftward-facing side of the garage as a pyramid of metal shingles was, quite logically, missing its fourth surface, its apex extending instead as a straight line toward the house; there was no ravine between the two in which anything might get lodged. From our vantage point now, we could see that the soccer ball had actually fallen quietly into the bushes just past the driveway, and we simply hadn't noticed.

There was nothing for us to do up there now, which made us linger longer.

Pretty soon we realized that the gap between the garage roof, at its high point, and the low-hanging eave of the house roof, that more glamorous peak, was probably small enough for us to surmount it with a running start and a vault. *Why not?* Taking turns, we dashed across the spine of the garage, one foot in front of the other, thinking of a squirrel's graceful scramble across a thin tree branch yet nearly slipping a few times before half-colliding with the gutter and hoisting our newly scraped legs onto the ledge.

At the top, we both felt good, although the view was not much—too low for us to see over the large trees in back, and the front-facing outlook ending where the street climbed a smallish hill about a hundred and fifty yards away. What I preferred was looking down, picturing the layout of the rooms beneath me and how they might look from my perspective if the ceiling had been glass—one-way glass, in my imagination, so that I could see downward but my parents couldn't peer back up at me. Luke and I quietly tramped around and spent most of the afternoon up there. From the roof, it felt interestingly small, this container for our lives. Without any walls or furniture in the way, I could traverse it end to end in a few seconds, almost without noticing.

On our eventual descent, it was Luke who realized that the distance from the lowest section of the garage roof to the grass where we'd been playing soccer was not so great that a jump would necessarily produce serious injury. Examining the drop, he explained to me—in imprecise, already goading terms—his belief that the downward slope of the section of the yard below us would in some sense "catch" us if we fell correctly: i. e., in a manner reminiscent of Olympic ski jumpers alighting upon their graded landing strip at an angle so perfect that the trajectory change between flight and touchdown became negligible and the otherwise hard thud of impact was avoided. The trick, he said, would be to hit the ground and immediately roll, allowing the momentum of the fall to resolve itself over time and space, instead of trying to absorb it in one stiff jolt.

I didn't totally trust this notion, but Luke had convinced himself, and abruptly I watched him dive from the garage's eave onto the grass below, a distance of maybe twelve feet. His feet struck the ground lightly, I thought, and then he tumbled with some greater roughness. But he jumped up immediately and, without dusting himself off, urged me to follow.

I intuited that the more time I spent staring fearfully downward, the bigger the drop would begin to look, so I counted my heartbeats and, on the fifth one, threw myself overboard, regretting it immediately and attempting, just after my launch, to halt the plunge by latching onto the gutter with my left arm. My arm banged into it loudly but failed to grasp it—fortunately, since it doubtless wouldn't have supported my weight anyway. I forgot Luke's landing instructions, but when I hit the grass, I pitched forward without meaning to and rolled naturally.

I stood up; my bare feet were stinging, but otherwise I was fine. By then it was getting late, and we went inside without ever retrieving the soccer ball from the bush, and by the time we came out again some days later to play again, we'd forgotten all about it and used another one from our massive spoiled-brat collection of sporting goods.

For all its apparent pointlessness, I can say without exaggeration that the rooftop excursion of that afternoon, the first of many, changed my life permanently—I don't recount the story for the purpose of reveling in carefree days of childhood exploration and wonder. It was the start of a common practice, and what I found within it was not wonderment but comfort: ultimately, mounting the roof of my house was for me not a thrill or transgression even in some minor childish way like watching TV past bedtime—I wasn't by nature a rule-breaker; on the contrary, I felt unselfconsciously within my rights, and as time went on, I climbed out there more and more frequently through my bedroom window, often at night, to sit and look at the sky. Sometimes, I brought a blanket and fell asleep outside and didn't come inside until the first small sharp rays of morning had woken me; the half-elevated angle of my body, held in place by the friction of the shingles' rough surface against my skin, felt more natural and soothing to me than the corpse-flat position of the mattress in my bedroom. It never occurred to me to wonder what my neighbors would think if they noticed a blanketed boy lying on the roof of a house in the middle of the night; of course, they never noticed.

This practice—which I now understand to have been strange, although I didn't realize it then—ended when I was twelve and, while asleep, accidentally rolled off the top of the garage onto the grass below. Fortunately I hadn't fallen asleep on the *upper* roof, whose dangers I vaguely registered in the dark; even so, the fall from the lower section—an unconscious reproduction of the leap that Luke and I had taken the first day we'd climbed onto the roof—broke my leg. I lay on the ground in a state of pure thoughtless pain upon suddenly waking; I had no idea where I was or what had happened, and I had spent a minute or two on the ground moaning before it even occurred to me to wonder. Once I'd figured it out—my body still pressed into the wet prickly nighttime grass —I felt a new shame potent enough to make itself known even amid the intense physical discomfort that continued to surge through me. Getting up seemed impossible, so I yelled louder—half an expression of agony, half a call for help: sometimes words, sometimes not. It took my sleeping mom and dad some time to hear me through the closed window of their bedroom. I couldn't tell how much time, exactly, had elapsed, but it felt as though I'd been there for a while when they finally emerged from the house in that pajama- and bathrobe-clad panic that would probably have struck a kid more rebellious than I as a hallmark of parenthood.

The bodily damage could have been worse, but that autumn of recuperation still wasn't great. The accident had happened at the beginning of September, and I missed the first day of the seventh grade as a result —I sat in bed with my cast, wondering what all my classmates' back-to-school outfits looked like that year. Because I hadn't been able to come up with an adequate lie to explain to my parents why I'd been out on the roof in the middle of the night, I'd simply told them the truth, which was that I didn't really know why, and to them this was a failure of explication so complete as to qualify as dishonesty—their sympathy for me throughout the medical and emotional ordeal of my injury was therefore slightly tinged with suspicion. Ultimately they gave up and began, I believed, to regard me as a somewhat stranger person than they'd previously known.

I missed the entire fall soccer season, although I later came to believe that this was to my benefit. It was, in a sense, the most important soccer season of my life: before breaking my leg, I hadn't taken the game seriously—it had been a fun diversion like any other, and although it was arguably my best sport from a competitive perspective, I didn't privilege it over basketball or tennis or, for that matter, video games. But once I'd temporarily lost the ability to play—at the very start of the season—I began to dream jealously about it, and in my bed, attempting to reckon honestly with what it would take for me to turn myself into a great athlete, I made a silent, serious vow to become the best soccer player I could possibly become once I could walk freely again: to practice every day, to endure the pain of strenuous exertion and the tedium of repetitive training, so that the ball would become a body part, and my body parts would do exactly as I wanted them to on the field—I would run faster and longer, kick harder and straighter, move relentlessly.

I missed more than soccer that fall—I felt embarrassed by my injury, mostly because the bizarreness of its origin prevented me from truthfully explaining it when anyone asked, which everyone did, and for that reason I spent a lot of time hiding in my room, thinking about myself and other people in a threatened, insecure, envious way that hadn't been part of my life before. This aligned with my later teen experiences: the more time I spent on my own, the more time I spent consumed by thoughts of other people—classmates who were smarter and more talented than I was, boys who had more friends than I did, the proverbial girls who didn't know my name.

Yet, long after I'd healed, I also came to doubt whether high school "society"—its cliques and hierarchies—really existed in any concrete and meaningful sense: adolescence in the suburbs, from what I could tell, was a significantly more inward-facing, family-oriented experience than popular culture suggested. Regardless of one's place in the popularity standings, and whether one had a broken leg or not, one inevitably spent a lot more time at home watching TV or doing homework amid parents and siblings than one did inside the common warzone of pep rallies and sweet sixteens. And within the more vivid and encompassing world of the home, it was hard sometimes to tell whether the supposedly all-important externalities of teendom—the put-downs, the crushes, the breakups—had genuine substance or whether the whole supposed social structure of middle school and high school was just a dramatic extrapolation from events that, in reality, were relatively brief and insignificant. Had I ever been bullied? Had I ever been loved? Did I have any true friends? I often couldn't remember. In the end, it was the short, evasive, almost spectral nature of the social experience that made it so intriguing and maddening: it wasn't like soccer, where at least to some degree you could determine your own destiny through hours and hours and hours of practice—over the course of my high school career, I'd had at most four or five brief, random encounters that had in some way communicated to me my nebulous, seemingly arbitrary station within an equally amorphous teenage caste system. It was more about what *didn't* happen, the slow way adventures and intimacies failed to accumulate. Since you didn't know what you were missing, you had to sit around for long time before you could be sure that you'd missed it.

Like every other teenager whom adults could instinctively identify as a minor misfit, I'd heard the idiotically dichotomous lectures about the ephemerality of high school popularity and the cosmically corrective course of the years that would follow: the heroes of grades nine through twelve would turn into fry cooks and gas station attendants, and the nerds would become CEOs and famous Hollywood film directors—in the male version of this story, at least, the ultimate arbiter of life-prosperity was career success and its attendant money and women, who, in both their teenage and adult incarnations, would be drawn like flame-hypnotized moths to men of status, shifting their interest from charismatic, handsome guys to smart, industrious ones only once the determinants of status had shifted. In fact, I wasn't a nerd, but my grades were good—not spectacular, just generically good. Still, even if I could expect to achieve some greater measure of capitalist prestige in mid-life than some of the guys who had been better-looking than my seventeen-year-old self, would that ultimately soothe my youthful pain? Would there really be anything so notably glorious about an upper-middle-class heterosexual white male achieving success in the corporate world? Did that qualify as a story of suffering, resilience, and ultimate justice? I didn't feel that way about the future, that its more predictable and supposedly meritorious triumphs would outweigh the ambiguous missteps and bruises of an adolescence in which, as a matter of fact, it was *not* only the taller, handsomer, stupider guys who were more loved than I was—it was those whose DNA contained in various forms the mysterious alchemy of likability, a sort of magic that no degree of career-based prosperity would ever convince me that I possessed. I had a sense that my future job promotions, irrespective of their effects upon my romantic prospects or material comfort, would feel no different from good report cards: if you studied some small reasonable amount, you got an A. There was no miracle in this; it wasn't like the love that some people inspired just by being themselves.

I kept the promise I'd made to myself at age twelve: once my leg had healed, I played soccer till my feet blistered and ran sprints till my lungs burned. Eventually I bumped up, honorably, against my natural limitations—I had no real innate gift for the sport, but still by junior year I'd earned a spot in the varsity starting lineup, as one of the five or six best players on the team. Even so, the narrative wherein my leg injury was a strictly positive "growth experience" from which I'd emerged "stronger and more determined than ever" began to ring false. Later, I thought of the fracture not as a bodily wound but as a kind of head injury, the sort after which one is never quite the same. Just an accident of timing, no doubt: the incident made me a temporary invalid at age twelve, and then of course adolescence, which followed, was its own invalidism—between quiet off-season emotional breakdowns and postgame bouts of repetitive masturbation, I was, though able-bodied, effectively bed-ridden much of the time anyway. It was here—perhaps specifically during those jerk-off sessions, prompted as they were by a horniness that, exacerbated by a more general loneliness, became a sort of hunger for anything human— that my edenic subdivision began, in my own eyes, to lack something, when I turned away from the glowing carnal computer screen and looked out my window and saw nothing—no neighbors, no friends, no movement whatsoever—and this no longer seemed completely natural. What if, for the rest of my life, when I looked out the window, I saw nothing? I still had the dull socioeconomic fact of my happiness: that and myself, somewhat at odds.

....

The day after Victor's party, I was on the roof of the house again, quietly recuperating from my hangover by lying exposed to the hot blue cloudless sky without sunblock, hoping that the boozy toxins inside me would dissipate beneath the unfiltered heat. After waking up I'd eaten an entire bunch of bananas (seven of them) and drunk a quart of water and then had immediately retreated to my isolated canopy and stayed there. The hideaway served three loosely contradictory purposes: to provide me with undistracted time and space to contemplate my deeds of the night before; to allow me to sink slowly and peacefully into a private world in which those deeds might no longer seem real or consequential; and to give me a bird's-eye-view of Caswell Road, so that, if the police arrived to arrest me for clothing theft or sexual assault, I'd be the first to see them coming—not that I would try to escape.

I'd woken up unharmed in my bed at around noon, almost as though it were a normal summer day. I didn't know how I'd gotten home or what had happened after I'd approached that strange house on Erwin Road. Even with my hangover I jumped rapidly out of bed and rushed across the hall to Luke's vacated bedroom, which had a front-facing view of the driveway: my parked 2007 BMW sat there unscratched, impassive. Although I wasn't a drinker, my memory lapse—from just one (large) cup of vodka—seemed unreasonably vast. I wondered whether someone else had driven me home in my car, and if so, whether he or she had come to the door and alerted my parents as to my condition. Yet my mother wasn't waiting for me with a lecture or an interrogation when I got up, so maybe I was in the clear—except, of course, with regard to my behavior at Victor's house, which surely would bear consequences, if not parental or legal, then at least for my mostly nonexistent reputation.

On the roof, eyes shut to the sun, I found myself wondering just how advanced and empathetic my male classmates' sexual politics were; how empowered my female classmates had become; and whether, by some luck, a degree of lingering rape culture inside our politically correct yet hardly *political* town might ultimately pardon my infraction against Alice—which, within a traditional paradigm of male supremacy, would be considered totally minor, harmless, and even kind of amusing. Hazily I remembered a few 1980s teen comedies that I'd seen on TV late at night, like *The Revenge of the Nerds* and *Sixteen Candles*, wherein the sympathetic "geek" characters implicitly or explicitly committed full-on penetrative rape, yet because their victims were teasingly elusive "popular girls" with whom the viewer, male or female, wasn't expected to identify, the crimes were presented as a feel-good comic moments: the underdog standing up for himself, finally receiving his due. In the year 2015, had we come so far from this time? Or was it still possible that the grotesque kiss that I (the endearing wallflower) had planted upon Alice Brubaker (the stuck-up beauty queen) would be interpreted in this misogynistic light, even though I was not endearing, and Alice was probably not stuck-up? If all but the top five percent of high-schoolers were in some sense losers, would I not receive the support of the majority?

Or would my jock status derail this narrative, rendering me not a desperate romantic but a brawny, entitled bully, and Alice the delicate victim of my excessive testosterone? Or, on the other hand, would it make my behavior seem *normal*—a rambunctiously masculine act for which I, the red-blooded sportsman, couldn't be blamed? We were all drinking, and boys would be boys, wouldn't they? It was my belief that a lot of people had witnessed what I'd done, and inevitably different people would have different takes: it wasn't clear what would coalesce. It was theoretically plausible but somehow didn't seem likely that the overall verdict would go my way, yet I knew that, every day, teenage boys got away with things far worse than what I'd done, even in liberal, well-meaning, well-to-do towns, usually because the violator's peers were at best half-informed as to what constituted a violation against someone who happened to be female, or non-white, or handicapped: someone whom they'd been culturally conditioned to regard as a natural and deserving recipient of male violence, as long as it wasn't anything *too* bad.

Part of me wanted to receive the full, justified brunt of some global feminist wrath—torture me for a few weeks, attack my small fearful testicles with pliers, I might actually emerge as a better person, it might be worth it—but most likely, I thought, my schoolmates would on the whole regard my behavior from an unserious yet nevertheless unflattering perspective, wherein, giving little or no thought to Alice's feelings about the matter (which might not strike her as a fun source of loud gossipy delight), they'd publicly ridicule me not as a criminal but as a pathetic, awkward dork: there'd be no righteous politics to their rejection, just a joyful cruelty. The verbal lynch mob would spot the easy target, and I'd become an outcast not because I'd done something morally objectionable but because I'd done something socially humiliating.

I heard a car turn onto my street and sat up: not a police car. I lay down again.

Would it matter if I *were* a detested outcast, rather than a nonspecifically unloved guy? Would I be able to tell the difference? It meant that people would ignore me face-to-face and then talk about me once I'd left, instead of just ignoring me altogether; the actual experience for me would be the same. Maybe my real error had been in not courting controversy earlier—I'd tried so hard to be "normal," and it had worked in exactly the wrong way.

It was my first time on the roof since my fall almost exactly five years earlier. The neighborhood had changed a little, in ways that hardly seemed worth noticing: the big tree in my neighbor's backyard had come down, the family two doors down had built an extra bedroom on top of their garage, different cars occupied the driveways. Would I someday own an overlarge house like these ones, love it enough to adorn it with pointless additions and demolish encroaching plant life? It seemed possible that I wouldn't: that, in accordance with newer trends within my privileged demographic, I would begin to yearn instead for man's historically communal habitat—higher-density living, walkability—and, in keeping with our country's diminishing greatness, end up purchasing a smaller home than my parents had, ostensibly as part of a growing morally and ecologically repentant effort to patch up the irreversible social and environmental rupture created by the advent of the undemocratic, pollution-spewing automobile; that I perhaps belonged to the last generation condemned to spend its childhood inside the sterile postwar dream created by the innocent self-entitlement of the American Empire at its zenith, a way of life that would soon strike younger people as an unimaginable Bizarro World within the ignorant past like the Jim Crow South; that I would, by some newer commercial deception, come to view my shorter commute time and the accessible farm-to-table restaurants of my overpriced, gentrified urban neighborhood as a solution to the spiritual trauma that my subdivision-bound adolescence had supposedly inflicted upon me. But then again, maybe not—ultimately, I'd go wherever they told me to go. In any case I tried to imagine my future—the days when, according to the standard-issue reassurances, I'd no longer even remember the humiliations of high school: what did I earnestly dream of for myself, the way my parents and grandparents had dreamed of classic American prosperity? What did I want? Nothing. Everything purportedly attractive looked like some kind of con that I was too dumb to understand. I would live a pointless life, would only ever make the world slightly worse, and would know it only in some obscure, nagging way, the problem unidentifiable and therefore unsolvable. Of course I dreamed of love.

My cell phone vibrated in my pocket. I took it out and, only when I'd answered the call, realized that this meant it had sprung back to life. It was Matt.

"Our phones are working again," I said.

"What do you mean?" he said.

"They weren't working last night. Now they're working again. It's weird," I said, realizing that it didn't sound that weird when I described the situation aloud.

"Our phones weren't working last night?" he said. "I don't remember that."

"Yeah, I mean—it was really strange. Everyone's phone stopped working. It didn't matter who your carrier was."

"Why would that matter?"

"I don't know."

There was a pause.

"Anyway," he said, "I'm in the middle of a kind of emergency. Can you help?"

"What happened?"

"I lost my dog. I mean, my dog got lost while we were at Victor's house last night. I guess the gate on the fence in the backyard got left open somehow. When I got home, my parents were out looking for him, walking around the neighborhood, but now they're at work, and I've spent the whole day kind of—I mean, I'm sure he'll turn up, he has a collar with our phone number on it and everything, but I haven't really slept. I've been wandering around, calling out his name, but, like —maybe we need to canvass a broader area? I don't have a car, but I printed out some posters . . ."

A lost dog: such a weirdly wholesome problem—distressing, obviously, but so removed from one's own internal issues that it sounded almost refreshing, a vacation from interiority. I had no recollection of Matt's having had a dog.

Moreover, I was a little surprised and flattered that Matt had turned to me, even if it was primarily, again, for the purpose of using my car. There were other plenty of other people with cars—maybe he considered me a better friend than I had thought he did.

I told him I'd be there in a few minutes, and then I hung up without saying goodbye, like a character in a movie—a self-promotional tactic to which I'd recently committed for all phone calls, avoiding saying goodbye in any form ("see you around," "talk to you later," and others were equally prohibited). I'd adopted this behavior not necessarily for its cinematic quality as for the cliffhanger nature of it, wherein, because the conversation hadn't properly ended, my interlocutor would be left in a nebulous unfulfilled state of suspense or expectation and therefore would be afflicted by a subconscious need to see me again soon in order to "fin-ish" the interaction. I kept them wanting more of me—that was the idea, but naturally it worked only if they'd wanted me in the first place, which they usually didn't, at least not in any meaningful sense.

And then, when I put my phone back into my pocket with my wal-let and car keys, I noticed—for the first time, incredibly—what kind of pocket it was: I hadn't changed since waking up, and I was wearing jeans. It took me a moment to ascertain that they were the same jeans that I'd thought I'd left at Victor's house. I was also wearing the previous night's beige shirt. Had I somehow gone back to Victor's home during the early morning hours and retrieved my outfit from his bedroom? How could such a transaction have taken place? It almost seemed more plausible that all that had occurred after some particular time in the party—a flip-switching moment denoted in some obscure but telling way, if I'd been perceptive enough to notice—had been an extended "dream sequence" of the sort that existed only in movies, or that I had "lost my mind" and could no longer distinguish fantasy from reality. But I didn't *feel* insane.

Did insane people feel insane? My longstanding belief was that the knowledge of their insanity didn't occupy the forefront of their brains —hence their ability to take their insane notions seriously—but deep down they knew and preferred to go along with it rather than fight it off. I had assumed that losing one's mind would be more fun than what I was currently experiencing, which appeared to me as the same unem-bellished reality that I would have to continue to navigate with my usual painstaking cluelessness: it *should* be more like losing control of a car, where ultimately you could do nothing but surrender to the exhilaration as you spun off the cliff.

If I wasn't insane—well, since I'd stolen Victor's clothes before taking a single sip of alcohol, there was really no reasonable way for me to be confused about what had happened there. Somehow I'd switched back to my own ill-considered garments: I couldn't invent the necessary chain of events to get myself there, but it'd happened. I decided to think more about it later and to get off the roof and drive over to Matt's house, as I'd promised, instead of freaking out, so I crept back to my bedroom window and slipped through.

I started to feel better on the way to Matt's house: he didn't remember the cell phone incident of the night before—maybe he (and by extension, others) also didn't remember my incident with Alice. In fact, he almost definitely didn't remember: as I mentally replayed our conversation about his lost dog, I couldn't find a trace of newfound disgust for me or any indication that in his estimation anything strange had occurred the prior evening until he'd come home. It was possible that he just hadn't been among the witnesses of my assault; even so, if *others* had processed it as a major event, its consequent reverberations would have traveled throughout the party, and he would have heard. I found myself beginning to believe that, yes, nothing of consequence had happened at Victor's house—the otherwise troubling reappearance of my discarded clothing now vaguely seemed to buttress this optimistic interpretation: I'd emerged without a single mark of my odd behavior upon me. And was my clothing's reappearance so strange anyway? My car, too, had rematerialized, so *clearly* I *had* gone back to Victor's at some point.

Matt lived about ten minutes away. I loved driving through Weybridge: my idea of heaven looked exactly like my own town—broad roads, green grass, nothing remotely interesting to see. The pleasure of my surroundings was something I received as a feature unique to this particular municipality, ending at the town limits, even as I recognized and consciously experienced every day the utter *lack* of uniqueness within Weybridge. I couldn't fathom the lives of adults here, how boring they must be, but to be a teenager in such a setting was some kind of god-kissed good luck: it was a world where, somehow, your stupidity was absorbed without repercussion, indulged, made to feel not like clumsiness or ineptitude but like a natural and infinitely extendable state. I *was* looking forward to senior year: learning nothing while getting more A's, wildly outscoring kids from less affluent school districts on culturally biased standardized tests, basking in the continued sanction of my ignorance of the entire world. Those moments of life in which I bumped up against my practical incompetence—at the post office, for example, when I realized I didn't know to mail a letter—struck me as unjust deviations; I had only to will them away, and eventually they went.

When I got to Matt's house, he hurried outside without my having to honk or text him. His face was shiny with the grease of fear, his hair flattened askew. He was wearing his clothes from the night before, just as I was, and he was carrying a backpack not on his back but in the top-crumpling grip of his left hand, as though it were a kitten he was holding by the scruff of its neck.

"Thanks for coming," he said. "I thought maybe we'd head over to Timberland Meadow or Wildwood Haven." These were the beautiful names of other nearby subdivisions.

"What'll we do over there?"

"Just keep looking for him, I guess. I brought the squeaky toy that Oscar likes. I've just been walking around, squeaking it, hoping he hears." He took a plastic cartoonish pink octopus out of the backpack. "And we'll put up more flyers. I already covered most of my neighborhood. We can put them up at supermarkets and other places, too."

"What kind of breed is he?"

"He's a Border Collie." His answer, I realized, would have been meaningless to me almost irrespective of what it was, since I didn't know anything about dog breeds, but he pulled a stack of flyers out of his backpack next and showed me what Oscar looked like: a black and white coat, a dog-like face—essentially what I would have attempted to draw in the first grade if my teacher had asked me to draw a dog. The flyers were printed in color.

I started to drive, although I was a little confused about our mission. Did it make sense to use a car to track down an animal that itself had escaped on foot, and therefore was logically within walking range? Was it really so strange, anyway, for a dog to go missing for fifteen hours or so? Wouldn't it eventually wander back? Shouldn't Matt stay at the house to receive Oscar when he reappeared?

"Do you think you should stay at home, in case Oscar comes back?" I said.

"Stephen is still at home," he said, "and just in case I left the back door open and put out some food for him."

"For Stephen?" Stephen was Matt's younger brother.

"No, for Oscar."

"Oh."

"I also let all my neighbors know what was going on."

Talking to your neighbors, for any reason—such a strange concept, but maybe not if you had a pet that needed to be walked every day. Matt probably knew everyone on his street: accidental encounters and "What a cute puppy!" comments had probably evolved, in some cases, into life-long intergenerational friendships like the one between Marty and Doc in *Back to the Future*.

"Sounds like you've done a lot already," I said, hoping to convince Matt that, his moral obligation to the pet having long ago been discharged, he didn't necessarily *need* to keep me out all night on the search. I'd already assumed that, regardless of Oscar's ultimate fate, we together would not find him: it just didn't seem plausible that I could be involved in a non-futile enterprise.

"Yeah, I guess. I called the *Sentinel*'s office to put an ad in this week's paper, too. I can't just sit around, though, you know?"

I was starting to wonder why my family had never had a dog. Was that (rather than the superior replacement-version of myself that I imagined in my waking nightmares) what my household had been lacking—some leaping, nonhuman, love-inspiring addition to our pallid nuclear family whose absurd presence (a normalized absurdity but one all the same, wherein a testicle-licking, anus-sniffing animal would be welcomed into a human home otherwise bound by social protocol completely incomprehensible to canines) would, for all its predictability as a middle-class accessory, have broadened the dimensions of our daily experience, its permanent happy uselessness subverting the perfunctory quality of our unspiritual, materialistic, goal-driven lives? A dog was a philosophical statement that living creatures could embody and inspire joy, and that joy was a meaningful part of life, worth cleaning up shit for—it existed for no other reason. I tried to remember the last time I'd felt upset about something that hadn't been directly about me: probably never.

Leaving Matt's cul-de-sac, I turned left on Pickett Road and drove a mile before turning left again at the enormous stone signboard for Timberland Meadow—probably not real stone but whatever gray material the faux-castles of Medieval Times venues were made from—and then slowed down, awaiting instruction. Matt didn't say anything, so eventually I pulled over at an arbitrary point along the endless looping house-lined road. I cut the engine, and we got out. He was still holding the squeaky toy, and now he removed a small plastic bag full of some brown organic-looking material that I immediately found frightening.

"Oscar likes boiled liver as a treat," he said.

"Tasty," I said. He didn't laugh.

Matt pointed to an intersection within the subdivision about sixty yards ahead of us. "Here," he said, "I'll go this way, and you go that way. There's a park in that direction that we sometimes take Oscar to—he could be hanging out over there." The phrase *hanging out* stuck out for me, as though Oscar were a deadbeat, alcoholic father, avoiding his responsibilities, whom we could track down simply by stopping in at his favorite "hangouts," the dive bars and pool halls.

Matt took a chunk of boiled liver out of its bag and gave it to me. I tried not to grip it, just let it lie on my flat, outstretched palm as though my hand were an inanimate platform. Even so, I could sense some of its simultaneously mealy and fibrous texture subtly depositing itself onto my skin.

"He might come if he smells it," Matt said. "He has a great sense of smell."

Didn't all dogs have a great sense of smell? We walked together for a minute or two, Matt squeaking the octopus the whole time, and then we diverged, he heading toward the park, I taking the less important route. We agreed to meet back at the car in twenty minutes.

Suddenly, I was alone, strolling down a blank street that resembled my own, holding out a piece of boiled liver as if it were an offering to the gods, and the aggressively pointless nature of our endeavor—whose purpose, apparently, was not so much to *find* a dog as to use one's mental powers to *conjure* a dog from the thin air of a blatantly empty suburban street—began to feel kind of enjoyable. I sniffed the liver; it was disgusting. Since the age of fourteen, I'd been a vegetarian for ethical reasons that I could almost no longer remember—where was the search-and-rescue mission for this organ-harvested pig or cow or chicken, my sanctimonious earlier self wondered?

Almost treeless despite its moniker, Timberland Meadow was a big subdivision, but eventually the dead-end road I was following ended in a broad paved loop, a sort of traffic circle to no purpose. The backyards in this development were small and unfenced: I could see behind the final house on the street to the no man's land—a shallow, soggy ditch and some uncut grass, the titular meadow perhaps—that separated Timberland Meadow from whatever neighborhood abutted it. Since I had nowhere else to go, I decided to brave the wilderness and forge a path to the other side.

But soon after I'd invaded the private property of the homeowner at the end of the street, I heard a dog bark. It took a moment for the otherwise insignificant sound to register as a detail of import, but as I heard it again, I jolted to attention. It was coming from the rear-facing deck of the house in whose featureless backyard I illegally stood. I looked toward the dog; it looked at me. It was not Oscar. It was a larger, brown dog. I didn't know what breed it was, but it wasn't the same kind as Oscar.

Even so, I found myself approaching this dog—I couldn't have said why: maybe a sense that, if I didn't recapture Oscar, kidnapping some other dog was the next best thing, that a dog was a dog. It was a mocha-colored creature, unaccompanied, with a thinly furred, boney face and pale blue eyes from which it stared at me with the annoyed, judgmental intelligence of an unmarried, childless man of forty—a human impatience so striking that when it stood up and barked now *at* me, *like a dog*, I was actually surprised. I was on the first step of the deck, and for a moment I had something like a flashback to the prior night, when I'd illicitly set foot onto the porch of another stranger's home, but the memory, though newly vivid, didn't extend beyond the point where it'd previously ended—in fact, it shot back in the opposite direction, to Victor's backyard and the faux-wood backyard deck that more closely resembled this one—thus serving no purpose except by its brief intensity to make the present seem abstract and unreal so that, when the dog barked for a third time, its pitch more violent, I again failed to process it correctly and continued to come closer.

It barked a fourth time. I was on the second step from the bottom of the deck, two from the top, so the angry dog still hovered over me like an abusive authority figure from a traumatic childhood memory, and I was wondering—as an extension of my earlier thought—whether people tended to love their dogs for the specific qualities of their dogs' personalities or simply for their general dog-ness, the quality of being a dog that they shared with all other dogs, so that the love one had for one's individual dog was only like the attachment of a child to the *specific* action figure in his possession, identical to all the others from the mass-produced batch from which it had been purchased yet personal enough to its owner that, if it were lost, the child would cry even if his parent promised immediately to buy him a new, identical one, since it wouldn't be the same, it wouldn't be *his* Batman ... and yet, ultimately, it *would* be the same, the new Batman would resume the lifespan of the first, the gap between the two would be forgotten, and the child would stop crying very soon: which meant that if I could lure this strange dog back to the car, I'd be a hero.

When I took one step closer, the dog—collared, groomed, well-owned, but it didn't seem to matter to me—lunged at me.

I stepped back quickly, slipped, tipped over backward, and fell from some small but not completely insignificant height to the grass behind me. I jumped up as fast I could, before I could tell whether I'd injured myself, for fear that the dog, whom I suddenly began to process as a threat, would otherwise begin kicking me (or pawing me, or biting me) while I was down. Turning around, I headed for the distant car, running and then slowing down slightly in order to turn and check if the dog was following, first disappointed that it wasn't, then frightened as it rounded the corner because it *was*—it was, and suddenly I felt bizarrely like the stereotypical hard-luck postman of the popular imagination, a creature of comedy, fleeing to some playful musical score, and yet also, within some other vision of the situation, still *leading* the dog back to my car deliberately, with a plan in mind. It looked very focused, its tongue not hanging out, no drool, just an expression of concentration and pursuit, like a very calm person with a very important goal. It was hard for me to decide whether it was chasing me or I was escorting it, but eventually, in my fear, I settled on the former interpretation, tossing the piece of liver in the opposite direction before reaching the car, getting in, locking the door, and then finally realizing that the dog had only wanted to play with me, this wonderful food-bearing stranger. After eating the liver, it came back to the car in which I'd stashed my cowardly self, looking a little forlorn, but I did nothing, speculating as I did that some alternate explanation for my friendlessness among humans had presented itself in my inability to receive here the corresponding pursuit of that which I'd initially pursued: I ultimately shrank from what I desired—the people whom I wanted to love and befriend noticed it, that I could fathom desire only as a one-way street, that I couldn't receive theirs if it did exist in some mild, fluctuating, dissatisfying state. I considered, too, a potential reason why I'd never had a dog, which would by its nature have adored me without reason, an affection I'd have failed to accept: better not to be reminded of my emotional inadequacies day after day.

....

Matt hadn't found Oscar either. We drove to one other subdivision, wandered around uselessly, and then visited two supermarkets and three strip malls to pin, tape, and staple flyers wherever we could find places for them. I felt oddly "connected to my community" while doing this, like someone in a shitty band promoting a show to which people might actually show up in an effort to "support local artists," even though in actuality I assumed that no one would call Matt despite the mention of a nonspecific reward on the poster. As the afternoon sun began to fall, I dropped Matt off at his house, still dog-less, and when he got out of the car I did too, for some reason, and with actual tears gathered in his eyes, he hugged me. I was sort of weirded out, still trying to understand how the emotional center of this usually normal, good-humored, unreflective boy, now a mess, had apparently been buoyed all his life solely by a furry family pet, but I hugged him back and felt proud of myself for doing so.

But when I got back in the car, I didn't feel sufficiently warmed by the interaction to go home with the sense of satisfaction traditionally begotten by the sort of failed quest or enterprise wherein, though the primary objective was not achieved, the human bonds forged along the way ultimately constituted their own consummation or fulfillment. I drove to Wawa, ate an egg salad hoagie in the parking lot while answering a text from my mom with the other hand, and then, on the way home, passed the turn for my street, instead continuing west on Morehead Avenue, eventually ending up on Erwin Road. It was starting to get dark, the window of possibility for a *Hangover*-like series of hilarious episodes leading me back to the forgotten truths of the drunken night before rapidly closing, which was sort of a relief: I had more or less resigned myself to the idea that anything that seemed to have happened during that evening may or may not have actually happened, that it didn't matter either way, and that whatever I couldn't remember was equally unimportant—I could sometimes do this type of thing because all of life was equally strange and painful to me. I almost didn't want to know more, except that I was semi-inadvertently driving in the direction of the spot where I last recalled standing that night.

I found the house. At dusk I saw that it was painted an insipid light blue, like the sky in a child's ugly drawing. I was still driving when I noticed this. I thought about pulling over, but the primarily nonresidential road was busy, and the shoulder was small. I passed by, which for a moment felt like all I was going to do. But at the first turn, I got off Erwin, parked on the side of the street, and walked back.

Standing on the front lawn of this house, I hesitated to come to the door—not so much for fear that I'd plunge once again into a bizarre unconscious trance as because I wasn't sure what I'd say to the home's occupant if my knock were answered, uncertain as I was whether this residence had played some pivotal role in the events of the preceding night or whether I'd only stood on its porch for a moment before some unrelated highway bandit had chloroformed me.

I was considering what to do when I noticed a small fluffy object in the grass, what looked at first like a brown hairball, dark-reddish at the ends. I wasn't sure why I bothered to examine it more closely, but it looked as though some small chunks of mud had been caught and wound into the furry miniature tumbleweed, and then I noticed that the dusting of maroon that touched the tips of the hairs was not only color but texture, a thickening toward clinging clumps. Then I saw the little black protrusions, like the graphite tips of pencils: little claws above the digital pads, not mud—it was a dog's paw, severed.

I came close but not too close. The object still looked strangely light, a weightless puff of fur with no bones visible, almost a fully independent object, as if it had never belonged to a living, loved creature. I suddenly felt very strange standing on this strange lawn; it was my stomach more than my brain that told me to leave. I left quickly.

Chapter Three

My doctor's office was located behind a Chuck E. Cheese in an office park whose cursorily decorative greenery and fountain—a sort of eternal burbling pond-bound flatulence that merely disrupted the surface of the shallow murky water more often than it surmounted it—seemed contrived and pitiful even by office-park standards. I'd had the same pediatrician all my life, a man called Dr. Steinfeld, who, like all pediatricians, had chosen his career solely to satisfy his urge to finger young boys' testicles, the lush scrotal skin like some expensive fabric between his ecstatic thumb and forefinger. He worked in a complex occupied entirely by medical professionals—dentists (including mine), chiropractors, dermatologists—where the flimsy trailer-like quality of the buildings gave the place the feeling of a miniature golf course.

I was there for my required pre-participation physical examination, a yearly ritual at the beginning of soccer season. I sat in the low-ceilinged, germ-ridden waiting room for fifteen minutes amid toddlers and their moms, feces-smeared toys and untouched *Highlights* magazines, before the nurse called me back behind the Dutch door.

She led me to a small room with thin walls and a heavy door, where I undressed in that peculiarly conscious, vulnerable way that for me recalled female-narrated stories of awkward virginity loss. I sat on the unrolled tissue paper with the cold vinyl pressing through to my exposed thighs and waited for the doctor, who ultimately gave me the usual battery of tests, which I seemed to pass. I put my clothes back on, and the middle-aged, mole-dotted nurse led me to a scale in the common area, where I took off my shoes again and let her weigh and measure me.

Adjusted for the addition of my clothes, my weight was exactly what I'd expected it to be—I monitored it at home as stringently as a bulimic girl—and when the nurse extended the metal beam to check my height, I waited placidly for the predictable news that I'd already ceased to grow, but then she looked at her clipboard and seemed surprised. I was still standing straight up, trying hopelessly to extend my spine an extra centimeter, and the nurse came back and examined the scale more closely, squinting at the numbers as though she needed glasses.

"That's so strange," she said.

I immediately felt alarmed. "What's so strange?"

She tried to laugh, but it sounded fake, a reassurance she didn't believe in. "Last year we measured you at five-foot-ten. This year you're only five-foot-eight. Teenagers aren't supposed to shrink."

Five-foot-eight? I was more outraged by the number itself than I was alarmed by the possibility that my body was undergoing some medically abnormal process: I had spent enough years praying for growth, dreaming of height, to believe that I'd *earned* my five-foot-ten, that I had *achieved* averageness—technical averageness rather than genuine adequacy, like having a five-inch erection, still somehow a failure but statistically common enough that the numbers provided at least some kind of refuge and comfort—by dint of my own hard work.

"There must be some mistake," I said, suddenly the disbelieving protagonist in the first act of a made-for-TV cancer movie.

"Well, yes, there must be," the nurse said, surprising me. "Like I said, teenagers aren't supposed to shrink—and there's no medical reason why you should, no matter how healthy or unhealthy you are. And you seem very healthy. But this scale isn't wrong."

"Are you sure?"

"I'm absolutely sure."

"So," I said, feeling defeated, "the nurse last year must have measured me wrong."

"That seems unlikely," she said. "It's kind of hard to mess this up, and I can't imagine how she would have gotten the measurement wrong by two whole inches."

"Maybe she got the measurement right but wrote it down wrong," I said, although I had a distinct memory of being verbally *told* that I was five-foot-ten.

"That could be," the nurse said, "but even if there was a mistake last year, you were already five-foot-nine *two* years ago, according to your chart, which means you've shrunk either way—which is impossible."

"So what does that mean?" I said.

"Maybe you should come see us again in a couple months."

"What for?"

"Just to check in, make sure everything's all right. We'll do another measurement."

She was holding my hand now, pulling me off the scale. She didn't seem all that intrigued by the bona fide medical mystery before her. I wondered, as I put my shoes back on, whether I ought to be naked under the bright lights of a lab somewhere, poked and prodded (if there was a difference between the two acts) by a team of fascinated scientists. But the nurse's basic indifference felt like an irreversible fact of where I lived, not particular to her: here, even the objectively interesting became uninteresting. I couldn't fight it.

....

As a returning player in good standing, I was nevertheless required to go to soccer tryouts, but for me and several teammates who likewise had played for Weybridge High since the ninth grade, they were only a formality—an opportunity to sharpen our skills together before the season and to see where we all stood. Every year some senior got a little worse instead of better, having neglected the sport the whole offseason or having gotten fat over the summer. More distressingly, the smarter, more interesting kids in the program—who, starting high school as jocks but, lacking the correct disposition for it, were ultimately destined to become more substantive human beings than the rest of us, often by virtue of forfeiting a measure of productivity in the present—tended to "lose focus" after their sophomore seasons as part of some morally or spiritually introspective, typically drug-related personal journey utterly incomprehensible to Coach Carrell, whose sports-cliché value system, from which sprung our hardworking team's identity, generally rang true for his best players even if they occasionally mocked it.

I had gotten better every year, including this year. I played on a USYSA team during the spring and had spent three weeks of the summer at a soccer camp, but mostly it was what I did on my own: studying the game on obscure *futbol*-devoted TV channels buried deep within my parents' deluxe cable package, working out, touching the ball every day. My greatest strength was a firm knowledge of my own limitations: in other words, I benefitted from what my guidance counselor had termed my low self-esteem. Because I knew what I couldn't do, I also knew what I had to be great at in order to compensate for those weaknesses.

I was never going to be a beautiful, transcendent soccer talent; my feet didn't manipulate the ball with the feathery grace of an expert musician handling his instrument of choice. I had never dazzled anyone with my tricky dribbling, had never made the impossible flamboyant play: the pass that no one saw coming, the physics-defying shot that curled from some obscure angle past three defenders and the goalkeeper. I'd encountered players whose cleats had magic in them, whose on-field decisions were guided not by studious good judgment but by poetic inspiration, who made mistakes and then made those mistakes beautiful. And by junior year, I'd learned how to be better than most of these players. I became the midfielder who never stopped sprinting, who never got tired, who understood and systematically exploited the weaknesses in every opponent's passing game, ensuring that the ball more or less belonged to us, not to them. I went after it ruthlessly. I became not a poet of the sport but a destroyer of poets, outrunning and outmuscling the gifted ones, maintaining a stricter focus, and once I had the ball, always making the safe, sensible play. I wasn't much of a scorer and thus went somewhat underappreciated by our local fan-base of inappropriately invested yet still ignorant parents, but my teammates recognized my contributions and viewed me as a significant part of the team.

By senior year, I felt that I'd perfected my particular brand of soccer, which remained devoid of greatness though I now executed it almost completely without error; there was no reason, at this point, for me ever to make a mistake. My contribution was positive on each play, and I played well throughout the first day of tryouts.

Somehow I didn't notice Adam Nordmark until the second day. I had never seen him before, which meant that he was a freshman, which meant that he was irrelevant—I didn't care remotely about the future of the Weybridge Bears beyond my four-year career, and even the team's success within my own tenure wasn't particularly important to me. I cared about every moment of every game but not its result, not our record, not our achievements—yet after some time I'd noticed enough of my teammates pointing at this boy that I couldn't help but look too. Watching him, I found that he obviously stood out among his mostly talentless peers, but soon enough I'd managed to dismiss him as another golden-footed weakling, performing magic tricks with his legs while remaining indifferent to all that occurred on the field beyond the tiny radius he occupied, consumed by that stonerish sensual fascination with the ball itself as though it were an oversized Hacky Sack: he had long hair—a male physical trait for which I harbored a sort of Vietnam-era suspicion—that, dampened by sweat, lent his skinny frame the malignant character of a wet rat. He scored a lot of effortless twirling goals against inept defenses.

At the end of the third day, I was peeling off my tall nylon socks and putting on those ugly rubber Adidas sandals worn only by postgame soccer players and college kids taking showers in grimy shared dorm bathrooms when I saw Coach Carrell take Adam aside. I moved closer to listen.

"Son," he said, "how come you didn't play for the eighth-grade team last year?"

Coaches, I thought: the last remaining humans still addressing younger men as *son*.

"Oh, I don't know," Adam said. It was the first time I'd heard him talk, since he was one of those silent players on the field, offering no warning to blindsided teammates, no helpful advice: proof that he wasn't interested in the totality of soccer as a team game, cared only about his own graceful maneuverings, an issue not of selfishness—I too was selfish, playing only for myself—but of missing the point of the exercise.

"Where have you *been* playing?" Coach said.

"I've never really played before," Adam said.

"You've never played before?"

"Well, in gym class a few times."

"In gym class."

"Yeah, a few times."

"A few times."

Silence.

"OK, that's all I wanted to ask, Adam."

Adam walked off with an air of cheerful cluelessness, and I rolled my eyes, hoping he would look at me and notice: it was all a lie, of course, some mystical make-believe—of course he was an experienced player, more practiced than any of the other freshmen, it was obvious.

Among the seniors, meanwhile, the one who'd gotten worse was Matt Spruell, not because he'd stopped practicing—we'd practiced together— but because he'd lost his dog for good (I hadn't told him what I'd seen on Erwin Road, but enough time had passed for him to guess that Oscar was gone), and he remained in some weird psychological slump because of it. Drained of vivacity, he kicked the ball as though it were a frustrat- ingly empty whiskey bottle. He sucked: for once it felt like a blessing that I'd never successfully loved anyone or anything—I felt relatively em- powered, verging on indestructible.

Chapter Four

The first few days of school were pretty good, and by the end of the first week, I still hadn't bothered to learn my teachers' names. I was engaged in a sort of negative learning—soothing my anxieties in the warm bath of thoughtlessness that senior year had enabled, I sat in the classroom not to absorb knowledge but to expel it from my brain. It was a cleansing experience: I became as vacant as a high-level Buddhist and processed my school surroundings as a purely sensual environment—sniffing girls' perfumes with beatifically flared nostrils, getting lost staring into the yellows and pinks of their T-shirts and blouses as if to extricate the secret three-dimensional image within a Magic Eye poster, absorbing the drone of my teachers only as the white noise to my waking naps. The first round of pop quizzes came in, and although I didn't care much either way, I did fine. School, apparently, was a skill like anything else: you could get good enough at it to figure out the correct answers without knowing them. It was largely a question of cadence, rhythm, musicality—aided rather than impeded by the emptiness of my mind, I felt it out and put down what felt right, and usually it was right.

It was when school and soccer were over for the day that I began to feel very nervous about things.

On a Tuesday night, Matt called me and asked if I wanted to join him and some other kids at the Denny's on Route 18. At first I thought he wanted a ride, but it turned out he was already there. He and his friends weren't eating dinner; they were just hanging out in that charming teenage way that would command three hours of the waitress's attention for a bill that ultimately would come to six dollars and 72 cents—I could meet them over there, he suggested. I got in the car immediately and drove at least fifteen miles per hour over the speed limit for the brief duration of the trip.

Once I'd entered the restaurant, I spotted Matt, George Antonakis, Karen Brennan, Annie Klosinski, and Jillian Heller in a giant booth in the back corner, visibly reveling in the semi-adult thrill of being out on a weeknight for no reason except that they felt like it. It was something beyond uncommon for me to get invited to casually purposeless group hangouts—rare enough that I occasionally wondered whether they existed only in TV shows, where it was dramatically impossible to allow the characters to spend any significant time alone—so naturally I was so excited that I didn't even notice the Denny's hostess until I'd already passed her on my way to the table. More teenage insolence, she'd think. Deal with it, lady: I had *friends*.

I knew all five people a little and in fact had briefly talked to Jillian at Victor's party—I believed that she (fortunately) had left earlier than I had that night. George didn't play soccer, and I wondered whether Matt had recognized his recent athletic decline and, needing a mental break from his own failures, was inching away from our team socially—none of the three girls were jocks, either. I had the impression that I'd been called in only in order to even the count: three boys for three girls, the deliberate symmetry contradicting the ostensible casualness of the occasion—they might do this sort of thing every night, but it wasn't so long ago that they'd never done this sort of thing at all. I said hello and ordered a glass of orange juice. Annie and Karen were shit-talking a girl not present, discussing rumors that her boyfriend was cheating on her. It took me a minute to understand that they were talking about Emily Pomeroy, whom I knew about as well as I did the girls here.

"I actually sat next to Emily last year in Spanish," Annie said. "She was really weird. I remember I once coughed in class—like, once, just a random dry cough, not some long wheezing mucousy string of coughs. And she literally got up and asked the teacher if she could change seats with someone else because she didn't want to catch my cold. I didn't even have a cold! Coughs happen for no reason sometimes!"

George flung down his fork in semi-mock outrage. "What if you *had* had a cold, even? What made her think that someone else should take the seat next to you? Why should the teacher have believed that it was more important to protect *Emily's* health than that of any of her other students?"

"Yeah, she has to accept her luck of the draw like everyone else," Matt said. "I once spent a whole year in English sitting next to Caleb Lemke, who passed the time by digging in his ear for wax, finding huge golden chunks of it, and then eating it openly, right in front of everyone. I never complained once."

"Wow, that's so much worse than eating boogers," George said. "Eating boogers I can understand. They really don't taste that bad, if we can all be honest about it. Earwax tastes awful."

"I don't even understand how Caleb had that much earwax," Matt said. "It would have taken me a year to produce the amount of earwax he unearthed daily."

"It was just cycling through his body on an endless loop," George said. "Ear to mouth to stomach to ear again."

"Can we please stop talking about this?" Karen said.

"Did your Spanish teacher let Emily change seats or not?" Jillian said to Annie.

"No," Annie said. "She told her to sit down and be quiet. It was hilarious. After that I forced myself to cough four or five more times before the class was over, just to torture her."

I was almost too afraid to talk; I just stared at everyone very closely. We were all the same age, yet I sometimes found myself dumbstruck in the distant covetous manner of the elderly by the youthfulness of my classmates—the whiteness of their teeth and the suppleness of their flesh, the way their skin glowed with life even under the grayish overhead lights at Denny's. They were all ordinary-looking kids: lanky, friendly-faced Matt; George, a hairy Greek boy, the pale thin central gap of his carefully severed black unibrow unconvincing though cleanly plucked, suggestive rather of a bascule bridge opened momentarily for boat traffic; acne-stained Annie, like the before-photo of a model in a Proactiv commercial; Jillian, her straight blond hair somehow more banal than glamorous; slumped Karen, uncomfortable with her largeness, her broad shoulders pinched inward. Yet I was captivated by the movements of their mouths and limbs, each shift and twitch miraculous to me. They seemed to know how they animated and redeemed the irredeemable corporate spaces of our suburb, this town that after all existed solely for them, relied on them, would be purposeless without them—they talked louder than the other diners, not as an impoliteness but as a favor unconsciously performed. I steeled myself.

"I went to elementary school with Emily," I said. "In the third grade, she spent the whole year insisting that everyone refer to her by her first and middle names. She wouldn't answer to 'Emily.' It had to be 'Emily Grace.' She even bullied our teacher into saying her full name, every single time." It wasn't a bad contribution.

"Wow, 'Emily Grace,' what a precious darling," George said. "I think parents who name their kids after abstract concepts really need to get over themselves. Grace, Destiny, Faith, Joy, Hope—those shouldn't be allowed to be names."

"It's just a girl thing, too," Jillian said. "None of those are guys' names. 'Hi, I'm Serendipity Essence Johnson; this is my brother Bob.' So dumb."

"We have to represent all the ethereal qualities that nobody can actually live up to, and you just get to be guys," Annie said.

"'Serendipity Essence Johnson' just sounds like a black girl," Matt said. "It's a perfectly fine name. Stop being racist against black people."

"My brother said he had a girl named Prudence living in his dorm last year," I said. "I think he said she was from Iowa."

"Emily's parents should have named her Prudence," Matt said. "'Prude' for short."

"Yeah, I've heard she's a virgin," George said. "Tyler isn't getting any from her, that's why he's cheating."

"'Getting any'? Do people still use that phrase?" Karen said.

"How would *you* know whether Emily Grace is a virgin?" Annie said. "Did she tell you?"

"No, of course not," George said. "I barely know her."

"I didn't think so," Annie said.

"But I have it on good authority. Leo Klattenhoff told me," George said.

"Who?" Jillian said.

"Leo. You don't know him?" George said. "He and I were sort of friends in elementary school. He's like this repulsive little troll of a guy who knew the names and definitions of all the most disgusting sexual acts in the world before the rest of us even really knew what a vagina was. I'm talking about the kind of stuff that exists only on the most horrible parts of the internet."

"You mean like the 'Dirty Sanchez' or whatever?" Karen said.

"Sure," George said, "the Dirty Sanchez, the Rusty Nail, the Flying Camel, the Alabama Hot Pocket . . ."

"I'm not going to ask," Karen said.

"He's also like an encyclopedia on the sexual histories and proclivities of our female classmates," George said. "He knows which girls give blowjobs versus which only give handjobs. He knows which ones have never gone past first base and which ones have banged, like, every guy at our school except me. He knows what their bra size is, whether they trim their pubic hair, and what their vaginas smell like. The level of detail is incredible."

"I don't get it," Jillian said. "Like he's supposed to have been with all these girls personally? *I'm* a girl, and I literally don't even know who this guy is. I've never heard of him."

"No," George said, "I know he hasn't been with any of you ladies *personally*. He's disgusting, like I said. He's just, like, the supreme aggregator of secondhand sexual information."

"He's like one of those guys who can't throw a ball more than two feet but know the batting average of every MLB player ever. I bet he knows exactly how many guys each of you have hooked up with," Matt said, looking at Annie, then at Karen, then at Jillian.

"I think even I've lost track," Karen said. "Maybe I should ask him. I'd honestly like to know."

"Don't you think he's just making it all up?" Jillian said.

"No," George said, "his information always feels right. I mean, Emily Grace *is* definitely a virgin. All girls with the middle name 'Grace' are virgins, it's a well-known fact."

"Her family is religious, right?" Matt said.

"Maybe," George said, "But based on what Annie said, it sounds like she's just too much of a germaphobe to get that close to anyone."

"Semen is basically just snot from your testicles," Matt said. "It's probably nothing but germs. Bacteria so powerful that it can get you pregnant."

"Virginity is definitely the safest route if you don't want to get pregnant *or* a cold," Annie said.

Matt seemed cheerful—it was a good conversation, the kind I always imagined non-jocks had when I wasn't present, and maybe he'd finally gotten over Oscar, his suckiness at soccer in fact an unrelated non-psychological phenomenon. He seemed engaged, his old joviality not merely returned but sharpened into a truer sense of humor by the others' wit.

"Man, virgins are the worst," George said. "They disgust me, honestly."

"That's kind of an obnoxious thing to say," Jillian said.

"Well, it's true," George said. "I can't believe there are people who still think that abstinence is a proof of moral virtue. It's just like this self-obsessive neurotic power play for closed-off, ungenerous people. It's actually morally repulsive."

"I really don't think that describes every girl who hasn't lost her virginity yet," Jillian said.

I tried not to look at the floor during this part of the conversation, but my eyes strayed, anyway, to the fuzzless green cheap-motel carpet strewn with stale gray French fries.

"Have you ever felt like it might be time for society to get rid of the word 'virginity'?" Karen said. "I mean, it kind of implies a specific idea of sexuality that almost no one holds anymore, but everyone still uses the word without thinking about it. 'I lost my virginity'—what exactly did you lose?"

"You're right, the whole concept shouldn't exist," Annie said. "I mean, do people still think there's an actual difference between someone who's had sex and someone who hasn't? We don't designate two whole separate states of being for, like, people who have flown in airplanes and people who haven't. Sex is presented in a way where you think you'll be a totally different person after you do it, but that just isn't true. You aren't magically transformed."

"I agree," Jillian said. "There are a million ways you can be experienced or inexperienced in life. Sexual virginity is basically irrelevant to being an adult. No one can even agree on what it means anyway—who qualifies as a virgin, who doesn't, how much touching of mouths and genitals you can get away with without altering your status."

"I was thinking more about how the term kind of equates sexual inexperience with, like, freshness and purity," Karen said. "Like women who've had sex are fallen, sullied, whatever. That's the offensive part to me. I feel like word 'virginity' was probably invented by a pedophile."

"Yeah, it's like there's something wrong with us now," Annie said. "We're broken and undesirable. *Deflowered*—gross! But of course guys all desperately *want* you to do this supposedly ruinous thing. It's such a fucked-up state of affairs."

I thought about this for a moment—how, in reality, the emotional experience of "virginity" played out exactly in reverse of the narrative implied by the word: it was being a virgin, in fact, that made you feel tainted, as though there were something wrong with you, as though you were infected with a disease that no one would risk catching, when all you wanted was nothing more than to achieve a state of human naturalness by participating in that most human of behaviors, that proof that you were a person just like every other person in human history. I hadn't believed Annie when she'd said that there was no difference between people who hadn't had sex and people who had; I was *counting* on this miraculous difference, counting on the rabbit hole of my unimaginable future partner's vagina to suck me into a new world of self-assuredness. Ideally, a chemical reaction registered by my whole body would take place the moment my dick made first contact; my internal organs would shift, click into place, find their stability. I knew it was this hyperbolic, high-stakes thinking that made the act seem impossible to me, made me feel hopeless and certain that it would never happen—but if sex was not magical (and therefore not impossible), what was the point of it, anyway? If the entirety of my mental distress—distilled suddenly to a serum intermixed with my come—was not going to discharge itself, never to return, during my first coital ejaculation, what did it matter? From my blind vantage point, it all seemed to matter *so much.*

I looked at my tablemates again, their faces, their fingers on the grease-spotted Formica. Did Karen, Annie, Matt, Jillian, and George really have the answers? Had everyone at Denny's but me actually had sex, or was somebody else harboring a dark dirty secret?

"You know, as a guy, I don't think any of those virginity-loss connotations apply," Matt said. "Losing your virginity is, like, purely awesome. No downside from any perspective."

"It's true. We men are already of this earth," George said. "That's why our parents don't name us Angel or Chastity."

"Latino guys are sometimes named Angel," Jillian said. "Stop being racist against Latinos."

Matt laughed; it took me a moment longer to realize that Jillian had deliberately referred back to Matt's previous line about racism—I felt socially unpracticed, too slow to comprehend basic jokes. Jillian took out her iPhone, pushed the circular button to illuminate it, frowned.

"Shit," she said. "I'm officially out past curfew."

I smiled involuntarily—I'd never had a curfew myself and was smiling not out of smugness but from the whiff of quaintness not only within the word *curfew* itself but, more generally, within the elaborate rules and rituals that parents (not mine) invented supposedly to maintain order and safety among their children but really, I suspected, in order to lend a greater tangibility to their family life and create a stronger shared interior world. I imagined, within the Heller household, embarrassing holiday customs and birthday traditions and their particular gravitational pull of sentimentality, comfort, and dread; a well-memorized list of ceremonial daily chores for the kids to do; a mandatory weekly family movie night in which everybody piled onto the couch together to watch a DVD (something terrible that everyone in the family had already seen twice, rented somehow from the ghost of the Blockbuster Video on Club Boulevard, as if Netflix had never been invented)—and then I saw a mental image of my own home, in which each family member wore headphones in a separate room, streaming superior content on his or her own iPad: not so much unhappy as inadequate, this image bore its own resonance, inseparable from its inadequacy and the way its happiness wounded and implicated me. My parents had never imposed a curfew because they knew I was incapable of having any real fun even without any strictures to prohibit it—but what if they'd had the kindness to pretend, the insight to realize that their love would have been more strongly felt if manifested as some pain-in-the-ass artificial system of domestic domination?

"Your curfew is nine?" I said. "That's a little harsh."

"It used to be a little less strict," Jillian said, "but I got in trouble over the summer for going to too many parties and staying out too late, and my parents started telling me once or twice a week, kind of arbitrarily, that I wasn't allowed to go out. So a couple weeks ago, I snuck out to Victor Bogdan's party and got caught coming back in. Now I have a nine o'clock curfew every night, except Friday and Saturday, where it's ten."

"How'd you get caught?" Annie said. "I remember how you used to climb in through your bedroom window whenever we stayed out late."

"Well, yeah, that was always the system," Jillian said. "Every night, my dad checks to make sure the doors are all locked, usually around nine. He's very consistent about it, like a security guard making his rounds or something—he kind of shuffles around the house with this air of purpose and authority, battening down the hatches, making sure that all the downstairs lights are shut off and that there aren't any dirty dishes left in the sink or any criminals lurking behind the sofa. There's no crime in our neighborhood—I think locking up just gives him an enjoyable feeling of being, like, a responsible homeowner, a man, whatever. So usually I leave the window in my bedroom unlatched if I think I'm going to get back later than I want him to know about. He doesn't really check my room, which is on the second floor, because he kind of respects my privacy to a weird degree, like he's actually sort of afraid of girls or something, the unknowable world of Barbie dolls and tampons that he thinks we inhabit. Technically I could go in through the garage door, because I know the key-code, but it's too loud. He'd wake up, so instead I climb in through my bedroom window from the railing on the front porch—it's pretty easy."

"That actually sounds terrifying," Karen said.

"It's not so bad. On the night of Victor's party, though, Melanie wanted to come with me—Melanie's my little sister," Jillian said, seeming to address me specifically. "She's a sophomore and doesn't really have any friends except for the boy who lives down the street, Aaron, who she's always been *desperately* in love with, but even though they hang out together all the time, I think he doesn't view her in a romantic way, and she's too afraid to tell him her real feelings—it'd actually be pretty adorable in a shitty-teen-movie way if it didn't cause her to spend all her time moping in my bedroom, asking me whether I think boys will ever notice her, and should she try being less of a tomboy or a geek or whatever. Anyway, Melanie was in my room when I was getting ready to leave for the party, and she asked me if she could come with me, and I said no because she's too young to be drinking, which obviously is unavoidable at that kind of party. She got mad, but I left without her anyway, and when I got back, I tried to sneak in through the window, which I'd left unlatched, and to my surprise I found out that it wouldn't budge—Melanie had locked it behind me."

"What a jerk!" Karen said.

"I know!" Jillian said. "It was unbelievable. I had to come in through the garage, and of course my dad woke up, and I got in trouble. The next day I confronted Melanie about it, and she just laughed and laughed like it was some kind of hilarious prank. Now she checks my window *every time* I go out to make sure it's locked—if it isn't, she'll lock it, trying to get me caught past curfew again. It hasn't happened, at least not till just now, maybe, but I really want to get her back for what she did that night."

"Get her back how?" Annie said.

"I don't know," Jillian said. "I guess I'm not much of a prankster. Melanie is always playing these awful practical jokes on me, and I never have any response. I feel like I don't have the creativity for it. I remember once, when we were kids, I was watching TV with Melanie, and I was drinking a glass of Diet Coke when my phone rang, and I answered it and went to my bedroom for privacy, leaving the soda behind. I was addicted to Diet Coke at the time and drank, like, at least a liter of it every day. When I got back to the den, Melanie was still there, and I sat down next to her and took a gulp of my drink—there were only a few ounces left—and this horrible intense salty taste suddenly hit me, and I immediately had to run to the sink and throw up. It turned out that Melanie had dumped out the Diet Coke and refilled the glass with soy sauce while I was gone. It was literally the most disgusting moment of my life."

"Wow," George said. "Your little sister is an evil genius."

"This is why she can't get a boyfriend," Jillian said. "She's totally lacking in, like, girlish sweetness. She'll be so delighted if I get in trouble for staying out late again."

"Maybe you can still get home before your dad locks all the doors if we leave right now," Karen said.

"Maybe," Jillian said. "Sometimes he doesn't do his nightly rounds till like 9:15 or 9:20. If I got back before then, he probably wouldn't even know I'd been gone."

I looked at my phone: 9:08.

"I don't want to make you leave early, though," Jillian said to Karen.

"I could just drop you off and come right back," Karen said. "It's not far."

"No, it's not that big a deal," Jillian said. "I'll probably just get grounded for a couple days. It's probably unavoidable."

A notion occurred to me, an idea by which I might make an impression at least on one person after a conversation in which I'd contributed virtually nothing. It was Jillian's story about climbing into her bedroom through the window—whatever the reason—that had made me feel, stupidly, that we might have a sort of kinship: I decided to try something.

"I'm going to have to get going in a few minutes," I said. "I have to do some studying tonight. If you want, you can come with me."

I looked at her. She looked back but didn't say anything.

"We can leave now if you want," I said, "and I'll drop you off on my way home."

"Really?" Jillian said. "You have to go anyway? But you just got here."

"It's no problem," I said, and before she could protest further I opened my wallet and pulled out a five-dollar bill and put it on the table and stood up.

"Well, OK. I think it's worth a try," she said. "Thank you. See you later, guys."

I waved to the others as we walked out, and she followed me into the parking lot. I considered opening the passenger door of my car for her but ruled against it—too formal, weird. We got in.

"Your car is so clean," she said. "It feels like a rental car."

"Where do you live?" I said.

"Eleven Branchwood Drive."

"I don't know where that is."

"It's off Montvale Road."

"I don't know where that is either."

"I'll tell you where to go."

She gave me directions, and I hastily turned on the radio to cover up my usual practice of driving in absolute silence, which struck me now as the habit of a serial killer. Staticky sports-talk burbled forth from my speakers; I had no idea which channel played music for young people. I spun the dial once or twice, then lowered the volume until the sound had no discernible content, was only sound. It took us less than five minutes to get to Jillian's house, and I parked on the street.

"I feel like I should stay until you get into the house safely," I said. "It seems like things could go badly."

"Actually, come with me," she said. "If the doors are already locked, I'll have to try the window, and if the window is locked, I'll need you to help me down. Climbing up is easy, but climbing down is actually pretty scary."

She exited the car, and this time I followed her. She lived in a beige, vinyl-sided house, squat-looking though two-storied, and she was moving quickly across its front lawn, not toward the front door but toward the side of the house, where we turned the corner once and then again, into the backyard, now almost running until we reached the patio. From there we crept silently to the backdoor, and I stood back in the dark as she pulled on it fruitlessly.

"Already locked," she said.

She was running again now, back around the house, slowing as she reached the front porch, climbed its two steps, and then pushed herself up (first with her arms, then swinging her right leg high) onto the decorative hand-railing. Again, I remained behind her, this time a little closer, acting vaguely as her spotter, wondering whether I would really be able to catch her if she fell.

From the railing, she moved her left leg onto the shutter of a downstairs window, grasping the bottom of what must have been her own bedroom's double window above with her left hand, and then pushing and pulling her way up—all pretty gracefully, I thought—until she could reach it with her right hand, too. I had shifted to the gravel ground below and watched as her right hand sought to raise the lower pane; it didn't move.

"Goddammit," she said. "Can you please help me down?"

"What should I do?" I said.

"Just, like, hold my foot while I transfer my weight back to the railing."

I took her sneaker in my right hand, and then I felt her pressing down, first a little, then a lot, and then it was over. She hopped down from the railing and retreated a little from the house.

"We need a new plan," I said. By now we'd wandered back to the opposite side of my car, a buffer between us and her parents.

"I don't have any other plan," she said. "I just hate getting into trouble with my parents. Not really even because of the consequences—it's just embarrassing and annoying to be reminded that I'm in a position where I can still 'get in trouble with my parents.' I feel like I'm too old to be grounded. It's mortifying."

"Everything about parents is always humiliating," I said. "Just having them at all."

We stood around for a little while. I surveyed her neighborhood: wealthier than Matt's, less wealthy than mine, the houses a little smaller though roughly the same distance apart.

"What was your sister's name again?" I said.

"Melanie," she said.

"And the boy she's in love with?"

"Aaron."

"Which house is Aaron's?"

She pointed at the home three doors down, on the other side of the street, a gray split-level. I was thinking very hard—I felt intrigued by Jillian's sister's crush, by the concept of a girl actually being in love with a boy who lived on the same street, a boy alongside whom she presumably walked home from the bus stop every single day: a trope of pop songs, I thought, not a reality I'd ever heard of before—teenage love borne of actual closeness and familiarity rather than of ignorance, not a product of the romanticized unknown that constituted adolescent desire as I had mostly witnessed and experienced it, in the form of a daydream of another person that, with any luck, might occasionally collide with another person's daydream of you ... without intermingling, even so. I thought of Melanie, who had a known object within view at which she could direct her bedroom-window longing during the night, and I wondered whether my own neighborhood might seem completely different if I loved someone inside it. The plan that entered my brain might possibly strike Jillian as insane; I decided to pitch it to her anyway.

"What if Aaron texted Melanie and asked her to sneak out?" I said. "Would she come outside?"

"Yeah, I guess," Jillian said. "What's the point, though?"

"Well, in that case, she'd have to leave some way for herself to get back into the house, which you could use to get back in, too," I said.

"OK, but how would we get Aaron to text Melanie?" she said, more engaged.

The fact of her talking, I thought—not as a performance or as a courtesy to me, but as an unselfconscious earnest effort to glean information, to figure out whether I was an idiot or whether I held an idea that could be useful to her: I loved this. I didn't care whether she got in trouble with her parents; it was her caring that mattered, and my being involved in it.

"Well, we could go over to his house and ask him to," I said.

"You mean just, like, ring the doorbell?"

"Sure."

"He's probably tucked away in bed."

"Isn't he a sophomore? It's not even 9:30."

"He's a very sweet coddled little boy. That's why he doesn't want to date my terrifying sister."

"Well, I'll try it if you don't want to. You said that one's his house, right?"

"Seriously? You're crazy."

With feigned confidence—or maybe real confidence, I couldn't tell—I plucked my backpack from the backseat of my car and marched down the street to Aaron's house. On my back, I felt Jillian follow me for a few steps, but she trailed off before I crossed Aaron's property line. I went straight across the grass for the front door and rang the bell. I couldn't believe what I was doing—even so, I was doing it.

I stood there for about a half a minute before a middle-aged guy in sweatpants opened the door. He was shorter than I was and probably weighed fifteen pounds less: adults were becoming more and more pathetic-looking as I got older—it was more sad than it was a relief. We looked at each other—I hadn't figured out what I ought to say.

"Hi, sir, I'm really sorry to bother you so late at night," I said, "but would it be possible for Aaron to come to the door for a second?"

He stared at me with mild contemptuous indifference, then shouted his son's name in the general direction of the staircase behind him and wandered back to whatever deep sofa recess he'd emerged from. Aaron —the boy who apparently was Aaron—appeared a moment later at the top of the staircase, looked down quizzically at the opened front door, and approached very slowly as I waved hello. He was a bespectacled, diminutive boy, a cuter version of his father, wearing a baby blue T-shirt and black gym shorts and flip-flops.

"Hey, Aaron," I said once he'd come close enough to hear without my shouting. "I'm here with your neighbor Jillian Heller, and we need to borrow your phone to contact her sister Melanie. Do you have her number?"

"I don't understand," Aaron said, in the recently and seemingly excessively deepened voice of a fifteen-year-old. "Who are you?"

"Oh, I'm Jeff," I said, and I motioned frantically for Jillian to come to me. Once she'd made it to the door, Aaron seemed to calm down.

"Hi, Jillian," he said, his voice suddenly now a shy prepubescent whisper.

"Hi, Aaron," she said.

"What's going on? Don't you have Melanie's number?" he said.

"Her phone is broken," I said. "She dropped it in the toilet earlier tonight. She needs to text Melanie to get back into her house because she stayed out past curfew, and her parents locked all the doors."

Jillian was silent for a moment. "That's right," she said.

Aaron wasn't convinced. "Don't you have a phone?" he said.

"Mine's out of battery," I said. "We just need to borrow yours for, like, three minutes. You can come with us if you want."

He still seemed skeptical, but he looked once more to Jillian. "Fine," he said.

He handed me his iPhone, and the three of us—all feeling equally bizarre, probably—marched back toward the Heller residence. I opened Aaron's contact list, found Melanie, and created a new text message. The cursor blinked at me, and I typed the first thing I thought of: "melanie, i love you, please meet me outside your front door."

I showed it to Jillian.

"That's really mean," she said.

"It's the prank you never thought of," I said. "It's perfect."

Was it? Probably not, but who knew?

Jillian smiled, first just a little, then more. "I like it."

The phone buzzed with Melanie's message: "when?"

I could almost feel the hot nervous breath of the girl on the other end —her shocked, frantically beating heart: she'd fallen for it. "right now, i am here," I typed.

We were all three still at the curb bordering Jillian's front yard.

"You should go wait by the door," I said to Jillian. "Make sure she doesn't see you."

Herself a little breathless, Jillian said again that I was crazy, this time definitely as a sort of compliment, I thought, and she dashed up the grass to the front porch, pressing herself against the wall beside the door as though she were a ninja-assassin waiting to slice the throat of whoever came out. I handed the phone back to Aaron and pulled him behind my car, at which point I ducked, and he was so confused that he could only follow my lead and duck too. We looked at each other: he seemed like a good-spirited kid, not especially annoyed even though he was smart enough to know that we'd lied to him, maybe even a little excited to be out on some inexplicable adventure with two *seniors* on a school night.

For a moment nothing happened. Then I heard a door open, and then the door shut, and there was nothing again. The silence was a little scary with the knowledge that we shared it, perhaps, with another, unseen person.

I could only imagine what had happened: Melanie had come out, Jillian had slipped in and shut the door behind her—it had all worked. Warily I rose up, my eyes now just above the hood of the car.

It took me a moment to notice a human form, hair brown, legs in pajama pants, standing alone, face pointed in one direction, then the other: Melanie, still looking for the boy, maybe, not yet fully comprehending our ruse. Possibly she hadn't seen Jillian slip past her, thinking a breeze had shut the door behind her. She craned her neck in one direction and the other. Then she sat down on the steps, her back hunched, and I ducked again and looked at Aaron; it occurred to me that the strangeness of the situation I'd invented was likely only beginning, and it had now become a very bad strangeness. Jillian was gone—Melanie was left.

But I couldn't stay down. I peeked out again: the same girl, the same posture—it was a posture of pain, I realized. I saw a slight shivering of the white arms that stuck out from a small gray T-shirt, heard what sounded like a small whimper. I wondered whether Jillian had *locked* the door after flinging herself inside—whether Melanie was not only lovelorn but now also stranded. Aaron was beginning to shift uneasily within his crouch. I bent down once more, put a hand on his shoulder. He had wonderful, kind eyes behind his glasses. I tried to think. Could he really not be in love with Jillian's sister? Could he really allow a girl three doors down—a best friend from childhood, a girl he'd seen laugh and cry—to love him without loving her back? Having seen her awkward lonely despair from a distance, I'd extrapolated an inner vulnerability that was sentimentally irresistible: he probably loved her and just didn't know it, could not make the imaginative leap between their chaste geeky hangouts—the jokes, the video games, the study sessions—and having his tongue or his penis suddenly inside her, this real person whom he cared about, not a movie star or a porn star or a model.

"Aaron," I said, "have you ever been, like, assigned to read a book for English class, like maybe *Catcher in the Rye* or *The Great Gatsby* or one of those types of books, and you really don't want to read it because it's kind of been forced onto you, so you're very resistant at first, but when you finally do read it, you have this very strange feeling that it's not only actually very good and interesting but that it's actually speaking *for* you—or, better yet, *from* you: that is, this author who's never met you or laid eyes on you is saying all the secret things that are inside you, that you didn't know were inside you or you couldn't admit to knowing?"

"No," he said.

"Me neither," I said. "I hated both of those books. But my English teacher once told us that that sort of thing happens sometimes. So with that in mind, please look at the text message I sent to Melanie from your phone."

He pressed the round button, slid the right-facing arrow, and pressed the green and white icon. His face slackened, then tightened.

"What the fuck!" he said, keeping his voice lowered. "Why the fuck would you do that?"

"It's kind of complicated," I said.

"Who the fuck *are* you?"

"I'm really not even sure. My name's Jeff Conwell. I'm a senior."

We stared at each other, then turned away. I peeped once more at Melanie in the distance, still crying, probably.

"I'm Aaron Grasso," he said.

"Maybe I'm kind of like your guardian angel," I said. "You know what I mean?"

I felt almost dizzy, like I was learning a new dance.

"Just stand up," I said. "She's right there. Just tell her how you really feel."

"Are you serious?" he said.

"Sure. There's never been a better time. Honestly, it shouldn't have taken you this long. She doesn't have to know that I was the one who sent the message."

"My parents are probably wondering where I went."

"It doesn't matter. They'll be fine. Listen: I'm helping you out. You just needed a little help."

His big eyes were on me again. I looked away, and then I looked back, and now he was rising up. He stood straight, looking surprisingly tall from where I was crouched. He didn't say anything. And then he waved, not to me, and then he waited, and his facial features changed in some indescribable way. I wanted to stand up too, to see Melanie, but it would have made no sense for me to do so: one side of their silent conversation would have to suffice. Now he was smiling with some mixture of nervousness and serenity, his eyebrows slightly arched upward. And then he stepped out completely from behind the car, walked toward the house, and disappeared from my sight. A moment later, I heard his voice, then the voice of a girl, both in whispers. I couldn't make anything out.

As quietly as I could, I opened the door to my car and slid inside. My head lowered, not bothering to buckle up, I started the car and drove away, terrified. How had I done this? It wasn't me. It was something so much better.

Chapter Five

I had my driving test on a Saturday—I drove myself there, unaccompanied. Nobody knew I was there.

It was my fifth time taking the road test, and after my first failure, I'd become so scared of failing again—and so unwilling to accept that failure—that, through extensive research, I'd found someone on the internet capable of creating a fake driver's license for me so that, if I messed up a second time, I wouldn't have to come home to my parents empty-handed once more, unable still to receive the ceremonial paternal handoff of the keys to the 2007 BMW 4 Series—the "Bratmobile," as I would someday call it if ever I became secure enough to make self-deprecating Batman-related jokes in public reference to my family's affluence and the degree to which it had made me a disgusting non-human—that my dad had recently vacated in part to upgrade to a new Lexus hybrid but also to give me an undeserved seventeenth birthday present, its extravagance owing less to his overwhelming love or generosity than to a kind of lazy disinclination to find an appropriate car for me. The first fuckup was just a fluke, but now my confidence was ruined—hence the fabricated license, which looked authentic except insofar as I'd chosen a more flattering headshot than the DMV would conceivably have provided. I believed that, in the hours leading up to my repeat exam, having it on me as a backup would create a sense of security that would allow me to pass the test for real: I'd gone to all the shady effort of purchasing the fake ID— PayPaling a stranger, emailing him to confirm that, yes, I really wanted the license to say that I was seventeen rather than 21 (I was the first customer to make this request)—not with any actual intention of using it but solely to give myself sufficient psychological wiggle room in which to parallel-park in comfort: my anxiety reduced, I expected to pass the test and throw the $200 falsification in the trash.

That didn't happen; I forgot to use my turn signal—not only on one turn, but throughout the test, on every turn. Out of sheer depression, I considered tossing out the counterfeit license anyway, but then again, I really wanted to drive—I still held that pre-seventeen romantic vision of life with a car, of freedom, most importantly of connection: an entryway into the world. If I ever got pulled over by a cop, I'd be in unimaginable trouble, but the forgery was more than convincing enough for my mom and dad. Three months later, I was still driving without an actual license —I'd kind of gotten to the point where I'd forgotten that my fake ID was fake, and I drove around in a dreamy state of suspended anxiety, occupying an alternate realm in which passing the road test was somehow not a prerequisite to lawfully operating a motor vehicle in the state of New Jersey: an illusion that came crashing down only when it came time for me to retake the exam, which I periodically did, with the full force of the built-up terror not only of the test but of the precarious situation that I inhabited day-to-day now crashing down on me as I prepared to face the examiner, making the ordeal impossible.

I kept failing. It was incredible: the missed stop signs, ignored speed limits—I even forgot to put on my seatbelt once.

I'd had the same examiner three out of the first four times: Justin, a genial black dude in his thirties who, by the fifth test, had become the guy whom I would have had to envision if, in some other situation, I'd accidentally said something racist and then had had to explain that "one of my best friends" was black. Our names were alliterative, and we'd now spent a fair amount of time in close proximity, under the sort of trying circumstances that forged deep bonds. On the day of the fifth test, a mild rain was falling melancholically, and in the parking lot of the Edison driving school Justin and I sat together in the car.

"I know you can do it this time, Jeff," Justin said. "Just take it easy."

"I appreciate your confidence," I said.

"I know you know what to do. It's just a matter of staying calm and being thoughtful and attentive. You can do it."

With earnest determination, I looked him in the eye, and then I started the car and exited the parking lot, waiting for a sizable gap in the highway traffic, and then we made the usual circuit through the quiet suburban streets hidden off the side of Route 27, stopping at that one weird empty patch near the railroad tracks where the cones were already set up to delimit a parallel-parking space for aspiring license-holders. I could feel all my movements, the blood in my fingertips, the contractions of my intestines—even so, I got it just right, gliding perfectly into the area between the cones with unhesitating buttery finesse. I actually wasn't a bad driver; I'd just temporarily forgotten how to drive four times.

As far as could tell, I'd done everything right, though I'd equally believed this once or twice before, until Justin had informed me of my errors. I could have gleaned my fate from the look on his compassionate face as we cruised toward the finish line, but I didn't dare take my eyes off the road for a moment. The test was almost over; we were driving down an empty stretch of Sycamore Avenue, maybe a quarter of a mile from the end of the course. I was feeling mostly good. And then something bad happened.

When I say that the Ford Fiesta into which my vehicle collided "came out of nowhere," I mean it not in the usual sense employed by careless drivers, who actually mean that, at least for a split-second, they failed to pay attention to the road and in that moment another car quickly emerged, or that it popped up from a blind spot they'd failed to check, or that it made an unlikely move and crossed their path from an odd direction. What I mean, quite literally, is that it was not there and then it was, that it appeared not quite as if by magic—not with a bolt of lightning or a puff of smoke—but rather as if spliced in by a film editor indifferent to continuity. I was looking straight ahead, yet somehow, allegedly, I failed to see this bright green Ford Fiesta—straight ahead, right in front of me—until I was about four feet away, cruising slowly into its bumper, brakes slammed only milliseconds before the minor crash: it was, in fact, not a failure of my own but a glitch of the world itself, as what had occurred was impossible.

I had to stay in the car while Justin got out and talked to the other driver, a pale gray-haired man in a wrinkled brown button-up shirt. As it turned out, there wasn't any damage, except possibly to my long-term will to live. Afterward, I could recall not so much the sound of impact as the look on Justin's face when I turned to him—yet his countenance of pitying disgust and sympathetic exhaustion should by all rights have been one of shock and terror, directed not at me but at the green car into which we'd smashed: hadn't he seen that it had materialized from nothing, as if it had arrived by teleportation?

I wanted at first to protest on behalf of the laws of physics, but I didn't: the fatalism was setting in. Of course I didn't get my license. Sometime later, as I left the facility, I realized I was destined never to get one, would instead have to pay for another fake ID when my provisional fake ID expired, would never get to be an actual documented adult person, would never have a black friend. What had happened? I was doubting my sanity more than my vision—or not so much doubting it, at this point, as hopelessly seeking to employ my own faulty brain to gauge the extent of the gaps in its soundness, wondering whether I could fight on with some weird semi-functional patchwork life of half-truth and half-hallucination, clinging to actuality as best I could, or whether I should just kind of give up and allow the remaining shreds of reality to fold, releasing me into the bliss of complete disconnection and incomprehension. Ultimately I shrugged: there had never been a time when everything about me had not been fucked in some way—just keep moving, I thought. Just keep driving.

. . . .

In the following days all I really wanted was for Matt to call me and ask me if I wanted to come out to another low-end chain restaurant or diner where we—along with George, Jillian, Annie, and Karen—would sit and drink refillable nonalcoholic beverages and discuss life. But after a couple weeks in which no one invited me out, I began to see that the evening at Denny's was meant to exist for me solely as evidence of what I was missing in my high school years, a one-time-only demonstration of the somehow unreachable network of low-key everyday friendship that sustained the intelligent, healthy adolescents who constituted the large part of Weybridge High's student body. My spontaneously spectacular behavior with Jillian and Aaron and Melanie felt like something that someone else had done, or else a kind of exception that proved the rule of my own shittiness. Meanwhile, I'd returned to my regularly scheduled programming of jerking off in the evenings to streaming misogynistic hardcore group sex videos: ten guys on one girl, that sort of thing—a preference that I came to see as an especially odd manifestation of my low self-regard, as a consequence of which I consistently failed while viewing one-on-one encounters to sustain the necessary imaginative act of pornography, wherein the male actor's dick becomes a re-embodiment of one's own, although this *was* possible for me during crude, horrifying gangbang videos in which the faceless male performers seemed not so much to have been personally selected by a discriminating female partner as to be benefitting from an open-door policy; essentially, I was incapable of picturing a situation in which a woman would want to have sex with me specifically, and the best I could do instead was to picture a woman who was willing to have sex with everyone and to imagine that I might be in the right place at the right time. I tried not to download anything containing explicit violence—real or simulated—or an excess of verbal abuse, and at least a modicum of enthusiasm on the part of the female performer—real or (almost certainly) simulated—was obligatory for me to be interested, or so I told myself. Even so, I was apparently a monster, and I felt it pre-climax as a sort of minor nausea that I forced myself to ignore and then as full-on despair that necessitated afterward that I watch several reruns of Nickelodeon cartoons from my childhood in order to return to a more innocent mental space. I continued to respond to these Nicktoons surprisingly directly, enjoying them as if I still belonged to their target demographic, even with the semen not yet dry on my tissue: being a teenager was weird—I'd become not so much an incipient adult as a repulsive, perverted, sad child.

Having completed this cycle on a Wednesday night, I was looking out the window into the autumn moonlight with a dumb, blank, mouth-open, hand-in-underpants bovine stare, my gaze as deeply vacant as that which it perceived, the filled-up nothingness of my suburban environs. I hadn't bothered to close the curtains during my private activities—the window was positioned so that I could see the backyards of my next-door neighbors and the edges of their homes, but mostly it looked out on a thread of trees and bramble that separated the properties on my street from those on the next cul-de-sac over, which was served by the same collector road: fake nature into which deer occasionally strayed, looking confused, and a thin reproduction of country-life seclusion that functioned only if you ignored the bluish TV glow that bled from the windows of the rear neighbors' homes through the branches and leaves of the oaks and spruces—and yet the seclusion also was real, simply because no one in our neighborhood was interested in anyone else: I had the total privacy of the world's indifference.

It was a landscape of shallow oily blackness punctured by small but inescapable electrical intrusions. I waited for some flicker of change, something that would have allowed me to say that I'd *observed* something, and then, shockingly, I saw it.

There was a fire in the woods. It had appeared as suddenly as the green Ford on Sycamore Avenue, in a spot I'd held in view the whole time—not a spontaneous wildfire but a small, controlled blaze, as steady as a lightbulb. I watched it for a minute, the gray smoke rising up against the darker sky, and then I put on shoes, left my bedroom, and went outside.

As I walked toward the trees, I tried to remember the last time I'd actually set foot in my own backyard; I couldn't recall—the rectangular green expanse was useless, neither large enough for recreation nor attractive enough for relaxation, existing solely in accordance with the mores of suburban living, wherein one *had* to have a backyard as a symbol of American prosperity even if it bore no function. In a few strides the property had ended, dirt and moss replacing the grass as I came closer to the flame. It made no sense: it looked like a campfire, sticks piled underneath the blaze, as though some Appalachian thru-hiker had wandered seventy miles off-trail and, like the deer that I occasionally spotted, had mistaken our subdivision's contrived suggestion of woodland for an actual forest, in which he might set up a tent and roast some hot dogs.

I was standing almost directly in front of the fire when I noticed that someone else was standing beside it. I turned to my right, a little too confused to feel alarmed, and saw a girl of roughly my own age—at first she was just a girl, and the shock and import of that felt like sufficient information, but she was looking at me, not speaking, and, looking back, I recognized her dark hair and her green eyes and the golden sunburst that surrounded her pupils within the minty irises, a detail I thought I'd invented. I'd seen her before, at Victor's end-of-summer party for a moment, had almost bumped into her and had regretted not doing so —and here she was again, illuminated by the fiery radiance, the same person.

"Hi, Jeff," she said, finally.

"Hi," I said. "What are you doing here?"

"I'm not doing anything," she said. "What are *you* doing?"

It took me a moment to notice that she had no business knowing my name, that indeed her insertion of my never-stated name into her greeting was intended to be an obvious and menacing tipoff that she possessed some detailed malevolent plan of which I was ignorant—I had failed to pick up the cue. But nothing about the situation *felt* malevolent; if anything, it seemed friendly, and so far I felt more physically comfortable in the proximity of this girl than I did around most girls.

"Did you start this?" I said, pointing to the fire.

She nodded.

"How?"

She shrugged. "Wood, friction, heat? It's not a big deal."

"But why?"

"I wanted to get your attention."

"By starting a fire?"

"It worked, didn't it?"

Something about the fire was unreal, I thought: the brightness and height of it seemed disproportionate to the tiny collection of sticks from which it supposedly arose, and the flame was cohesive and unwavering to an unnatural degree.

"I don't understand," I said. "Do we know each other?"

When I'd seen her at the party, I'd assumed that we went to the same school but had never had a class together—it was a big place, with more than 800 kids in my class alone, and it was therefore nearly impossible to know everyone, which was really the great joy of Weybridge High: the false but enticing promise of its undiminishing potential for new discovery and self-reinvention. I almost couldn't imagine going to school in a truly small town, where by the fifth grade, you already thoroughly knew everyone you'd ever know until college, and they all knew you, and no new face would ever emerge to see you differently or to be seen differently. (But on the other hand, there was in the small town perhaps the comfort of being known, of not being anonymous, as well as some greater likelihood that, if your peers were truly stuck with you in their orbit forever, they might be inclined to dig deeper, to forgive certain things, to look past the surface—none of these phrases meant anything real to me as it was—instead of subjecting you to the usual quick dismissal of those who had plenty of other options. I wondered.)

"Well, I know you a little bit," she said, "but you don't seem to know me all that well. You don't seem to know anyone that well."

"What's your name?" I said.

"I'm Catherine Harding. We were in the same technology elective in seventh grade. You don't remember?"

I knew the class she was talking about and tried to reimagine the classroom itself, the teacher, my chair, the light fixtures above us and their glare on the aged desktop monitors, the students beside me. I could recall a cute dark-haired girl on the left side of the room but nothing about her.

"Maybe," I said. "What do you want with me now?"

"I just wanted to talk a little," she said.

"About some class we were in five years ago? I honestly have no idea what is going on here," I said, somehow grinning as I said it—inadvertently, possibly with genuine pleasure.

"We're talking," she said.

"About what?"

"About anything. I just wanted to talk to you finally. I've been kind of watching you a lot. Haven't you noticed?"

"I don't think so. What was I supposed to notice?"

"You haven't noticed that things have been kind of strange for you lately?"

"I don't know. They seem kind of normal for me."

"Seriously?"

"Yeah, pretty much."

"Well, if you think this has been normal, that's kind of fucked up."

"I don't see what any of it has to do with you anyway. You've just been, like, spying on me for entertainment?" The idea of this—which didn't strike me as fully plausible in any case—didn't anger me; in fact I kind of liked it.

"Not exactly. I mean, it's more than spying, and it's more than entertainment."

It felt as though I were imagining her: the vagueness in her speech was the vagueness of dreams, the paltry half-information, blindly accepted, that one's unreasoning brain supplied within its illogical oneiric narratives—it went nowhere, like my own thoughts.

I reached out and touched her arm. It was real: bone and skin and soft hair on top. She was a shorter-than-average person, I noticed: small, dense-looking, tightly constructed, I could tell somehow, despite the bagginess of the orange shirt she wore above her jeans.

"Why aren't you saying anything?" I said.

"Why are you *touching* me?" she said.

"Sorry. What do you know about me?"

"I don't know what there is to say, exactly," Catherine said. "You seem really unhappy and weird and self-conscious and prone to masturbation, I guess. Do you think that's why your life has been going so badly lately?"

"I am happy," I said. "And my life is going pretty well."

"Or do you think it's because you're ugly?" she said.

"I'm not ugly," I said. "I'm average-looking."

She seemed to appraise me. "Yeah, I guess that's true. Average-looking. I don't know what it is, then. Can we talk more later?"

"Sure, whatever."

"What's your phone number, Jeff?"

Dumbly I told her my number, like a four-year-old reciting the alphabet.

"OK," she said, "I'll send you a text so you'll have mine. We'll talk more later."

"All right," I said.

She turned and started to walk away.

"What about this fire?" I said. "Shouldn't we, like, douse it with water or something?"

"Nah," she said. "Don't worry about it."

She continued walking, keeping to the wooded area until it ended at Morehead Avenue, and I watched her till she disappeared. I looked at the flame again—it was starting to shrink, I thought, retaining its shape but getting steadily smaller as I looked at it until it was more or less just a candlelight and then nothing at all. Again, the whole thing felt imaginary: how many times had I wished that a beautiful girl would appear outside my bedroom window? Had I finally invented one?

I considered whether I should ask my parents to hire a psychiatrist for me. It would be more responsible to trust in modern medicine than to trust in myself, but the madness that had lately inflicted itself upon me was by far the most interesting and enjoyable aspect of my life. And my own very sane cognizance of my insanity—as a consequence of which I fully recognized that the scenario that had just unfolded could only have been an apparition—suggested that I wasn't all that insane after all, which meant that maybe the whole thing was real, in which case something cool might finally happen to me. I looked out the window for a few more minutes, saw nothing, masturbated again, went to sleep.

Chapter Six

Things were getting really strange in Weybridge, not only within my own immediate experience but more broadly, in ways that felt too disconnected from me to be products of my self-involved brain. Honestly, I didn't even care that much, but more and more people seemed to be losing their pets, as Matt had—not only dogs but cats and frogs and hamsters and iguanas. I saw the Facebook posts and the posters around town: a deaf parrot, a one-legged guinea pig, a snake named Marlon Brando, all vanished. These, I eventually realized, were not animals that had wandered off on their own; more troublingly, they'd been stolen from people's homes, during burglaries executed apparently for no other purpose, since no electronics or jewelry had gone missing. No one seemed to know what was going on. My classmates showed up to school with tear-streaked cheeks, and I was just as surprised by their tenderheartedness as I had been by Matt's: I'd sort of assumed that, for most kids, pets existed only for the practical purpose of generating cute and/or humorous social media content. Supposedly the police were looking into the disappearances, probably spending most of their time making dorky animal-related puns to one another—about how this pet-napper wasn't *kitten* around, his crimes were truly *paw*ful—as they poked around uselessly in the horror-stricken families' homes, none of them having ever solved an actual case before and possessing no real idea how to go about it. I kind of just felt somewhat distantly amazed by the number and variety of strange critters that, unknown to me, had previously occupied my antiseptic commuter suburb; it was not so much their departure as their initial existence, of which I'd just now learned, that struck me as surreal.

I had my own mysteries to ponder. Adam Nordmark, the graceful free-spirited fourteen-year-old who had wandered onto our soccer field like some kind of enigmatic troubadour, had made the varsity team as a freshman and, in practice, was outplaying everyone to a degree that I found extremely disturbing. I not only had accepted but indeed had come to rely on the idea that no one from my town could be *truly* gifted at soccer or at anything else—the idea, more generally, that at some point in the history of Weybridge we'd accepted a trade-off in which, receiving our bland all-encompassing prosperity, wherein every family was cheerful and materially comfortable and every child bound for college, we'd dispensed with both suffering and its rare, unfathomably interconnected compensations, the sublime parts of the universe that couldn't exist without their inverse, and thenceforth kids here would possess only those purchasable "talents" that could be forcibly instilled by professional lessons and tutors and stay-at-home moms: boys reciting pi to the millionth decimal point, girls playing Bach without any obvious errors. My peers might be better than I was at anything or everything, but as long as they possessed no genuinely remarkable inborne facility—and, by the nature of the situation into which they were born, could not—my own inadequacies felt unimportant: if the best any of us could do was only respectable, it didn't matter so much if I wasn't the best.

We'd always had a diligent soccer team, studded with the occasional dull spark of minor natural ability, but we'd had no geniuses of the sport —at least until now. Part of me hoped that, if Adam was the most brilliant soccer player I'd ever seen, he still wasn't one-thousandth as good as the most talented boy in the slums of Rio de Janeiro, and that what struck me as transcendence did so only because I'd never even come close to experiencing the real thing. But there was something about the way he dribbled, the way he anticipated and effortlessly avoided tackles so that it was impossible to take the ball away from him no matter how long he luxuriated in its possession, the way his shots hooked perfectly into the tiniest vulnerable corners—something about it made me physically sick. I got distracted; my own efforts seemed stupid. My own game was based entirely on gumption, of which I suddenly felt drained on the field as I did in the rest of my life. I was terrified that my entire approach to soccer was in fact worthless, and I tried to find the productive end of this fear, the kernel of motivation within it that would make me try even harder —I knew that, if despair was primarily an agent of paralysis, it also contained an evasive yet uniquely powerful and desperate impetus toward action, the only energy that propelled me through life—but I couldn't locate it, Adam had so elegantly yanked the ball away from me.

In our first game—where Adam physically resembled the middle-schoolers serving as our ball boys more than he did his varsity teammates—he scored two goals coming off the bench. In the second game, our rigidly hierarchical coach hesitantly inserted the freshman into the starting lineup (an unprecedented move for him), replacing me. By that point I wasn't even upset; I was more curious to see what Adam could do than I was determined to preserve my own meaningless stature. I was hypnotized. Oddly, I now felt that my teammates were underreacting to his greatness—that they were still treating him as though he were a very good new player, rather than a wholly new kind of player, a creature we'd never seen before. He scored two more goals.

At school, I looked for Catherine every day, believing at first that I wouldn't find her—that she was a figment of my imagination who would appear only nocturnally. But no, I ran into her occasionally in the halls, and she appeared to be a normal girl, visible to others, carrying books and interacting with friends. Once or twice I asked her how she was doing, as though we were old friends, and she said she was fine. She had never actually texted me, so she had my number, but I didn't have hers.

I felt at times that life was on the verge of being interesting but somehow still wasn't, at least not quite yet, and this was in some ways worse than it being completely and obviously boring. I found myself taking long drives in the afternoons, intrigued by whatever strangeness had improbably descended upon my town but of course turning up nothing.

And then, stopping at Wawa for food on a Friday night, I spotted Jillian Heller in her car by the gas pumps, her blond hair silver behind the reflection of the fluorescent lights on her driver-side window, her face whitely illuminated by the screen of her phone as she looked down. I approached and tapped on the glass; she looked up and rolled down the window, the deliberateness of the automatic descent like the slowness of an escalator upon which one was spatially prohibited by fellow occupants from making manual progress via walking.

"Hey, Jeff!" she said.

"Hey Jillian," I said. "You aren't grounded nowadays?"

"Nope, I'm free. You saved me."

"Oh, that's good!"

"Even Melanie leaves me alone these days."

"You're an independent woman. No one holding you back. Master of your own fate." I had no idea what I was saying.

"Do you have any plans for the weekend?" she said.

"Not really."

"Want to get breakfast tomorrow?"

"Sure." Was this a thing people did now—"getting breakfast" on weekends?

"Cool," she said. "I'll text you when I wake up tomorrow."

We shared our phone numbers. For the second time in the same month, a girl had initiated with me an exchange of contact information, with the suggestion that she would like to communicate further—what the fuck *was* going on in this town?

· ·

There was something very exciting about the prospect of Jillian texting me upon waking on Saturday morning. That evening, I couldn't sleep for the thought of her contacting me—thinking of me—while she was still in bed, still in her pajamas, not yet fully disconnected from the private world of her sleep and her dreams, inviting my disembodied presence into the intimacy of her feminine dishabille. I'd recently BitTorrented the entire *Land Before Time* film series—all thirteen feature-length installments—

which I watched on my iPad in bed while waiting for the night to pass, finishing the first six movies shortly after sunrise, dozing off for a couple hours in the thick toxic stew of my farts and body odor, waking at ten, showering, and then waiting another hour for Jillian to text me.

My phone buzzed—she was asking if I was awake. I told her that I'd just gotten up and asked where she wanted to go; she wasn't sure. I suggested the IHOP on Route 18, where families with screaming four-year-olds would inevitably surround us on all sides (reasserting, no doubt, the anti-sexual backward tug of our own absent families), but our town didn't have much else, and the International House of Pancakes was arguably a step up from the Denny's where I'd previously encountered her—among a friend-group large enough, however, to become its own setting, the restaurant around them forgotten. She said IHOP sounded good and wondered whether I remembered how to get to her house; I said I did —in fact, I had no conception of where, geographically, her house was located, but out of sheer creepiness I'd memorized her address, and when I got into the car half an hour later (she needed time to shower, she said, which meant, for some period, that she *was* naked at the same time I imagined her naked), I put it into my phone for directions. On the way there I nearly rear-ended two drivers, and I hit a curb on a right turn, not quite hard enough to puncture my tire.

Her home, in the daylight, was more elaborately landscaped than I'd noticed at night, with flower arrangements, purposefully placed stones, and rigorously geometric bushes occupying the front yard together like a maze for garden gnomes. I texted Jillian again as I waited outside, and she emerged in a green long-sleeved shirt, a blue skirt, and a thin useless gray scarf, ritually signaling her awareness of the start of autumn despite the warm weather. She hopped in next to me with an energy that I found reassuring.

"The inside of your car is still very clean," she said.

"I don't clean it that often," I said. "Are other people's cars all dirty inside?"

"Mine is," she said. "I leave all kinds of stuff in there—dirty old hoodies, papers from school, empty Wawa ice tea containers. It's awful."

"Well, my dad let me have this car on the condition that I really take care of it—wash it, vacuum it, change the oil, replace the windshield wipers, install new brake pads every once in a while." This was a lie; no one cared what I did with the car, and I did nothing in the way of upkeep except cleaning, which I was meticulous about because my car was, from some traditionally misogynistic outlook on "what women want," the only desirable thing about me, and I didn't want to ruin its air of luxury by leaving junk scattered around—although apparently I'd gone too far in the opposite direction, making myself look fussy.

"That makes sense. It's a really nice car. You know how to change the oil yourself?"

"Sure, it's not that hard." I resolved to look up a YouTube demonstration later at home.

We got to IHOP late enough to be able to get a table by the window, looking out onto the Red Lobster next door, recently remodeled in the Cape Cod style with gray faux-weathered shingles and a gabled roof: why did they bother trying? Its ocean was a parking lot.

"Have you ever been to that Red Lobster?" I said.

"Yeah, a few times," she said. "I like their biscuits."

"I've heard that before. That's what everyone says."

"It's true. Their biscuits are the best."

"They should ditch the whole seafood theme and just become a biscuit restaurant."

She laughed a little.

"I mean, have you ever actually had the lobster there?"

"No."

"I bet no one has. They've just had the same sad decrepit lobsters wandering around in the fish tank with their rubber-banded claws for the past two decades, while people eat biscuits."

"They all must be really good friends by now."

"Who?"

"The lobsters."

"Oh. Yeah." I laughed a little now. "Or they all deeply hate one another."

I looked at the IHOP menu, full of glossy interchangeable photos as though we couldn't be trusted to know what a pancake looked like—in each image, the pooled syrup seeping coyly over the lower-left corner of the plump, golden stack, obviously staged like the pint glass's strategic overflow of foam in a beer commercial. All the grownups in our town had completely given up on being thin, which to me felt correct and reassuring (for soccer games, my team had occasionally traveled to trendier North Jersey suburbs where the moms were all disconcertingly sexy women in tight designer jeans or yoga pants—I didn't approve), but since our local restaurant options, culled from the lesser national chains, reflected this local resignation, the food available in Weybridge was invariably kind of gross. When the waitress (a middle-aged woman wearing a nametag: inherently sad) came to our table, I asked for the Spinach and Mushroom Omelette. Jillian ordered the Bacon Temptation Omelette. We both got pancakes on the side, even though I would have preferred the fruit.

"You can tell this place is fancy because the menu puts an extra *t-e* on the word *omelet*," I said. "Very French."

"Spinach and mushroom, huh?" she said. I'd been hoping she hadn't noticed.

"Oh, yeah, I'm a vegetarian," I said, almost whispering the final word.

She was smiling but seemed incredulous. "A vegetarian? Why? Are you, like, religious?"

"You mean, like, Hindu?" The only other vegetarians in Weybridge were Hindus—literally, they were the only other ones I'd ever encountered.

She laughed, not seriously discomfited. "Well, I don't know."

"I guess I just kind of decided a few years ago not to eat meat—because, like, animals are sentient creatures that experience pain and fear?" I wished I had thought of something else to say; even so, I was pleased with the tone I'd managed to contrive, rendering the unavoidable self-righteousness of my explanation into a kind of question, as if to express a consciousness that the sentiment therein was a little kooky, reflecting a personal belief of which, for all its clear illogic, I couldn't quite rid myself. Obviously animals *deserved* to die (facts were facts); I was just an oddball.

"That's, uh, cool," Jillian said.

"Yeah," I said. "I mean, I still eat eggs and dairy products from tortured, factory-farmed chickens and cows, so it's not that big a deal."

"Do you have a lot of pets? It sounds like you really care about animals."

"No, I've never had one. Do you have any?"

"We have a cat named Banjo. He claws me every time he sees me, so we're not the best of friends, but lately I'm just glad he's alive. Marilyn Downey and Cheryl Goldenberg both had their cats disappear this month. It's so strange."

"Yeah, it's a definite trend—the numbers have gotten too big to think of all these pet-related incidents as coincidental. There's some kind of local conspiracy."

She bit a fingernail. "Honestly, I think it's the weirdest thing I've ever heard about in my life. I mean, I guess it's actually kind of scary or something, but since we can't really figure out what's going on, it's hard for me to know what we're even supposed to be afraid of."

"We don't know for sure that anybody's pet has actually died, though."

She nodded. "That's true."

"Maybe the animals are just, like, fed up with their lives here, on leashes and in cages—it could just be a coordinated mass exodus. They've all left Weybridge and moved on to the Great Valley."

"Well, I guess you couldn't blame them."

"No? What about all the heartbroken owners they left behind?"

"Still—I wouldn't want to make anyone stay in this town forever."

I didn't understand. "Why not?"

"It's so boring here. Don't you think? For humans, at least. I don't know how dogs really feel about it."

"I don't think it's so bad."

We paused; she seemed to be weighing whether to continue.

"I mean, it's a totally fine place," she said, "but it's hard to feel like you're doing anything special around here, like you're having an adventure—except maybe the other night with you and Aaron. That was legitimately crazy."

"Where would you rather be?" I said.

"Well, everyone I know wants to move to New York eventually, which I guess makes sense, since New York is amazing, but it also feels kind of too predictable to me—like, they want to meet a lot of interesting people and do cool stuff, but they also want to be close enough to their parents to come home for dinner any given night of the week. I was thinking more like Paris or Tokyo."

"But it has to be a big city?"

"No, not exactly. It could be anywhere—it just has to be somewhere kind of incredible, you know? I think, like, there are a lot of nice things you can say about Weybridge, but you can't say that it's *incredible*. You don't want to get out of here sometimes?

I had no thoughts on the matter—I wanted to escape myself, not my town—so I knew I would have to make up something. "I think I'd enjoy traveling," I said, "and I'd like to travel a lot, but I don't have any strong feelings about wanting to get out of Weybridge specifically. I don't have any problem with it."

"None? Not a *single* problem?"

"Well, I think, to some extent, every place has to be sort of the same —we don't have a lot of cool stores or restaurants here, but what makes any place magical is the people inside it, and I think the people here are probably no less capable of being inspiring or beautiful than the people anywhere else."

"I guess that's true."

"I don't know—spending too much time dreaming of some other place may lead you to miss the value of the real experiences that *are* accessible to you. I believe that the full range of human emotion, love and amazement and joy, is available to us here—we just kind of have to make it happen, the way we would anywhere else."

"Wow. Do you really feel like that? Even in school, when you're completely bored?"

"I don't think I'm ever bored in school, actually."

"Seriously? I mean, I know it's a cliché, but high school feels very institutional to me. Not like a prison, exactly, even though that's what everyone says—it's something way more benign. But I don't see any kind of opening into the infinite universe there, if you know what I mean."

I nodded sagely. "Well, I think I see it there as much as anywhere else. Maybe more. I guess I kind of love it, honestly. I almost can't imagine a deeper or more interesting experience than the time we've spent there. It hasn't been *exciting*, maybe, but that isn't really the point."

What *was* the point, then? I had no idea what I was talking about, but I sensed that the inexplicable events of our previous outing, with Melanie and Aaron, were guiding my words, influencing my self-presentation. Jillian knew me only from that one out-of-character night and its several minor miracles, each one a something made (by me) from nothing, the nothingness we shared—could I not extend that version of myself after all? The food came, and we ate our omelets, and the conversation slowed, but I caught her occasionally peering at me from across the table with something that seemed to resemble actual curiosity.

Chapter Seven

Five wins, zero losses. We were unstoppable—and by "we," I mean an entity not actually including myself, because I had by then settled fairly comfortably into my seat on the bench next to Matt. When I thought about it, I realized that losing my starting job and then, gradually, almost all of my playing time along with it was the best thing that could have happened to me. Whatever benefits were to be gained from a modestly successful high school athletic career, I'd already accrued them: it had given me a sense of identity and purpose, had taught me what it meant to work earnestly at something and get incrementally better at it (as well as the essential futility of such an effort), had beefed up my college application, and had basically functioned as the sole non-vagina-related motivating force that had pushed me through my freshman, sophomore, and junior years —and now it was pretty much over, regardless of how well I might have played in the remaining days of fall if Adam Nordmark had never shown up. In a couple months, like most of my teammates, I'd have no reason ever to touch a soccer ball again, and I felt now that I was being weaned off it gently, was being introduced within a familiar and comforting context to the physical idleness that would later characterize my soft-bellied college life.

With Matt beside me, the games were pure pleasure—blowouts, mostly, in which we sought to invent ever goofier ways to cheer on Adam when he scored. For the first time in my life, I felt some of the glorious active detachment—simultaneously above it all and below—of the classic class clown. Matt and I "cracked jokes" from the cozy perch of our irrelevance; our coach started to hate us, but it didn't matter, and in fact it seemed like a sign of our healthful maturity that neither of us craved his approval anymore.

During our sixth game, Matt and I were both deliberately wearing our jerseys backward. No one had noticed, or else no one cared.

"How many times so far do you think players from opposing teams have gone home and committed suicide directly after seeing Adam play for the first time?" Matt said. "The number has to be in the teens by now, doesn't it?"

"I like to think that the spiritual crisis brought on by the encounter ultimately inspires them to redirect their lives onto a more positive and meaningful path. I think it probably turns most of these preppie jock assholes into philanthropists and saints," I said.

"Maybe. In a way I feel jealous of the people who have to play against him. To be deconstructed in that way, broken down, every illusion you had about yourself shattered—it's probably liberating in a sense."

"You can start anew. Build yourself up again from scratch."

We watched as, seemingly trapped within a tight circle of defenders, Adam released from his left foot a ball that bypassed opposing legs and torsos, soared into the air, and finally landed 40 yards downfield at the toes of a streaking right-winger whom we with our superior vantage point had failed even to notice, the trajectories of the run and the pass meeting at exactly the perfect point, a knotty physics problem effortlessly solved.

"Do you ever wonder what Adam's early life was like?" Matt said.

"His early life?" I said.

"Was he ever just a normal boy like us? Did he have a happy home life? When did his parents first notice that their son had been touched by greatness?"

"That's an interesting question. I wish he had a Wikipedia page."

"I want to see, like, a made-for-TV biopic about him, where at first it seems like he's a normal boy and maybe even has some problems at school or at home or whatever, but then he sees a soccer ball for the first time, and suddenly there's this kind of shimmery light and music, and both he and the audience know that life will never be the same."

"And the entire rest of the movie plays in slow motion."

Even now, Adam didn't talk much to the rest of the team—this, too, struck me as an affectation, a reflection of his awareness of his own status as *the chosen one*; he knew his sublimity would to a certain degree be compromised if he went around acting like a normal kid, saying dumb stuff. So largely he remained silent, as enigmatic as the gift with which he'd been blessed, and when he did speak, his voice leaned toward a sort of otherworldly murmur. But we played along; it was more fun—and probably necessary for our sanity—for us to do so. Who knew: it was possible that he just was mildly retarded, but then he had—arguing in the opposite direction—these oceanic old-soul blue eyes that bespoke long centuries of upward reincarnation, building toward the greatness now contained within his otherwise ordinary and not especially lovely teeny-bopper frame. Or was that just my imagination? I wasn't fully a dummy, so I knew that a person's eyes—the elaborate crochet of the iris and the particular color of its crystalline yarn; the watery film of the cornea; the stirred half-submerged threads of immiscible red in the milky sclera; that weird chunk of pink meat at the inward end—were really the least important feature of a person's body, possessing less capacity than any other to render him or her beautiful or ugly. No one ever cared about your eyes until they cared about *you*—and then, suddenly, your eyes became the imaginary nexus not only of your elsewhere-derived attractiveness but also the physical manifestation of every internal quality you supposedly possessed. Of course human eyes in this sense were a fiction, like most of the internal qualities they purported to reveal—but then the entirety of Adam felt fictional, too.

"I wonder if he actually has parents," I said. "I don't think I've noticed them at any of the games."

"I see him more as a phenomenon of nature," Matt said, "like a hurricane or a flood."

"A weather event."

"No—maybe more like a meteor shower? An astrological event."

"Where does he live? Does he live in a normal house, like you and me?"

"He lives among the stars." He said this in a deliberately goofy awestruck poetic diction that he'd been steadily working on during these conversations; it almost didn't feel like a joke at this point—I nearly felt the wonder in my bones.

When the game ended, our team was still undefeated, and I was wondering which one would earn national media attention first—our town's ongoing string of pet kidnappings or Adam's flawless goal-scoring streak —or whether they both might somehow fly under the radar due to some reasonable unwillingness on the part of the world at large to believe that anything of interest could be occurring in my hometown. Yet dozens of animals had been stolen and presumably dismembered, one by one and limb by limb, by some kind of satanic heavy-metal pseudo-cult (or whatever), and then a freshman had scored more goals in boys' varsity soccer than any other player in the Greater Middlesex Conference— both seemed surreal enough to warrant a gravely voiced *20/20* segment or a *Today Show* puff-piece or *something*, but maybe I had just gotten so accustomed to the formerly unbroken uneventfulness of my town's history that any slightly remarkable goings-on consequently struck me as front-page-worthy news. It seemed possible that Weybridge's previously relentless inactivity—as though, without knowing it, I'd spent all my life within some kind of miniature mid-century utopian model of suburbia created by racist autistic scientists—had in fact constituted the most bizarre phenomenon of the three ... or else it'd been the most ordinary thing on the planet: my own lack of perspective could be kind of annoying in these situations—being a teenager sucked sometimes.

Adam regularly walked home from practices and games—it was possible that he actually lived very close to the high school, yet I kind of assumed, instead, that this practice, too, reflected artifice: he probably trudged eight or nine miles every day solely that we wouldn't see him get into the backseat of his mother's minivan like a normal child, preferring to walk off into the sunset like the silent solitary hero of a classic Western. So, after our team meeting in the locker room and some words of celebration, I started to drive home, and I saw Adam on the sidewalk, seeming to make deliberately snail-like progress. I had driven for a few minutes when—in a fit of curiosity—I decided to turn around and follow him.

By the time I'd finished backtracking, he'd reached the intersection of Buchanan Boulevard and Sedgefield Road and had turned left. Following and then quickly surpassing him, I employed the same technique I'd used inadvertently before, namely driving beyond sight of him, at standard speed, and then doubling back to see where he was headed next. When I'd returned to Sedgefield Road, I thought I'd lost him until I saw him make a right near the Temple B'Nai Shalom—one of our town's several Jewish places of worship—onto Carver Street. I pulled into the temple's lot and watched him as he plodded past Elmira Park and then some houses. I restarted my engine when I saw him veering left toward Barnwell Street (I knew the roads' names only because I was tracing his progress on my phone's Google Maps as he walked). Slowly, but not too slowly, I drove past him once more. Even though I'd initially felt clever for utilizing this tactic instead of lingering noisily behind him at two miles an hour until he'd reached his destination, it struck me that, fairly soon, he might notice that the same car had driven by several times from both directions, and this time I thought I might just keep going instead of risking embarrassment, but fortunately, through my rear-view mirror, I saw him at that moment diverge from the sidewalk, straying onto the driveway of a brown-shingled house and then disappearing into its open garage

It turned out that he did live very close to the high school. I drove around for about five minutes before returning to the vicinity of the house that Adam had entered and parking across the street, not quite directly across from its front door but close enough for me to have a good view.

I was sitting in the car as if I were involved in a stakeout. The house was normal, of course—what else could it be, and why would it matter either way? It occurred to me that, if I'd wanted to see where Adam lived, I could have just offered him a ride home. We were teammates—it would have been normal. In fact it was strange if no one had offered *already*. I felt very stupid, but I kept staring at Adam's house, as if willing my espionage to yield something, as if I might yet see something spectacular, some hint as to what his soul possessed that mine didn't.

I recognized, more or less, that it was dumb to venerate athletes at any level. Adam was undeniably talented, but I saw too how the difference between a "talented" person and an "untalented" person was primarily only the difference between a profitable talent and an unprofitable one: I could easily imagine an alternate universe in which the person who sneezed the loudest earned international superstardom—in our universe, that popularity and renown happened to belong to our elite sportsmen, but there was nothing inherently more useful at this stage of human civilization about the oddities of *their* bodies, which allowed them to excel on the soccer field or the tennis court. But of course I'd never notice who sneezed the loudest, or whose fingernails grew the fastest, or whose natural smell was the most pleasing—we were all stuck noticing the things we were supposed to notice, valuing the traits that our society had, for the moment, deemed valuable: sports happened to make for entertaining television and thus were monetizable, and thus the people who played them well had value. Did this make them more magical than the rest of us? No—but, if they weren't, then who was? As I said, Adam's gift— whether intrinsically or contingently valuable—was real, and what other gift would I ever be able to witness so clearly?

So I continued to peer through my car window at his home, the source of it all, the place where all that strange miraculous energy inside him had developed over the course of years, presumably. When one thought about it, every house was like an ancient tome, written in a lost language: it contained more than one would ever know. Gradually I fell asleep to the vagueness and stupidity of this thought.

When I woke up in my car, it was dark outside. I didn't know what time it was, but I felt embarrassed and turned the key in the ignition and put on my headlights. And then, in the distance, I saw Adam—I thought it was him, and then I thought maybe it wasn't, and then I was sure it was. He was coming toward me—not quite toward me directly, since he was on the opposite sidewalk, but toward his house, as though he'd gone out for some period while I was asleep and was now returning. I froze in the car, for some reason now too scared to drive; to lurch into movement now, in the silence of night (as opposed to the equal silence of day), was unthinkable—he'd notice me. I just sat still and watched him.

He was holding something in his hand, and for a moment, by the way his fingers wrapped around its grip, it looked like a small pistol, but the shape was wrong, rounded without the pointy panhandle of a barrel. It was only a leash, in fact, the kind with a plastic handle into which the cord could retract. Strangely, I couldn't make out any pet attached, but as Adam came closer I saw that he was tugging something with his arm, and eventually I noticed that the dog was behind him—not taking a walk but being dragged, its paws clawing at the sidewalk beneath. And yet Adam continued on, his pace unwavering, a certain blankness in his stride.

There was something disquieting about the scene: the lonely street; the silent relentlessness of the boy pulling at the dog, as if he were drawn hypnotically toward their destination, unable amid his trance to register the dissent of his cargo, at which he never looked back; the tenacious resistance of the animal that seemed to intuit some horror ahead. And so the question occurred to me: was this *his* dog? I pictured a normal boy walking a normal dog—Matt and his beloved late Oscar formed the image in my mind—and I couldn't imagine that this was what their outdoor play sessions looked like. What sinister thing was going on here?

Were the two bizarre currents in Weybridge—the supernatural boy and the kidnapped pets—directly linked? *It all made sense.*

Or did it? It seemed unlikely that I would be the one to discover the connection if there was one. The idea that the dual mysteries of my town would ultimately converge into some kind of coherent interrelated conspiracy, in which all the pieces would fit together, was hard enough to accept—I'd have predicted instead that, eventually, the pets would stop disappearing, and Adam would stop scoring goals, and both phenomena would remain unexplained until they were completely forgotten, as if they'd never existed. But the idea that I, of all people, would uncover the conspiracy if it *did* exist: that truly exceeded the bounds of my credulity. In a few hours, I'd probably be laughing mirthlessly at myself for having had the audacity to process my observation as a potential "clue," as if I were inhabiting an actual story, a thriller traveling toward a satisfying solution.

Yet was I a poor detective if I didn't look further into the matter? Well, maybe—I'd already seen plenty else that I'd failed to follow up on; one might plausibly infer that the mystery of our town was in fact hurling itself into me, only I was both too slow to dodge it and too clumsy to receive it. Again, I had no idea what to do, so—the whole thing was probably nothing: Adam was walking a dog. The most banal explanation was always the correct one. This idea had never failed me before.

....

Jillian let me into her house; I didn't have to sit outside. I had taken her to the movies on a Friday night, not specifically stating that it was intended to be a date but hoping that, by selecting an outing that clearly existed less as an actual activity that boys and girls did together in the 21st century—I had no idea what they did, but it wasn't this—than as the outmoded but somehow irreplaceable Platonic ideal of a date (a notion self-servingly perpetuated by the film industry itself, through the continued production of movies and TV shows in which modern teenagers went on first dates to the movies as if living in 1955), she'd get the message. Asking her to go with me to movies felt like an old-timey euphemism —the whole evening had weird quotation marks around it, and I realized midway through that, given the symbolic nature of the endeavor, we probably could have called it a night directly after my request and her acceptance, since those were the only parts that had mattered. We hadn't needed to drive to a theater, literally, and buy tickets and watch a movie, yet that was what we were doing—I had to pay the fair price for whatever interpersonal disfluency had forced me, like some fedora-wearing bozo toting red roses to a woman's doorstep, to rely on an outdated cinema-derived romantic trope in order to communicate to Jillian my interest in her. How did normal guys put themselves forth as potential boyfriend material? Some particular tilt of the head, an especially emphatic blink of the eyes . . .

Knowing that I'd require conversational fodder for the rest of the evening, I paid probably too much attention to the movie, seeking out "interesting" details, flaws, and conundrums in order to build a set of discussion points, so by the time we emerged from the auditorium in that awkward stumbling post-movie fashion—herded out like cattle by the blare of the closing credits, slowly re-accustoming ourselves to the harsher and uglier rhythms and surfaces of real life—I had formed such a detailed (and probably mildly insane) analysis of the film's themes and problems, punctuated by such complicated reader-response questions for Jillian (all of which tumbled out with agitated rapidity), as to destroy any possibility of a conversation on the subject of the movie; obviously Jillian felt like she was being quizzed, and she retreated. Also, she—understandably, but incorrectly—got the idea from my intensity that I was a "movie buff," and later, as if to reassure me of the normalcy of my passion, she talked with greater comfort about some of her own favorite movies. She seemed very disturbed that I had never seen an early-2000s classic called *Mean Girls*, which she owned on DVD, and she invited me over to watch it the next night. This idea, an at-home hangout, felt more organic (even if people didn't really watch DVDs anymore, either) —and she'd come up with it *on the spot*.

I came over on Sunday. Her family had an expensive basement-den "media room" that looked somehow like an elaborate death-machine, with a menacingly large TV, surround-sound speakers, and a sofa so deep your feet didn't touch the ground. On the way there, ushered toward the downward staircase, I'd looked frantically in all directions, taking in as much domestic detail as I could manage, memorizing the artwork on the walls and the faces of her younger cousins in the magnet-hung photos on the refrigerator door. No sight or sound of her parents. Alone in the basement, Jillian and I sat on the sofa close enough that our elbows touched, not quite snuggling.

The movie—a sociological teen comedy whose TV advertisements I still vaguely remembered from my childhood, though I'd never watched the movie itself—was good enough that our watching it didn't feel palpably like an artificial excuse to create bodily proximity. I was mildly but genuinely entertained by the early comedic charms of Lindsay Lohan as a homeschooled naïf flung into the treacherously shallow waters of a popularity-obsessed public high school in the same bland bourgeois expanse of Chicagoland that Molly Ringwald and Anthony Michael Hall had inhabited two decades earlier. I wasn't sure I fully understood what the movie was about—it felt like an instructive, moralistic satire on a real-world "problem," except for some reason the problem being addressed, primarily in earnest after-school-special style despite all sarcastic asides, was the cattiness and superficiality of suburban white girls, as if their backbiting and conformism constituted a self-perpetuating system of real destructive force that ensnared the lives of innocent young people across the country, thus constituting a serious social ill. Had I been a *victim*, all along?

"What'd you think?" Jillian said.

"I liked it," I said. "It was funny." No lie, at least: it was.

"It's *so* funny," she said. "I think it's the most accurate high school movie."

Was that right? Was high school really a social jungle—half puzzle, half adventure—in which one navigated a perilous obstacle course of friends and enemies, fluctuating trends, snap judgments and crafty deceptions? Wasn't it kind of more like that movie *Gravity*, with Sandra Bullock floating alone through the endless blackness of outer space?

"Does our school have a Regina George?" I said.

Regina George was the evil queen bee of the high school in *Mean Girls*. Rachel McAdams had dyed her hair blond for the part; I wondered whether Jillian, as a blonde, objected to the stereotype but didn't ask.

"I don't know if we have anyone that bad," Jillian said. "Maybe Sienna Page?"

"We have a girl named 'Sienna' at our school?" I said.

"For real? You don't know her?"

"I don't think so."

"She plays field hockey? She has *huge* boobs. They're extremely renowned."

"I'm not sure."

"You almost can't get past her in the hallway."

I laughed. "That is impressive."

"Well, there probably isn't ever any one girl as powerful as Regina George. We all have our moments of status. And the accompanying bitchiness, probably. I was popular for like a month in the sixth grade, and I'm sure I was insufferable about it."

"What happened?"

"I think Jay Rifkin liked me instead of Allison Reagan, who was in love with him at the time. And people found out about it. And because Allison had been the most popular girl in our class before that, and Jay was the most popular boy, somehow Allison's popularity got transferred to me for a little while."

"What was it like? How did you know you were popular?"

"How did I know? I don't know. I just knew."

I paused, shifting to face her more directly so that our upper bodies no longer touched, as if to signal a change of topic. "Have you ever seen that movie *Clueless*? It's an old movie. I think it came out in the '90s."

"Oh, yeah, the one with all the valley girls, right? That's a funny movie too."

"It's kind of the same movie as *Mean Girls,* but from a different perspective, isn't it? It's the same subject, I mean: popular, materialistic, vapid girls at a suburban high school. But in *Clueless* they're totally lovable, because the Lindsay Lohan character isn't there to show us how awful they are. With the morally superior outsider removed from the equation, the story becomes a romantic comedy instead of a cautionary tale or whatever. It's kind of interesting, right?"

"But that's also why it's less realistic. In real life those girls aren't lovable at all."

"Well, I think in real life they probably don't exist anyway. People usually make them up in order to despise them, because they know they'll never achieve the ideal that they represent—they'll never look that good or be that important socially, they'll never take up as much space in other people's minds as they want to. But all the qualities they supposedly hate in these imaginary people—the vanity and shallowness and attention-seeking—are qualities they themselves actually possess. The despicable 'cool kids' are just a fictional projection of what they're too afraid to admit they want."

It was all a risk—the word *projection*, like I was writing a paper for school (the whole thing like I was writing a paper for school)—but after a moment Jillian nodded thoughtfully. She was even better-looking than usual in the professionally dimmed light of the basement media room.

"Well, I think that's true to an extent," she said. "We imagine that some kind of perfect life exists, and we attribute that life to someone else, someone who looks like they have it all, and then we hate that person for it. But in reality the person we hate probably is just as messed-up as we are."

It seemed a little neat the way she put it, and I found myself resisting, even though she'd agreed with me. The TV was stuck on a loop of the animated main menu of the *Mean Girls* DVD; Jillian had turned down the volume instead of shutting it off.

"It's basically the relationship we have with celebrities," she said, "worshipping some made-up version of them that we see in the movies and simultaneously despising some other made-up version of them we read about in the tabloids. 'Popular kids' are just a kind of localized version of the same phenomenon. We create them so that we can be jealous of them, or live vicariously through them, or more likely both."

She was smarter than I was, but I didn't want to be having an "interesting conversation" about human psychology that somehow didn't apply to us—it wouldn't take us anywhere. *I* wanted to take her hand, stand up, and fly—impossible in a windowless basement.

"Definitely," I said. "It's like what we were talking about the other day. The notion that there's something so much better outside our own lives. And we can dream about it or resent it, but we can never have it. And I think that's a self-destructive, life-denying idea. I guess I'm weird or something, but I can't really understand how any of us can be jealous of anyone else or how we can ever believe that we don't have enough right in front of us, that we don't already have everything in the universe we could ever want. The only problem is how we receive our lives, what we get out of them and what we let slip by even while we possess it."

Life-denying? Was that a word? The whole thing was bullshit, the exact opposite of how I felt every moment of every day. But I believed that I'd felt Jillian's feelings so much more harshly than she herself had—the emptiness and longing, the looking hard and finding nothing—that I'd begun working on a fictive solution: not an escape but a digging-in of the heels, the hands, the eyes, the mouth. I would learn to rhapsodize like Emily in the last act of *Our Town*, renewing Jillian's belief in the magic of the everyday, as some lame-ass creative writing teacher would put it, and thus instilling a belief in the magic of my own uninspiring averageness. Would she ever fall for it?

Jillian stood up to retrieve the disc from the DVD player and put it back into its case. The TV went black except for a NO SIGNAL graphic.

"What should we watch next time?" she said. "Any recommendations?"

Had watching movies together now become our "thing"? It seemed arbitrary and silly and boring, but it felt good for us to have a "thing" together. That itself was huge progress.

"Oh, I don't know," I said. "What else do you have?"

"I have a big shelf of DVDs in my bedroom. Want to come take a look before they're so obsolete that I have to throw them all out?"

"Sure." I stood up, and we started to walk toward the stairs.

"It's already pretty embarrassing. I don't have Netflix or anything like that."

"I just download everything illegally."

"I don't even know how to do that. It's like I'm somebody's mom or something."

From the basement stairs we crossed the tiled floor of the landing to the beige carpeted staircase leading to the upstairs hallway. The first door at the top was Jillian's.

"It's probably very messy—just to warn you," she said, her hand on the doorknob.

"I'll hold my breath and try not to touch anything."

When she opened the door, finally, I saw that the room wasn't messy at all, or that it qualified as messy only by some female standard with which I was unacquainted: she had meant the unmade bed, maybe, or the one-quarter open drawer at the bottom of the dresser, or the smudged makeup mirror on her desk—not my own disarray of semen-crusted tissues and dirty dishware from solo meals. She led me over to the bookcase next to the window overlooking her driveway and my own car in the street. The first shelf was lined with DVDs, and as she returned *Mean Girls* to its slot, I noticed that the DVD cases occupied the shelf perfectly from end to end without extending into the books' space on the shelves below, as if she'd deliberately purchased exactly the right number of DVDs for the space allotted to them, or else had obsessive-compulsively thrown out one DVD for every new one purchased after reaching the correct number —or else this was just how girls' lives naturally worked out, devoid of chaos and ugliness.

"Not all of them are actually good," she said. "I have explanations if you need them."

The selections seemed normal to me. Her peak movie-buying (or movie-receiving) period had evidently occurred between 2011 and 2013

—she had *Toy Story 3*, *Midnight in Paris*, *We Bought a Zoo*, *The Hunger Games*, the Hugh Jackman version of *Les Misérables*, *21 Jump Street*, *Wreck-It Ralph*, *Cloudy with a Chance of Meatballs 2*, and *Warm Bodies*, as well as a few movies from our earlier childhoods, like the first *Pirates of the Caribbean* and *The Notebook*, two from the '90s (*Titanic* and *Mrs. Doubtfire*), another pair from the '80s (*When Harry Met Sally…* and *The NeverEnding Story*), and a copy of *Gone with the Wind* that her grandmother or some similar relative had probably given to her. About half of the movies were actually Blu-Rays, which came in thinner cases than DVDs as if to signal a superior futuristic sleekness of objecthood even though the discs were actually the same size.

So I knew what movies Jillian liked, what her house was like, what she liked to eat when she went out for breakfast. Did I know Jillian now? What was the difference between knowing someone and not? Was it anything but an accumulation of information?

I stared at her and wondered: where were the people inside people? At some point would I learn that she had chronic toenail fungus, that her uncle was in prison for first-degree murder but no one in the family talked about it? Would I know her *then*?

I looked around the room again—an enlarged poster of the original *Great Gatsby* dust jacket art, a promotional poster for Lorde's *Pure Heroine* album, a corkboard stuck with photos and illegible notes, a MacBook on her desk, a zip hoodie draped over her chair. She was a normal, smart girl—wasn't there sublimity in that itself? Maybe *too* much; I trembled. How can we ever believe that we don't have enough right in front us? And wasn't she putting herself right in front of me?

"Where's the first *Cloudy with a Chance of Meatballs*?" I said "You only have the sequel?"

"The sequel's better than the original. It's like *The Godfather: Part II*. One of those situations."

"Or *The Empire Strikes Back*."

"Yeah. I've actually never seen either of those. My dad always talks about how the second *Godfather* is better than the first. It's like his favorite way of demonstrating that he has nuanced views on things, it's great."

She sat down on the bed. I sat down next to her, with almost deliberate awkwardness, not saying anything for a moment, introducing the necessary *idea* of awkwardness so that we might proceed *from* it, into those things that made one feel awkward. I liked her.

I would have liked anyone, it was true. Her blond hair was somehow more yellow than blond, I thought. Even so, what was there not to like? She was intelligent, lively, nice, attractive. If she liked me, it was astonishing—uncomfortable even, like being the spectator who gets pulled from the crowd to attempt the half-court shot for a million dollars: an instance of incredible luck, but maybe you'd rather just stay in your seat and do nothing, depending on how emotionally enfeebled you were. I was sure I'd throw an air-ball.

We looked at each other, and I wondered what she saw—could I possibly be enough, right in front of *her*? I was a normal-looking person. Was that acceptable? How could *acceptable* possibly suffice in this situation? Or did she even care what I looked like? Could she imagine that there was more to me than what she saw? Would she know how to kiss not my unremarkable lips but *me*? I imagined it as the secret ability girls held, the only way their affection could be tolerable. We were looking at each other.

In the expectant silence, there was a sudden thump. Then a moan. Then another thump, another moan. It was coming from the wall.

We both turned and looked at it, the clean white paint. It was an unmusical beat that came through, the disjointed sounds of actual human conduct. *What the fuck.*

"Is that your sister's room on the other side?" I said, my voice gentle.

"Yeah," she said. A touch of disbelief in hers.

The sounds kept coming, not urgent or demonstrative but still fairly loud: a male grunt, a female purr.

"Is she, um, having sex?" I said. She clearly was; still, given her sister's age, it seemed wrong for me to imply it, the inserted *um* a demonstration of my sensitive hesitation to do so.

A pause. Still more.

"I guess so," Jillian said.

"Huh," I said. "Are your parents home?"

"No," she said. "They went to my dad's boss's wife's funeral today, actually."

We listened awhile longer, not because we wanted to—we were paralyzed. A philosophical mood had invaded our space: a woman buried on the one hand, teenagers fucking on the other—death, life. And us somewhere in the middle, not quite engaged in either. About two minutes later, the sounds stopped.

"Well, that was incredibly awkward," Jillian said. "I've never listened to anyone have sex before. Let alone my little sister."

"I think we should watch *We Bought a Zoo* next time. I haven't seen that one," I said.

My erection having withered (almost a relief), I understood that in some sense Melanie Heller had "cock-blocked" me—and also that I deserved it, that whatever I would have amounted to if I'd beaten her to the punch would have been less than what this fifteen-year-old girl had managed. Jillian and I talked a little while longer, and then I got up to go, mentioning dinner at home.

I opened the bedroom door, walked out, closed it quietly behind me. And then I heard the door open again, and I turned, thinking it might be Jillian calling me back for some beautiful reason—but it wasn't her, and it wasn't her door. It was another departing male, scrawny and glasses-clad, quietly shutting the door to Melanie's room behind him and then looking up, surprised and embarrassed to see me.

"Hey, Aaron," I said. "How's it going?"

"Oh, hi, Jeff," he said, not making eye contact. "I'm fine, how are you?"

"Pretty good," I said.

The boy followed me to the front door. Had I been an aural witness to someone else's virginity-loss? And not just a witness but, as the couple's prophetic matchmaker, a sort of spiritual participant in that which I myself would apparently never participate in? In a sense this was just as good: more amazing, really.

How had Aaron and Melanie, those dorky sophomores, started having sex *already*? Amazing. Life was spectacular: how could we ever ask for more?

Chapter Eight

In early October, Weybridge Public Schools were canceled for a day due to "mechanical problems" with some of the buses. It was the sort of good luck that seemed purposeless for us to question, like a twenty-dollar bill found in an old pair of jeans, but the next day there were stories, told to us by our mystified teachers themselves, that in fact *all* the school buses had been found inoperable the day before, their engines unwilling to start, for reasons still unknown—and that the following morning they'd just as inexplicably returned to working order, without repair. I was only half-listening, wondering as I did whether such a phenomenon could be attributable to the necessarily (and somewhat lovably) quirky—borderline shoddy—nature of the technology and machinery of the public realm even at its most prosperous and functional, alongside our school's erratic air conditioning system and glitchy computers, or whether, like our missing pets and our freakish freshman, the all-at-once failure of an entire fleet of buses was another genuine sign of the uncanny in our midst—which, however, seemed frustratingly stuck in low gear, amid the trivial mysteries of a sci-fi or horror movie's early atmosphere-building scenes, still no real plot in sight. Would ours ever take flight, or was this the whole thing? If the latter: temporary transit dysfunctions? Wow, *scary*.

I kind of didn't care whether sorcery had begotten it; I was just psyched to have an unsick sick day, at least until I realized, about an hour after the cancellation, that the period of my life where staying home from school felt like an incredible treat—a near-endless expanse of daytime hours to do *whatever I pleased,* among endless possibilities—had passed for me. I was bored, mopey, did nothing, realized I would have rather been at school, ceding to its salubrious impositions, my skin washed and my teeth brushed so that I might impersonate a functional human: that was half the battle. At home I was stuck with myself as I really was, melancholically cupping my smelly testicles, reflecting on how adolescence had turned out to be a process of impoverishment, a stripping-down, the one-by-one robbery of every childhood joy. I'd seen even in my better-adjusted peers how the stupid pleasures of a few years earlier survived only as affected displays of a retained purity of spirit: consuming excesses of candy and ice cream, climbing trees, stomping like a tyrannical toddler on the crinkly leaves of autumn—none of it was done unselfconsciously anymore. Where were my classmates now? Tweeting about the lazy bliss of a day off from school rather than experiencing it. It was hopeless.

The first day back was the first day Emily Grace Pomeroy didn't show up to school. I didn't know about it then; it wasn't till two days later that every last person at school—including those who didn't particularly know or care about Emily—found out that she was actually missing in the milk-carton sense.

Dimly I wondered whether I somehow had murdered her at some point without realizing it. In any case, there was a brief but emotional assembly on the matter during second period, during which Principal Tambakis encouraged us to come forward if we had any information, no matter how innocuous or irrelevant it might seem to us. Her family had last seen her in the kitchen of their home, making a peanut butter and jelly sandwich.

I tried to remember whatever I could remember about Emily, not in order to help the investigation but to forge a sense of personal participation within her mystery or tragedy or whatever it was. I'd once served as her spotter during the gymnastics unit of our eighth-grade gym class—did that count? She hadn't ever fallen. Still, the moments of anticipation, my protective hands hovering near her butt as it soared above me on the balance beam, were somewhat significant in my mind. The closest

I'd come to a meaningful interaction with her in recent years, however, had been listening to Karen Brennan and Annie Klosinski talk *about* her. Had they actually hated her enough to kidnap her—the horrifying finale of a high school rivalry taken too far, a darker *Mean Girls*?

Had I just cracked the case?

In the following days, people talked about Emily, college applications, Lily Gallner's rhinoplasty, Emily some more. Peculiarly, nobody seemed to connect Emily's disappearance to the pet disappearances of September—when I brought those up, people seemed puzzled to how I could think they might be related. It felt almost as though everyone had already forgotten about their lost cats and dogs until I'd mentioned them. Had our local detectives, too, been diverted from the domesticated animal beat in order to search for Emily? We had only so many policemen in Weybridge. There was a candlelight vigil for our vanished angel of prudery the following week, but I stayed home, feeling like a parody of a surly teenager, forever averse to any display of heartfeltness or piety: *those jerks, acting like they care*—except probably they did care. Why wouldn't they? An innocent girl had disappeared, was possibly dead.

I thought TV news teams might finally swarm the school when they caught wind of the case—missing white girl, honor-roll student, the wholesome smile on her school portrait now a haunting reminder of the hideous perversions lurking inside all men—but as it turned out Emily was a little too old for all that: almost eighteen, she had probably just run off with some secret boyfriend. Of course, that didn't sound like her—or at least it didn't sound like Annie and Karen's description of her, or the collective description put forth by those few reporters who, unnoticed by me, had come to town to file stories that would ultimately fail to grasp the top spot in the national news cycle.

I tried to care about the whole thing, but in the end I genuinely couldn't. Any movie about a missing white girl was more interesting: here, we had the initial fact of Emily's absence—which for me was functionally the same as her presence, since I never especially noticed her at school anyway—and then nothing to fill the space, no developments, no forward momentum. No one knew anything; there was no blood on the windowsill, no torn scrap of dress in the driveway.

Was the event responsible, however, for the advances I'd made with Jillian? Everyone was a little scared in the aftermath, huddling closer for comfort and security, and Jillian as much as anyone else seemed to need a warm body of pre-established safety to cling to. I couldn't be sure, but I sensed that I was now Jillian's boyfriend. Even if it wasn't yet official, the mere idea of it made *me* feel very official as a human being—it was like signing up for a library card, registering to vote, seeing my name in the phonebook: I now had a tangible presence in the life of another. It (almost) couldn't be denied.

So what would happen to us? I realized that I couldn't very well imagine now the full course of something that I had never previously dared to imagine on any realistic level. What would make her break up with me, if we were together?

Why did anyone ever break up?

I'd first kissed her—very successfully by my standards—after watching *We Bought a Zoo* in her basement. Her mouth bore no taste of gum or mouthwash, no minty cover-up; there was only the genuine and appealing intimacy of human saliva's warm flavorlessness. Nevertheless, in that moment, I registered instantly her devaluation in the back of my mind as she yielded to me, reciprocated, and asserted her own untraceable hunger, simultaneously betraying her muddled powerlessness to satiate it correctly: she'd settled for *me* instead. She couldn't tell the difference between an actual boyfriend and *me*, or else had ignored the difference out of desperation—even as I couldn't figure out any reason why she should be desperate. Visually, she wasn't rare and perfect, but she was objectively attractive—not in some niche way but in the normally appealing everyday sense. Yet somehow I couldn't be happy about what had happened until I'd left her house and went on Facebook and spent ten or so minutes looking at pictures of her. Then I felt very happy. That night I jerked off while looking at those same pictures, the first time

I'd ever masturbated to an image of someone I knew in real life. It felt bizarrely virtuous.

Emily Grace's disappearance had put a damper—a damper composed in large part, albeit, of veiled excitement—on my class's collective senior year even as I was obviously experiencing the best period of my own teenage life, and I kind of had to go along with the determinedly somber mood. It seemed probable that no one had especially liked her; still, her prim self-regard notwithstanding, she wasn't so disliked that the thought of her dismembered corpse floating in a river somewhere was not a reasonably heartbreaking image for her peers, who of course imagined *themselves* in her position. In any case, they recognized a need for restraint. As far as I knew, there weren't any major parties for the senior class until Halloween, when that hero Victor Bogdan stepped in once more to fill the void. It was still too soon, but it was Halloween: we didn't have a choice, right?

Once the party had been widely announced, Jillian wanted to go, and I couldn't think of a way of explaining to her that I couldn't go back to Victor's house without also explaining that I'd once stolen his clothes and then forced my tongue into his girlfriend's mouth—an incident that, even now, no one in my presence had yet remarked upon or even implicitly suggested knowledge of and so had become unreal to me, but what if I returned to scene of the crime? It might become real again. Just in case, I'd done my best to sidestep Victor and Alice at school, never making eye contact with either, which was easy because I was scared of eye contact anyway and avoided it in virtually all situations.

But then I remembered: it was a Hallowee*n* party. If you were cool, you weren't supposed to take the dress-up part too seriously—something sexy if you were a girl, something marginally funny if you were a guy— but there were always a few people who, with geeky fervor, embraced the opportunity every October to showcase their creativity, both conceptual and practical, in public. I'd always viewed cosplay as a sign of weakness— genuinely happy people logically wouldn't have fantasy lives—but it was also, I realized (in a stroke of minor genius), my passport to Victor's party.

After looking at Halloween outfits online, I ordered a very thorough Chewbacca costume, figuring that I'd wear the mask all night, revealing my identity only to those who asked. Victor would never know; it would be a huge event with lots of more important people, and he'd never bother to wonder. On the night of October 30th, for homework, I watched *Star Wars* for the first time, in case my costume prompted anyone to make reference to the iconic film series. It seemed like an OK movie, although I realized while watching it that Chewbacca was supposed to be very tall, which I wasn't. In any case it didn't seem necessary to watch the sequels or prequels; I'd gotten the idea—I was Harrison Ford's nonsexual life partner, and I could groan but couldn't speak.

A fairly elaborate concoction of rubber and stringy faux-fur, the costume had cost $185.00, and it was very hot inside. I was so drenched in sweat by the time Jillian and I had arrived to the party that, even if I hadn't needed to conceal my identity, I probably would have stayed behind my mask in order to hide my wet salty hair and flushed cheeks.

Technically, the party was probably just as good as the previous one, but some of the magic had worn off—on Halloween, I inhabited Victor's house, now mostly an indoor venue, not as a place of superior beauty and glamor but as just a house full of people with whom I had no especially powerful friendly connection. But I had a woman counting on me now, and in an effort to be more of a man, I drank alcohol, carefully this time, sipping Keystone Lights through the mouth-hole of my Wookie mask until the beer supply ran out, spilling a few drops every time.

I'd never come to a party with a date before, but I believed I was managing it well—breaking off from Jillian occasionally and equally allowing her to break off from me, but always returning and happy for her return. Hand in hand, we were on our way to the kitchen for another drink when Matt—whom I hadn't yet seen that night—stopped us. He was dressed as a banana, an oversized chiquita sticker on his chest.

"Hey, Jeff, how's it going?" he said.

I halted my stride, dropped Jillian's hand as if I'd been caught in the act of kidnapping. My hidden stream of sweat suddenly became a river.

"How did you know it was me?" I said.

"Sweet costume," he said. Then he made some ambiguously bird-like sounds that I realized were supposed to resemble Chewbacca's noises from *Star Wars*.

"Seriously," I said. I was now terrified: was there a hole in the mask, somehow unnoticed by me? Did everyone know who I was? Were they recognizing me by my shoes, not completely covered by my false Wookie paws?

"Seriously what?" he said.

"How did you know it was me? Is it obvious? Can people tell?"

He laughed. "Relax, man. I just figured it was you because you and Jillian were together. I mean, who else would she be holding hands with?"

My mood brightened in a tangible and instantaneous way that I was sure I'd never experienced before: I was part of a recognizable high-school couple, if only to one other person—Jillian and I had hung out with Matt and his friends a few times now, though never as a certified item. The terror vanished. I'd never felt so normal in my life: it was a feeling of incredible security.

Jillian and I got our drinks, found a couch, and drank them, my furry arm wrapped around her. We talked for a while. She was dressed as Dorothy from the *Wizard of Oz*: a blue polka-dotted dress, red shoes, pigtails. It was almost as though we'd mutually chosen a classic-cinema theme for our outfits—not an overly cutesy matching combo but appropriately connected, purely by chance. I liked the way she looked as a rosy-cheeked Kansas farm girl, but there was only so much I could do as Chewbacca; mostly I kept hoping that she wouldn't ask why I hadn't taken off my mask yet, why I was so extraordinarily *committed* to this *Star Wars* fantasy even though I'd previously never even mentioned liking *Star Wars*.

Matt approached us again.

"There's something weird about this house," he said. "My cell phone's doing the same thing as last time."

"What thing?" I said.

"Don't you remember?" he said. "Everybody's cell phone stopped working the last time we were over here. We all lost our signal. It was bizarre."

"Oh, right," I said, disappointed that this facet of the earlier party—like, perhaps, various events that had followed—was not after all a fiction of my mind; Matt now had remembered it. I took out my cell phone and saw that its reception had disappeared, too. I tried to check my email, and the loading sign—that elegant symbol of indeterminate waiting, of things possibly happening or possibly not—churned helplessly.

Jillian was looking at hers as well. "This is so weird," she said. "Do you know how to get home from here without your phone?"

"Probably not."

"Jeff can't get anywhere without Google Maps," she said to Matt, laughing. "Even if we're just driving to his house from my house, he has to put the address in."

I shrugged good-humoredly. Already I'd become the lovably incompetent husband of TV commercials: the pleasure she was taking in my small failings seemed like a sign of real attachment. I considered inventing more foibles—I could get food stuck in my teeth on purpose, forget to tie my shoes.

"I probably shouldn't be driving any time soon anyway," I said.

"Good point," she said.

With that remark we felt entitled—or even obliged—to another drink. But we didn't mix our beverages too strongly: the vodka like a melted ice cube in her orange juice, the rum a cautiously discreet poison in my Coke. Neither of us had any desire to get shit-faced; we wanted only to be pleasantly drunk. At the rate we were going, we would probably end up sliding anyway down the slippery slope to incoherence and nausea, but as we pursued this end less feverishly than did our desperate vulgar peers, we felt superior for our restraint and the adultness of our implicit goal: a gracefully lubricated evening out for two, not a bacchanal.

We were on the couch again, left alone in our bubble of coupledom by the other kids, and I felt only slightly lonely and left-out but otherwise good. I looked at Jillian, wondering what had made her dress as

Dorothy, her skirt just a little shorter than Judy Garland's. *The Wizard of Oz* wasn't in her DVD collection, but whether she liked the movie or not, she must have deciphered a sexual component to Dorothy's innocence and vulnerability, that exaggerated wholesomeness born of a male director's imagination—a girl surrounded on three sides by men twice her age, otherwise alone and defenseless in a strange land: the erotic possibilities there were more provocative, really, than those put forth by the French maids and Playboy bunnies in our midst.

Something, too, about her facial expression—Jillian's, not Dorothy's —expressed sexual potential for the evening. Was Chewbacca sexy? Despite his sidekick status, he had undeniable alpha-male characteristics, namely his impressive height and body hair, combined with a certain teddy-bear cuddliness that women might find appealing. And there may even have been some implication in the movie that Chewbacca allowed Han Solo to operate as the top dog only as an act of tolerance and kindly condescension—a hands-off approach attributable to the self-confidence of one whose superior physicality and firmness of character ensured that, if he ever needed to take the reins, he could. Copilot or not, Chewbacca wasn't getting bossed around by anyone. I was struck by the possibility of an irony wherein my superficially geeky costume might, owing to the visual effect of its man-beast hybridity if not to the mythology of the specific character it represented, ultimately help at some subconscious level to communicate to Jillian my own animalistic side, a necessary deepdown caveman reality of inarticulate growling and fur. What had I, as a bench-warming soccer player and "normal kid," done to show that hot red blood flowed through my veins? Now I was touching Jillian's arm, her leg, my paw on her bare skin.

"Don't you want to take your mask off?" she said.

Shit. Well, maybe it wasn't Chewbacca she wanted; maybe it was me, and I didn't fully like the thought. Being wanted was surprisingly similar to not being wanted; either way, the other person and her desires remained a total mystery—Jillian was responding to something in her own head, embodied by me but not me. It wasn't exactly a turnoff to wonder what this thing was—there were many things going on inside me when I looked at her that I didn't understand, a lot of doubt and confusion and misplaced yearning, but when I tried to reduce the situation to its simplest terms, my hunger and her body parts, removing her mind and its perception of me from the equation, I was cognizant of the losses sustained: I wouldn't get what I really wanted that way. Nevertheless, it was probably too much for me to consider while sustaining an erection.

"Let's go upstairs," I said.

She smiled big, a little drunkenly but also playing it up ever so slightly, embracing it. "Upstairs?"

"Sure, we could probably find a private spot. It's a big house."

"That sounds OK."

I took her by the hand at first as I pulled her up, but like a gentleman I delicately let go and allowed a foot or two of separation as we approached the stairs, lest it be too obvious that I was leading her up there, on a sort of preemptive walk of shame, to an unoccupied bedroom. I glimpsed Victor, grinning and laughing in the kitchen, as we mounted the steps. I realized I wasn't afraid of him, and in full view of him (though he wasn't watching), I peeled off my mask, holding it in my hand as I made my way upward.

It was of course my second visit to Victor's bedroom—I took her there immediately—and I sat down on the bed as if it were my own. We hadn't turned the lights on, so it was dark in the room despite its uncurtained window, and I hoped that my moist skin glistened in a sexy way, its fat-lady-on-a-hot-day sweat-swollen redness lost in the forgiving starlight. I put my tongue in Jillian's mouth and then pressed my body against hers, Wookie-fur against cotton. She received the whole gesture warmly, and I was struck by the possibility that my entire life of self-pity—that primary fact of my daily experience—was ridiculous. I had a *girlfriend.* And maybe she was going to have sex with me in someone else's bedroom at a party, the way every person who had ever lived had at some point dreamed of.

Determined not to be a Cowardly Lion, I was working up the courage to reach under Dorothy's skirt when I felt a buzz in the pocket of my Wookie pants. I ignored it at first, but when I remembered that my phone *was supposed to be broken*, my curiosity became irresistible. Pausing and retracting halfway through a tongue-swirl, I removed my face from Jillian's and took out my phone and saw that I'd received a text— yet, strangely, the words NO SERVICE still appeared at the top of my iPhone's screen.

"Is your phone still broken?" I said. No transition from the kissing: I couldn't help it.

"My phone?" Jillian said.

"Yeah, does it work?"

A good sport (I started to wonder if she was too good, her agreeableness a secret flaw: a pushover), she retrieved her phone from her purse and looked at it for a moment.

"No, I think it's still broken," she said.

"I just got a text," I said.

"Oh, so yours is working again?"

"No, I think it's still broken, but somehow the text went through anyway."

"It doesn't take that much reception for a text to get through."

"Yeah, I guess."

I turned slightly away. The text was the first I'd ever received from a theretofore unseen number: "it's catherine. come meet me now. 113 erwin road."

I felt sick and frantic as I read and reread it, knowing that I would have to heed its request, realizing as I realized this that I would have to lie in some necessarily suspicious way to Jillian at her most generous and therefore her most vulnerable. I would have to *reject* her, and within that veiled rejection she'd receive from me a feebly cushioned insult from which, in what now struck me as a crucial moment in the early development of our romance, some natural preexisting seed of beginners' unease would begin to flower into a more potent life-destroying force of insecurity and doubt. I had a still-hard dick—slick no doubt with its own independent coat of tangier nervous sweat—and, with it, perhaps, the capacity to nip this whole terrible situation in the bud, but I knew that I couldn't stay put after receiving Catherine's message. Was I afraid of her? I wasn't certain.

Who was this girl? Why was she more important than the girl right in front of me? If normalcy was what I wanted, why spurn the happily normal situation before me for a surely bizarre and upsetting evening at the junction of my own private hallucinations and the subtle violence that had crept into my ever-safe suburb? I couldn't say, and I didn't have time to wonder because, very quickly, I had to come up with a lie.

Putting the phone away, I said, "It's my dad. He says to he needs me to come home as soon as possible."

"That's weird," Jillian said. "Is everything OK?"

"I don't know. I texted him back, but he hasn't answered it. It kind of sounds bad? Like some kind of emergency?"

"Oh, man," she said. "Maybe we should go?"

"You should stay here. I'm pretty confident I'll be able to get home safely, but since I've had a few drinks, I'd rather not put you to any unnecessary risk."

"Are you sure you have to go? If your dad knew you'd been drinking, he definitely wouldn't want you on the road, regardless of whatever's happening at home."

"I'll be all right. I'm just kind of worried—I don't usually get texts like this from him, especially not in the middle of the night. Can I come back and pick you up later? Or maybe you can get a ride with someone else? I'm really sorry about this."

"It's fine. I'll get a ride or something. Just let me know as soon as you can that everything's OK. And please be super careful getting home."

"I will. Have fun here at the party."

How would a non-pushover girlfriend have reacted? Would she have gotten angry? Would she have physically prevented me from driving home in a state of obvious and irresponsible drunkenness? Jillian was too easy.

And it was amazing how something that only weeks earlier had seemed as unattainable as the highest red-stoned peak on Mars now felt *too easy*; amazing how, all of a sudden, I glimpsed here, in this still unfinished task, a hint of that same paucity of external struggle and substance that had defined my life in Weybridge, its unhappiness the unhappiness of a void; amazing how rapidly the biggest something, too, could become nothing—although it hadn't, not yet, and if I could prevent it, I would. In my reality, *nothing* was amazing; my only hope was to become in real life the person I'd pretended to be with Jillian, that false locator of the beauty and specialness—the amazingness—within the mundane nothingness of our lives. But what if my life, suddenly extricated from its usual reality, was not mundane after all? What if Catherine Harding was some kind of goddess or devil, the only one of her kind on earth, and she'd just called out to me?

With Jillian still sitting there pitiably on the bed in her uncertainty as to what to do now that her inebriated boyfriend had abandoned her mid-frottage, I left Victor's room and almost fell down the stairs in my fogged excitement, managing to find my balance just in time to avoid a tumble. I'd be all right.

Despite my obvious intoxication, I made it to my car before any goody-goody teetotaler could snatch my keys in an effort to thwart our town's yearly teenage drunk driving fatality (they were all probably rooting for it to be me). I started the engine, exited Victor's cul-de-sac, and started for the strange old house on Erwin Road that I now knew to be Catherine's, if I hadn't known all along. It wasn't until I was nearly there that I noticed that I hadn't needed to ask my phone, broken or not, for directions. Had alcohol unearthed my deep doglike directional instincts, normally jumbled by higher-level anxiety? Driving under the influence felt great, like skiing through fresh powder—effortless.

When I got to the house, I was drunker than I had been when I left, or so it seemed because the odd orange glow that I'd perceived the first time

I'd visited the house had become the larger ambience of a monochromatic disco ball, swirling without any obvious source in the vicinity of Catherine's home. I realized that I was still wearing my Chewbacca suit —a Wookie with a human face, the mask deposited like a fur-sprouting defecation on Rob's pillow.

I stepped out of the car and was led, I thought, by this orange light, the world otherwise dark around me, and it brought me not into the house, which I could barely see, but past it, into the unfenced backyard, which, extending indefinitely in three directions, was not a backyard as I knew the term. Now as bright as the outside of a Creamsicle, the colored luminosity somehow resembled nothing more than a stationary tornado of light: an upward-extending, self-contained beam, turning in place like a top, its glow limited to the space just in front of me—and with Catherine at the center of it—like Dorothy when she hurled through the stormy plains of Kansas, if Dorothy had been a rooted statue instead.

She seemed to be beckoning me toward her—was she, enclosed in an incandescent cyclone of otherworldly energy, better-looking than Jillian? It was hard to say: it was close, but in the end I wasn't sure it mattered. In a somewhat disconnected flash I was struck by the ridiculousness of that carping male obsession with the relative flaws and merits of women's bodies, the practice of holding one girl up against another and comparing them feature by feature as if it were possible, ultimately, to create a mix-and-match Frankenstein-babe from the two. Thinking of Jillian (and of Catherine, too), I almost couldn't fathom the pettiness of any guy who possessed the capacity to *care* that his girlfriend's nose was too big or her legs too thick—it wasn't so much the moral repugnance of the concern as the irrelevance of it: were we only protecting ourselves from the essential, scary truth that that pretty much all female humans were desirable and that, as long as they met some basic minimum standard, it didn't matter by how much or how little they exceeded it, if at all? We needed reasons to be dissatisfied, to justify our lack of love. I wondered whether I would love Jillian or find my own reasons not to—reasons like the other girl now in front of me, drawing me into her circle of inexplicable light.

I came closer, and then closer still—she put out a hand and stopped me before I could walk right into her. I paused and looked around. The light had disappeared; we were standing in the dark. I turned back to Catherine, half expecting her to have disappeared. But she was still there.

"Jeff," she said, "you're the worst."

I said nothing.

"You can go home now," she said.

Chapter Nine

The first unambiguous public instance of witchcraft (or "weird shit" as the student body seemed to prefer to call it) came in early November, when, for a single day, the Snapple cans in the school cafeteria were found to contain whiskey—floral, oaky, elegantly aged—instead of their usual range of artificial juices and iced teas. Our teachers and administrators didn't catch wind of the substitution until midway through the final lunch period, at which point they confirmed via taste test what every boy and girl at Weybridge High already knew or at least suspected —for, if there had been any debate, it had been as to which *type* of spirit had infiltrated the sealed aluminum cans of our lunchroom. As normal teenagers, we were more familiar with vodka (pronounced locally, by girls especially, for some reason as *vah-kah*, the *d* dropped), our philistine preference for its relative flavorlessness—and, to a lesser degree, with cheap spiced rum packaged to make us feel like we were on spring break in Cancun; disgusting sugary liqueurs like Southern Comfort and Jägermeister; and, among those who really wanted to make trouble for themselves and wanted everyone to *know* that they intended to make trouble for themselves, the neutral spirit Everclear. But there lurked, too, somewhere within the school halls, an elite cadre of would-be sophisticates who were supposedly grown-up enough to savor the more complicated palate-based aggressions and seductions of expensive liquor, and from them we learned, mostly through secondary word of mouth, that what we were drinking—or, more often, what we were spitting out—was some type of Tennessee whiskey or Kentucky bourbon; no one was completely sure. They may have been off completely, but we had nothing else to go by. Fake knowledge was better than no knowledge; at our age it was all one could aspire to.

I overheard one Snapple-craving girl describing the whiskey's taste, from one large gulp undertaken wholly in ignorance, as "like getting mouth-raped by Satan," and by half past noon, a standard prank had emerged, with those in the know buying cans for their oblivious friends and waiting for the priceless reaction, a sitcom spit-take brought to real life, filmed for YouTube.

Still, on the whole, our student body proved its scruples on that day perhaps more than any other; we were suitably amazed by the whiskey's appearance at lunch, but hardly anyone drank enough to get drunk, and I didn't see anyone puking in the halls or passing out in class in the afternoon. The teenagers of our town had compartmentalized their bad decision-making, turning it into a decision unto itself, knowing that they could fulfill their youthful obligation to irresponsibility and realize its potential for meaning and personal growth within the multifaceted narratives of their life-journeys without allowing it to exceed certain reasonably determined parameters. School wasn't the place for such stuff, not even when an apparently magical force had, with what struck me as an undeniably charming sense of whimsy and mischief, implanted such stuff directly into the school routine, forming by any reasonable reckoning a special circumstance by whose implied dictates one might expect a sensible but nevertheless fun-loving person, possessed of some normal level of sensitivity, appreciation, and adaptability with regard to life's surprises and winks and whispers, to abide—but, in their covert way, the imperturbable young androids of Weybridge High refused to do so, for all their prankish lunch-hour fun. It was depressing.

Still, our teachers seemed to find us culpable for the incident, as if we not only had participated in it but had somehow effected it—as though any of us had the technical knowhow, let alone the materials, to penetrate dozens of seemingly unmarked, unopened cans and replace their contents with more Jack Daniels than any local liquor store had in stock: each can (of multitudes) held twelve ounces, a lot of whiskey. Was it a manufacturing error? Presumably our angry, baffled principal was on the phone with the Dr Pepper Snapple Group of Plano, Texas, demanding an explanation, but it was fairly clear that none would materialize and that the student body collectively would receive the indeterminate blame for the hijinks of the day—as if "hijinks" could explain it.

Was whiskey really so bad? I wondered. Why had they been selling us Snapple, that corporate-produced sugar-water, in the first place, instead of, say, freshly squeezed juice? Who was the real villain here? School lunches in America were a disgrace; everyone knew it.

Personally, I'd done nothing wrong—I had to take everyone else's word for it that the whiskey substitution had really occurred. When I bought my Snapple at lunch, fully informed by that point of the trick that Catherine had played on (or for) us, I opened it and discovered the usual lemon-chemical-flavored iced tea. Miffed, I bought a second one and found the same thing. I asked around as to whether anyone else had come across an unaltered Snapple that day; it seemed I was the only one.

I pondered whether I was, additionally, the only one who knew that in some way Catherine Harding was likely responsible not only for the Snapple incident but also, loosely, perhaps, for every strange thing that had happened to me and to my town over the past several months. I didn't know her well enough to know whether she was, to those who knew her, a regular girl with regular interests—cat videos and volleyball—or whether she surrounded herself with a group of equally spectacular and possibly sinister friends who participated in her animal sacrifices and kidnappings, affixing SQUADGOAL hashtags to photos from mass murder scenes and other violent cult rituals. As far as I knew, she had no particular reputation at school as a "weird girl"—not like the retro-goth Kelly Anders or the asocial math genius Lacy Ramos—but then again my knowledge didn't go all that far. Frequently, in the days following Halloween, I questioned what, exactly, I'd seen at her house that night: the orange light around her had reminded me, in the manner of a slightly cheesy special effect, of the *ki* auras with which the superheroes from the TV cartoon *Dragon Ball Z* had surrounded themselves while "powering up," a manifestation of their burgeoning life-force and, for the viewer, a sort of fantasy of emotional tangibility, each wavy glowing outline expanding and contracting according to the fluctuations of anger and grief within the impassioned heart from which it emanated, shaking the ground and breaking through walls. But Catherine had looked so cool, so impassive, and then the light had vanished, her subsequent dismissal of me suggesting that somehow I was to blame for its disappearance. Well, whatever—I hadn't drunkenly crashed my car, and once I'd made up some story about my mother having been taken to the hospital for chest pains (with no serious consequences, however), Jillian had forgiven me.

These were the things that mattered. I thought about Jillian more than I did about Catherine, in part because Jillian gave me stuff to think about: I'd smelled her feet, listened to her pee through the bathroom door, met her parents—this last a gradual process, an accumulation of household encounters rather than a staged, formal meeting over dinner. Her mom treated me with effortfully accommodating pleasantness, the exertion of her politeness somehow visible, as if accompanied by sweat on her brow, whenever she asked me how I was doing or whether I'd like a glass of water. Her dad was more aloof, exuding primarily an air of protective fatherly suspicion, which, however, seemed mixed at times (and increasingly, as time went on) with a kind of jealous curiosity, its covetousness manifested as a conspiratorially male inside-jokiness into whose intimacy I was, on occasion, discordantly invited because (I guessed) all fathers actually wanted to have sex with their daughters, or at least to know what it might be like—he didn't know that so far I could only wonder, too. Once in a while, quietly, he told inappropriate jokes, like the one about the guitar teacher who got arrested "for fingering a minor" (it took me hours to realize the pun, as I didn't know much about guitars or music).

Families in general were gross to me—there was something inherently terrible about them: even the idea of a bunch of people who all looked vaguely alike, ate the same food, and shat in the same toilets day after day, building all the while some impenetrable mythology of love, happiness, resentment, and sacrifice around the collective survival mechanism whose outmoded practices formed the crux of their lives, genuinely creeped me out. When I looked at the Hellers as they watched *The Voice* or some other intergenerationally accessible television program together in the upstairs den (the downstairs media room seemingly reserved for "movie nights")—Mr. and Mrs. Heller, Melanie, and Jillian, their identical eyeballs affixed to the screen—I was reminded of my own family and wondered how anybody could ever want this, why one would ever choose to perpetuate the cycle. But when Jillian and I adjourned sneakily to her bedroom, the core miracle of human life was at least a little clearer to me, even if I'd missed my one potential opportunity thus far for actual sexual intercourse, the miracle's purest distillation: her body still had a lot to offer—not from any particular area as from its overall humanness.

My own body was improving. On a Wednesday after school, I went back to Dr. Steinfeld's office for another physical, and by some unknown process I'd returned to my normal height of five-foot-ten—a full two inches above my September mark. Had I just been having a bad day, my spine compressed by the weight of some imaginary stressor? The reversal of that shrinkage felt part of a larger trend of life-improvement for me —not a consequence of anything special I was doing, just a lucky streak. The nurse never apologized to me for what, by any reasonable conclusion, had to have been her error. The next time she saw me, I vowed, I'd be six-foot-one: fuck her.

My restored height notwithstanding, things were not "back to normal," whatever that might mean. In fact, the second significant instance of "weird shit" at school was a bigger and more impressive event than the first.

October and the first days of November had been almost summery, with global warming—my generation's anemic A-bomb—asserting itself more powerfully than ever before in our state, snatching the Pumpkin Spice Lattes and J. Crew sweaters away from our outstretched fingers, unwilling to allow the seasonal patterns of our consumerism to run their natural course. The temperature crept past 80 degrees—this lame rerun of summer, with all the good parts edited out, refused to go away. We couldn't move forward—it was like repeating a grade. Within our newly stagnant climate, the leaves withered not from chill but from boredom, and we watched, powerless not only to stop the progression of our planet's death but even to stop contributing to it, as the greenhouse gases wrenched New Jersey from its established borderland position within the dignified Northeast—land of covered bridges, Ivy League schools, and fall foliage—and nudged it gradually into the characterless temperate non-region of the Mid-Atlantic.

In what resembled, then, an act of triumphant reversal (the climate like an aging athlete, written off by the sportscasters, reclaiming the top spot if only for a single game), a snow day—or at any rate a partial one —occurred in the second week of November: the earliest in the history of Weybridge Public Schools. But, abnormally, it didn't extend to the entire district.

When I'd left my house that morning, the weather had been mild, not cool enough in the early hours even to chill the leather upholstery in my absurd luxury coupe. During first period, however, I looked out the window, as I often did during school hours with something less thoughtful than contemplation and uglier than yearning, and out of nowhere I saw the first snowflakes of the season falling like pixie dust from the gentle blue skies above. Had the temperature really dropped 30 degrees, for no apparent reason, in less than an hour? I felt instantly that something magical was happening—without in that moment connecting it, mentally, to the more dangerous voodoo of prior events—and began to evaluate my capacity to appreciate its magic: i.e., whether I would be able to take advantage, spontaneously and effortlessly, of its joy-inspiring potential. By perceiving it as an *opportunity* for joy, like a shopper noticing a major sale at a department store, had I already missed the point? Yet in the midst of these thoughts I experienced what I believed was an authentic urge to open the window, jump outside, and allow the white crystals to accumulate on my skin.

The period was almost over; in the final minutes we all gathered on the left side of the room and watched, *ooh*-ing and *ahh*-ing earnestly. When the bell rang, we rushed to apprise our friends who'd just emerged from windowless classrooms (all of us suddenly cognizant for the first time of the difference between the spaces in our school that looked out on the natural world, never before a subject of wide interest, and those that didn't), and by the time we'd finished talking to them about the meteorological miracle, we had to head to our next classes, having missed our chance to check out the event itself by stepping outdoors for a moment.

But in second period, the snowfall intensified to blizzard conditions, and my teacher made no attempt to hold a normal class. It got thicker and thicker, as though the air itself were a heavy white blanket in the process of shredding itself. I was on the wrong side of the classroom for observation this time, but ultimately I gravitated toward the window along with my classmates and even the imperturbable Mr. Salmon, suddenly unstuck by this bizarreness of weather from the unnoticing trance in which he'd surely been delivering his invariable civics lectures for generations.

Principal Tambakis's voice animated the classroom loudspeaker: the remainder of the school day was canceled—buses were on their way to pick up the underclassmen, and those of us who had arrived by private transportation were urged to use caution while driving home. Everyone had by then figured the announcement was coming, yet the consequent departure from what felt like primeval routine set us briefly into a state of mild bewilderment, as if we'd sat down at a restaurant and been served a shoe. *School was over already?* As we packed up our books, released abruptly from our roles as students and educators and returned to ourselves at this odd hour of the morning as private citizens, it took us a moment or two to realize that we could actually just leave.

Once I'd exited the room, I walked slowly through the halls, still beating most of my clustering social classmates to the doors. And then because the comfortable outdoor temperature accorded so well, in its surreal way, with the images of feathery softness that I'd observed from inside, I didn't immediately notice that anything was truly eerie—apart, of course, from the atypical earliness of the autumn snowstorm, upon which everyone had already commented. Without thinking about it, I'd expected, while venturing forth into the whitened outdoors, a world of tranquil beauty, not the frigid string that ought to have met somebody wearing a thin cotton shirt, without a coat, in harsh winter weather. And somehow the world *was* soft and gorgeous, the ambient drone of its usual misery smothered to silence by the cumulative pillow of the new snow. So I felt, first, something that, for me, had to qualify as joy, and then some very minor form of horror—a surprisingly small shock with which, nevertheless, my joy vanished—as I realized that it was still about 60 degrees outside.

Had I wandered onto a movie set, the snow composed of instant mashed potato flakes to mimic a white Christmas? Finally, I looked out into the distance, and the impression that I was inhabiting the artificial climate of a film production only increased: the snow ended at the school's property line, just past the soccer fields. The traffic out on Buchanan Boulevard whizzed by unimpeded and oblivious, no cars skidding.

I looked up. The snow was still falling, more gently now, but somehow it was coming down around me rather than on top of me, as if I were encased in a cone-shaped force-field. Bending down, I scooped a handful of the icy powder and saw it dissolve on my palm faster than sugar on a moist tongue—melting with such mirage-like quickness, in fact, that, by touching it, I could ascertain its materiality no more convincingly than I had by looking at it on the ground. I continued more slowly still in the direction of the parking lot, wandering past the tennis courts, pausing, waiting for my classmates to tumble out of school building in a fever of oblivious excitement, and then realizing as they failed to turn up that I was inhabiting my own solitary dreamscape of colorless confetti, the pale ash of reality's explosion. But of course this was wrong: time passed in the warm haze of white, and I became alert again as sound crept into the silence and the sight of my peers frolicking in the gleaming fluff, as if wholly unaware of the impossibility of granular precipitation during warm weather, soon asserted itself in my peripheral vision. They caught downward-twirling flakes on their tongues, rolled snowballs, threw them at one another—it seemed to be only for me that the snowstorm belonged to the diaphanous realm of fantasy; for them it was real life.

Free booze and snow days: it all felt a little pandering to me. Who was Catherine trying to win over, and why? Was she trying to come across as "relatable"—just another average teenager who "hated school" (as all teenagers supposedly did, though of course it wasn't true), exceptional only in her ability to do something about it—or were these *gifts* to us, attempts to make up for her various kidnappings, those thefts of life both human and animal? Would it work?

I looked around and saw a vision of pure adolescent happiness as the yellow buses slid uneasily into the lot, ignored by hundreds of kids who had no wish to go home—and, amid the teenage revelry on the lawn, a single set of tracks in the snow, seared into the soft new outdoor carpet as if the soles of the shoes that had made them had been hot irons: my own, penetrating to the ground below. Whatever she was doing, it seemed to be working—somehow it just wasn't working for me.

Chapter Ten

The more I spied on Adam Nordmark outside his home on Barnwell Street, the more I felt impelled to conclude that, removed from the soccer field, he was actually a pretty normal kid. I didn't have a lot to base this on, as I couldn't see much of him from the vantage point of my parked car across the street, but I watched him walk his dog again and again, apparently a daily post-dinner chore, and from that act of normalcy I couldn't help but extrapolate a similarly benign daily life surrounding it. The dog *was* his, as it turned out—it was just a bad walker, stubborn and lazy. Yet he loved his immovable pup; he was no pet-killer.

After school, whenever I wasn't with Jillian, I was at Adam's—I came to see that particular stretch of Barnwell, just past Elmira Park, as my hangout, almost independent of Adam and my increasingly pointless self-determined mission to gather information on his private life, the street like a dingy corner bar to which one might return each evening in order to take refuge not so much in alcohol as in routine. My snooping was almost comically boring, like a parody of *Rear Window* where Jimmy Stewart discovers absolutely nothing amiss among his neighbors and has to sit idle until his leg heals. I kept hoping that someone on the block would notice me there and, with a hint of hard-edged suspicion, question the purpose of my lurking in their neighborhood—if it contained no villain, then the villain had to be me—but this never happened. More than anything, I wanted Adam to approach me and acknowledge that he'd seen me there every time, night after night. Where would we go from there? Somewhere: that was the important thing.

I was sleeping one or two hours a night during the week and then sixteen or seventeen hours a day on weekends. When, on school-nights, it was time for Jillian to hang up the phone and doze off, I pretended to have the same plan, but instead I stayed up and watched old episodes of *Sabrina the Teenage Witch* and *Charmed,* for Catherine-related research, on Amazon Prime and Netflix. Both revolved around a central dishonesty that served to flatter their non-magical audiences, doggedly implying that the pleasures of ordinary life, outside the exotic territory of science fiction and fantasy, were in fact so greatly superior to those of the paranormal realm that, for wizards or sorceresses, the most important day-to-day challenge was to subdue their powers stringently enough to allow them to blend seamlessly into the general happy crowd and to participate in the dull human rituals (like making a living and going to school and falling in love and getting married) that, existing in service to laws of nature that obviously didn't apply to prophets or immortals, should logically have struck these heroines as pointless—so, while viewers sought by watching these shows to escape the inescapable realism of their reality, the characters they watched sought the inverse, thus ultimately reassuring their hopeless audiences that being a witch was nothing much in comparison to being a normal person, even as, in each case, the inherent inadequacy of normal personhood was the very reason for the show's creation and popularity. I didn't know what witches cared about specifically, but it seemed hard to believe that their thought processes were the same as mine, that living outside the bounds of reality didn't cause them to perceive life differently.

How did anyone else perceive life? Shortly before the whiskey incident and the snow day, a more "serious" but obviously less important event had occurred within the high school community: the disgraced ex-boyfriend of Emily Grace Pomeroy, a guy named Tyler Hankin, attempted to kill himself on a Wednesday by swallowing a few handfuls of prescription sleeping pills in his bedroom, where he was discovered by his mother, home unexpectedly early from work, just in time to call an ambulance. Tyler was apparently not responsible in a criminal sense for

Emily Grace's vanishing, as investigators had early on and without diffi-culty confirmed his alibi for the night she'd disappeared, but he still bore some slightly more abstract quality of guilt or blame, perhaps intrinsic to the role of the lover or ex in these cases but also partly a consequence of specific meaningful actions on his part that may not have amounted to murder but nevertheless constituted the only traceable storyline relat-ing to Emily Grace's case: if she had run off deliberately, his betrayal of her might have propelled her—as he allegedly had cheated on her, in reaction to her well-known prudery, in the months preceding her disap-pearance. I didn't know all the details, but like everyone else I wondered whether his sense of shame over the infidelity had led him to attempt to take his own life.

If so: a little melodramatic, no? I felt defensive around kids who had tried to off themselves (Tyler's was the third failed suicide in our class to my knowledge, albeit the first since sophomore year), the same way I'd once felt defensive around kids whose grades were better than mine, privately insisting in each case that the outer reality was not necessarily an accurate measurement of the inner quality it purported to represent. Had Tyler Hankin truly experienced greater psychic distress than I had, if I had never attempted such a thing? Not necessarily, right?

Well, why *hadn't* I ever tried to kill myself? Somehow it was outside my range of behavior—not just suicide but the whole lifestyle that ac-companied it. With a powerful jealousy, I watched my school's overtly troubled, black-clad victims of adolescent depression, drifting visibly in and out of catatonia with greasy hair and scars on their wrists, and I thought: I could do that; I could be them, if only I weren't me—if I weren't stuck playing soccer, getting good grades, practicing adequate hygiene, and dressing like a surprisingly homely Gap model. But my outside would never match up with the inside; I was incapable of liv-ing in harmony even with my disharmonies. For this reason, Tyler was more intriguing to me than his predecessors in botched self-slaughter: he looked even more normal than I did, had not by the looks of it worked his way up to the act of suicide with the normalizing consumer accessories of mental illness, the faux-vintage Smiths T-shirts and Sylvia Plath poetry collections.

I tried to imagine Tyler, a boy I knew hardly at all but who seemed cheerful in passing, secretly inhabiting the day-by-day misery of my own ridiculous, frantic, jumbled point of view. Was it possible that suicide attempts like his were more like random events than culminations, the misfires of overexcited teenage brains operating not in a state of despair but within their usual erratic incoherence—their ADD, like a roulette wheel, landing on sleeping pills as easily it might have landed on ice cream? It was the only way I could conceive of it.

Still, I wanted to know more. About a week after Tyler's return from the psych ward (or wherever they temporarily stashed teenagers who had tried to kill themselves—it sounded like my kind of summer camp), I saw him walking through the halls in a conspicuously normal fashion, without any observable self-consciousness, as if he were unaware that we were all looking at him. Possibly because he was wearing a pink shirt, the thought of him contemplating self-annihilation seemed implausible, like the idea of a Muppet shooting heroin. Yet it had happened: Matt had told me first, and then Jillian, whose mother was friends with a woman who was friends with Tyler's mother, had confirmed it. I'd since heard at least a dozen other people talking about it, even though barely anyone talked to me at school at all.

On an impulse (or maybe something more than impulse, as this was in fact a fairly complicated maneuver), I opened my backpack, retrieved a notebook, and ripped out a sheet of paper. Keeping Tyler in sight, I wrote very quickly, before I could chicken out: "Tyler, I know we don't know each other well, but please call me if you ever want to talk. 908-208-2231."

And I walked up to him and handed him the note, just like that, smiling earnestly and walking away before he could read it. Not a Snapchat or a Facebook message: a real letter, the authenticity of its sentiment proved somehow by the archaism of its medium.

I'd never done anything like it before, and I wasn't sure what had empowered me to do it now. Was it the presence in my life of Jillian, to whom I could confidently point if the act of handing my phone number to another guy were construed as "super fucking gay"? In any case, I didn't think Tyler would really call me, but amazingly, my phone buzzed later that day at about five o'clock, displaying an unknown number. I picked up.

"Hello?" I said.

An enthusiastic voice on the other end: "Hey, Jeff! It's Tyler. What's up, man?"

"Oh. Not much," I said, wondering what was going on, whether he was somehow mocking my invasive attempt to "help out"—it was clear from his tone that he wasn't reaching out for compassion in a moment of deep distress. But he didn't sound annoyed, either.

"It was so cool of you to give me your number," Tyler said. "I don't know why more people don't do that sort of thing—I mean, like, at school, we all just enclose ourselves in our little friend groups that we've had since freshman year or junior high. There are all these other people around who are probably nice or cool or whatever, but no one wants to take the risk of talking to someone new."

"Thanks," I said. "Yeah, um, I figured, why not."

"Most guys would probably be too worried that other dudes would think they were gay if they ever tried to be friendly." He laughed. "Not that it's a problem if you are gay. That's cool, too."

"I'm not," I said. "I have a girlfriend. But I also condemn homophobia."

"Nice. So what are you up to tonight? You want to grab some pizza? I was just about to head over to Vinny's Pizza on Hillsborough, I'm totally starving right now."

"Pizza sounds all right."

"Awesome, bro. Let's meet there in like fifteen? Sorry to rush you, but like I said I'm super hungry right now."

"Yeah, I guess I'm hungry, too."

"Right on."

A pause. "OK, see you there."

I ended the call and, after using the bathroom, grabbed my car keys. How had this happened? I left the question silently hanging, realizing it didn't need an answer. En route to Vinny's, I left the windows of my car open, basking in the November warmth of our doomed planet. The roads were clogged with returning commuters, the misery of their happy lives unimaginable: the ugliness of their wives, the whininess of their children, the burdens of their mortgages and the property taxes on their discombobulatingly tasteless homes. I had only a vague idea what a mortgage *was*—it was so much better to be a young person in a stupidly expensive car that I hadn't paid for. *Never get old*, I reminded myself.

I sat in traffic, genuinely curious as to what Tyler and I would talk about and why he wanted to meet me, yet somehow not negatively consumed by this curiosity, embedded as I was in the strangely soothing pleasure of being on my way, on a nice day, to meet someone of whom I had no hopes or expectations. Idly I considered Tyler as if he were not about to appear in front of me: what did I know about him? From what I could recall, he had ruptured his spleen in the sixth grade during a BMX accident, was now on the swim team—those sorts of things: the usual nothings of which we were all composed. Ten minutes later, I was at the pizzeria, parked.

I went inside and spotted Tyler, sitting at the booth in front (one of three in the tiny space), even before the shop's perma-smell of hot dough had entered my nostrils. He jumped up energetically and shook my hand, smiling.

"Hey, Jeff! You like mushrooms?" he said.

"Yeah, they're good," I said.

"Good. I already ordered a pizza with mushrooms on it. *So* hungry, man."

Why such an intensity of appetite? Was he just now coming off a successful hunger strike, all of his demands ceded? He was wearing a sleeveless shirt with black and white stripes—inappropriate for November even at this stage of our planet's irreversible descent into the inferno. Still, he looked comfortable in own private Southern California, his shoulders large and tan.

"You ordered a whole pizza?" I said. "How much was it?"

"Oh, don't worry about it, bro. My treat. I'm just relieved you like mushrooms, man. Mushrooms are the best, but for some reason everyone hates on them."

"Yeah, they're good." Had I already said this?

"There's just too much hate in this world, you know?"

"Like, with regard to mushrooms, or just generally?"

"Both, man."

A lot of *man*s and *bro*s in his speech—as if to relieve, through constant acknowledgment, the embarrassment of being a male talking to another male. Or maybe that was just how he talked—maybe he called his grandma *bro*. I sat down.

"So how's it going?" I said.

"Pretty good. Solid day at school. Stat test—aced it. French Club meeting afterward. And now I'm about to eat some pizza. Can't ask for more than that."

"Our school has a French Club?"

"Hell yeah, man. It's fucking great."

"What do you guys do?"

"Watch French movies, bake croissants, talk in French, shit like that."

"That sounds fun."

He nodded. "You're still on the soccer team, right?"

"Yeah, more or less."

"What a season so far, huh? From what I've heard, you guys are incredible this year. Just destroying everyone."

"Oh, yeah, we're undefeated, but it's basically just because of this one kid, a freshman named Adam Nordmark. The rest of us suck."

"Seriously? I haven't heard about him."

"Yeah, for some reason no one is talking about him. Everybody's just pretending that we've been playing exceptionally well as a team. It's a conspiracy."

He was still smiling. "There are a lot of those lately. You know that girl Catherine Harding? Supposedly she was the one who slipped all that booze into the cafeteria the other day. The school administration just can't prove it yet."

My mouth opened well before any words came out. "Shit, I thought I was the only one who knew about that."

"Oh yeah, you know her? Everyone's talking about it. They say she was responsible for all that snow, too. Apparently she can manipulate weather—pretty spooky, huh?"

In truth he didn't seem at all spooked by this breach of our reality. His light brown eyes, the same shade as his sun-cooked skin, radiated calm.

"But," I said, "that's literally impossible."

"I don't know, man," he said. "I have a cousin who can always predict when it's about to rain. Like, before a single drop has fallen, she'll always tell us it's about to happen, and she's always right. Some people are weird like that."

"I think there's a pretty big difference between predicting the weather and altering it. Humans can't alter the weather."

"What about global warming? Liberals always say it's manmade."

"Yeah," I said, recognizing that the point was irrelevant but temporarily lacking the language to prove it. Why bother? Logic had been rendered invalid already, and not by him.

"Personally, I'm loving this climate change stuff," he said. "I don't need winter in my life. I just love to be outdoors—going for walks, playing sports, or even just lying down in the grass with my thoughts, you know? It's the best. I hate being cooped up inside."

"Bummer for the polar bears, though," I said.

"Shit, you'd think they'd be the happiest of all. The North Pole must've been a pretty rough spot before all this. At least now it's not *completely* ice, you know? Pretty soon they'll all be hanging out in, like, a nice warm meadow up there."

The doughy smell intensified. I looked up, and the guy from behind the counter—possibly the eponymous Vinny himself—was lowering the pizza on its silver platter to our table. With his other hand he dropped a stack of paper plates. We each took one and carefully extracted a slice of the pie, its cheese still liquid.

"Don't you hate people who have to dab all the grease off the pizza with a napkin before they can eat it?" Tyler said. "I mean, where's their *joie de vivre*? It makes sense from a caloric perspective, but sometimes you have to just *live*, my man."

"Totally," I said, surreptitiously letting the napkin in my left hand drop. I allowed the pizza to cool a moment longer, then bit: it was noticeably better with the grease still present. The mushrooms had obviously come from a can, but it didn't matter much—I was fairly sure that the slice tasted good, a quality I could appreciate only abstractly.

"Wow," Tyler said between ecstatic bites. "I love pizza."

He loved pizza: were uncontroversial opinions the key to happiness? Then again, hadn't this boy just tried to kill himself? Yet he seemed so content, brimming with the pleasure of his hearty male hunger as if he were in a commercial for a steakhouse chain. I thought about texting Jillian to ask whether I'd somehow gotten my information wrong: had it been Tyler Lannister, the junior with the weirdly long fingernails, who had actually attempted to commit suicide?

"I think, sometimes, when life seems totally crazy, you just have to appreciate the small things," he said, "like pizza."

Was this how I sounded when I talked to Jillian? It seemed so stupid.

"It's actually a pretty big pizza," I said. "You think we can finish it?"

"Oh, hell yeah, bro," he said. "You've just got to believe in yourself."

I finished my slice and, with time, ate one more, as I watched him eat the other six.

"Man," he said, "I feel like my appetite has been insane ever since I got my stomach pumped at the hospital. It's like I never stop feeling hungry."

Whoa. "Yeah, uh, that makes sense," I said. It didn't, but who cared? I was bowled over less by what he's said than by the equanimity with which he'd said it.

"So what's next for us, man?" he said.

"After high school? I guess college," I said, suddenly struck by the rigid predictability of our course, thrust by nothing in particular into an unexpected comprehension of the typically drug-induced perception of the covert earthly openness existing beyond the purview of our guidance counselors that compelled some of my alternative-minded classmates to view life with a goggle-eyed belief in its wonder and possibility: why *did* I have to go to college? For a moment I considered whether joining ISIS, for example, might give me a stronger sense of purpose and direction than majoring in communications or some such bullshit—whether the spiritual certitude of Islamic fundamentalism might have been what was missing from my life all along. I shrugged it off, but not without some effort.

"No, I mean tonight," he said. "You want to go to the Copper Monkey?"

"What's the Copper Monkey?"

"Oh man, you don't know? It's a bar in New Brunswick where they never check IDs. It's a well-known thing."

"It's a Tuesday night."

He grinned big. "So what? We're seniors, bro!"

"You want to go all the way to New Brunswick?"

"It's on Easton Ave. We can be there in fifteen minutes."

The swiftness of the proposal had knocked me further off balance, and I realized I would have to answer it without really thinking about it. "Yeah, OK," I said. "Let's go."

Tyler clapped his hands and then punched me on the shoulder. "Yes! Let's do this!"

I was committed, so now I could wonder only uselessly whether it would be a good idea. In truth, the experience might fill some void in my adolescent experience: wasn't being a teenager primarily about participating in high-spirited hijinks? What other source of meaning was there? The only alternative to being trivially naughty was being boring —that or falling in love with someone who had cancer. There was really nothing else to do during high school. Why didn't anyone in *my* school have cancer?

Still, it seemed impossible that a bar could exist where high schoolers could freely obtain alcohol, without fake IDs, on a Tuesday night. Such a place would get shut down, especially in a college town like New Brunswick, where underage drinking was doubtless a concern, wouldn't it? If it were possible to serve minors there without penalty, every bar would do it, but surely not every bar did: hence it wasn't possible. Maybe a few eighteen-year-olds had scored some booze once; maybe there was one negligent bartender who had yet to be disciplined for his negligence. Tyler and I, however, might encounter a different bartender, and we might get caught. What would happen if we were? How bad did the penalty have to be before our mistake could no longer be interpreted within the rubric of hijinks?

And what would happen if we *weren't* caught? I could see that Tyler wanted to have fun. I had not only never had fun—I probably had never even successfully convinced someone else that I was having fun. Would drinking in a bar underage intrinsically qualify as a "hijink"—the noun had no singular form, I was the first person in the world whose life was lame enough to require one—or would we need some additional misadventure to issue from our illegal intoxication at a bar within the most urbanized section of Central Jersey? If the latter were the case, what would we do? It struck me how much of life was artistry—creating a story, a tone, an atmosphere. I couldn't do any of it.

"Want me to drive?" Tyler said. "It probably makes more sense to take one car. Parking can be a pain in the ass over by Rutgers."

We had stood up and were carrying our trash over to the pizzeria's garbage can, its swinging slotted opening marked with tomato sauce at its edge like the mouth of a sloppy child.

"We can take mine," I said, making a calculation on the fly: by controlling our transportation, I would retain some control over our evening, or so I reasoned.

"Sweet," Tyler said.

I unlocked the doors with my electronic key fob—the Bratmobile had a better unlocking sound than my friends' lesser cars did, a sort of pneumatic unsealing as inviting (in its subtler way) as the fizzy pop of the opened top of a Coke can—and we got inside. Had I ever ventured beyond the town limits of Weybridge in my own car? I'd had such big plans before I'd gotten my own car but of course had ended up doing nothing. I input the name of the bar into my phone.

"Whoa, your car is really clean," Tyler said. "I dig it."

"Thanks, bro."

Now *I* was saying it. But why not? Why not say it all the time, to everyone?

Traffic had thinned, and in fact it took less than ten minutes to reach the New Brunswick border. New Brunswick sat directly north of Weybridge, its population roughly the same but its character entirely different, its streets dominated primarily by higher-density housing for the lower middle-class. It was Middlesex County's only stronghold of ethnic diversity—not counting the Jews and Asians of Weybridge—and hosted various big-city amenities (hospitals, a train station, non-chain restaurants, concert venues) for the barren surrounding suburbs, forming a localized, miniaturized urbanism for Central Jersey while still existing within the larger orbit of New York City, not a true destination unto itself and aware of it in some vague but obvious way. It was also the site of the large main campus of Rutgers University, the respectable public safety school for virtually all of my classmates. I'd seen a performance of *The Nutcracker* at the State Theater on George Street with my parents when I was eight but hadn't been back much since.

I drove directly to the address of the Copper Monkey, forgoing several viable parking spots on the way before remembering that parking worked differently outside of suburbia: I'd already forgotten the reason Tyler was in the car with me—I'd never before driven to an establishment without off-street parking. I circled back and parallel-parked a few blocks away, not too badly.

And then, outside, on the sidewalk, I felt excited—this was *definitely* a hijink. We were in a city (of sorts), going to a *bar*. I was as cool as anyone else.

"So you've been to this place before?" I said.

"Me?" Tyler said. "No, I've just heard about it a lot."

This made me feel better rather than worse: he and I were both greenhorns, equally eager for some experience, some joy and redemption following the traumatic experiences of his suicide attempt and my whole life, respectively. I walked in, observing almost nothing, anticipating only the make-or-break moment, approaching it amid a whirl of internal butterflies and external barstools and stale beer smell. I looked at the bartender, a scuzzy guy in a Rutgers hoodie, the puffy blackish rottenness beneath his eyes showing that he was too old to be a student— probably the kind of guy who had loved college life so much that he had decided to stay on after graduation and yet now, regretting his choice to stick around campus, hated college kids above all else: it felt as though he might deny us our drinks even if we *were* over twenty-one.

Tyler spoke up before I could back down. "Can I get a Sam Adams?" he said.

The bartender grabbed a glass. "Five dollars," he said, and he poured the beer, cocking the tap handle, releasing the bubbly liquid as if from an underground well: so much mysticism in that foamy ambrosia—I focused on it and finally comprehended the general fascination with alcohol, somehow.

As he set it on the bar, I said, "I'll have the same, please."

I reached into my wallet and put a ten dollar bill on the bar, wondering whether I had spoiled our presentation of self-assurance and belonging with the wimpy entreaty of my *please*.

"I'll cover both of us," I said to Tyler.

Tyler pushed his face close to my ear. "Thanks, bro," he said, "but you have to tip a dollar for each beer." Not as green a greenhorn as I was, apparently.

"Oh shit," I said—speaking aloud, not whispering as he had. But the bartender, dispensing my beer from the hidden keg, hadn't collected the cash yet, and I added two Washingtons. Then, when he returned, we took our beers and sat down at a table nearby.

There were only three other people inside the bar, a college-aged couple and a random older guy. I felt drunk already from the relief of our success, and in a fit of reckless energy I downed the pint of beer almost in a gulp. Tyler did much the same, guzzling surely less from nervousness than from his aforementioned ceaselessness of appetite.

Was I drunk for real now? Whatever—I sensed that I was in as altered a state as I would be that night, whether from alcohol or some other force. I looked Tyler in the eye; he looked back as if unaware that sustained eye contact was meaningful in human culture rather than a default setting.

"Tyler," I said, my courage at its height, "was Emily Grace the reason you took those sleeping pills?"

"Emily Grace?" he said. "You mean Emily?"

"Yeah," I said. "Grace was her middle name."

"Really? I didn't know that."

"I thought everyone called her Emily Grace."

"I've literally never heard anyone call her that."

"Well, anyway, was she the reason you did it?"

I looked at him more intently but sensed no tensing-up on his part. I leaned forward in my seat, and he slumped back casually in his as though he were a Copper Monkey regular.

"Well," he said, "at some point I realized that I was never going to see her again, and that got me pretty upset. I mean, obviously, it's all still up in the air, but that's how I feel—I just don't see her ever coming back. And I know everyone thought I was a shitty boyfriend to her because I cheated on her and stuff, but I really loved her, bro. Have you ever been in love, Jeff?"

"Yeah," I said. "Maybe."

Was I in love with Jillian? It seemed unlikely that my desire would ever register fully as a love-like euphoria for me: unlikely that I would ever be rendered unable, through sheer joy, to break down the agglomeration of feeling into discrete parts, its uglier urges and selfish needs. Even so, did I not deserve to call it love? Tyler had used the word—so could I, if I wanted to: weren't people always talking about themselves, really, when they said they loved someone else?

"It wasn't like I really wanted to kill myself. I just wanted to be closer to her again. Somehow, at that moment, that seemed like the only way. I know it doesn't make sense."

He was a moron; still, it did make sense, and as I tried to imagine the sensation of being pharmaceutically pulled (at first willingly, then half-willingly, then unwillingly, then willingly again) into a deeper kind of sleep—not to the usual callow stopping point, on the nearest border of unconsciousness, but toward a more remote and vivid home, amid the loftier scenery granted only on the condition of a firmer commitment— it seemed, in my own moment of imaginative illogic, almost irresistible, whether a girl waited on the other side of the journey or not.

"Why'd you cheat on her?" I said.

"Well, she didn't believe in doing a lot of the things that other girls are willing to do—it was like a morals thing for her. So cheating was basically a necessity."

He alluded to his dick as casually as he had to his heart, as though each constituted a third (and perfectly respectable) person in the room, its needs and opinions as valid and worthy of consideration as anyone else's. Why couldn't *I* believe in either, my dick or my heart?

"But you regret it now?" I said.

"No, not really," he said. "I guess I feel bad about the way life's set up, you know, like there's no really perfect solution to anything. But jerking off is so fucking boring, bro. It's like having a conversation with yourself. What was I supposed to do?"

I pondered his metaphor, or simile, or whatever: hadn't every conversation I'd ever had felt like a conversation with myself? What did it feel like to talk *with* someone? I couldn't imagine it: maybe that was why I couldn't imagine having sex.

"How many times did you cheat on her?"

"I'm not sure. Lots, I guess. You think I'm a bad person, man?"

"No," I said, knowing that there was no other possible response to the question, regardless of the circumstances: I imagined Hitler morosely sipping a mug of beer, asking his pal on the next barstool whether he thought he was a bad person just because of the Holocaust. "Who'd you cheat on her with?"

"Man, I can't even remember at this point," he said.

"Aw, c'mon, bro," I said, struggling a little with the informal contraction of *come on*. I was the worst teenager: didn't understand social media, had no idea which bands were cool, was now somehow losing my grasp on basic colloquialisms.

Still, it seemed the *bro* had swayed him: "There was Sharon Hillman first, I think. Then Nadia Scott. Lauren Rosenberg, Amy Ross, Cathy Yang. Oh, and Bree Paoletti. Also, I once got a handjob at a party from Shirley McDermott, but, like, I'm not sure it counts because I didn't *do* anything. I didn't kiss her or even flirt with her. She just grabbed my dick and went to work, for no reason at all."

"But you didn't stop her," I said.

"Yeah, I mean, wouldn't that have been kind of rude?" he said.

"I guess so. So you had sex with all those other girls?"

"Sex? No, I don't believe in sex before marriage."

"So what does it mean to cheat on somebody?"

"In my case, mostly non-penetrative sexual contact, with occasional oral or digital penetration, sometimes orgasm. No big deal, really, but it definitely hurt Emily's feelings when she found out."

"Yeah, I mean, that was a lot of girls you mentioned."

"I also finger-fucked Patricia Biondi one time. And Trisha Metcalf, Kylie Hinkle, Brenda Shapiro . . ."

"You finger-fucked all of them?"

"Yeah, all of them."

"Wow. Any others?"

"Let's see … Lizzy Solomon, for sure. A few times. Tara Wolfe, Cara Riddick—same night. Sarah Prosser, Jillian Heller, Christina Cogswell, Taylor Barker. That might be it."

I'd almost missed Jillian's name in the near-endless list. Maybe none of it was true, or maybe all of it was—I was leaning toward the latter. But did it matter? I'd decide later.

"Want another beer?" I said.

"Sure," Tyler said.

Fearless this time, I stood faced up to the bartender, my shoulders square, and ordered a second round. A minute later, I was back at the table, taking a hearty gulp of my beverage. After two more gulps, I felt unmistakably good, my mission already accomplished in some sense: nothing else to do but enjoy the small things in life. Tyler had been onto something: daily pleasures, the natural (or augmented) sensory joy of the moment. Nothing transcendent, nothing sublime: this happiness was probably enough, the whole point of everything. In a minute or an hour, I'd let it slip away, of course.

"Why didn't you just break up with Emily Grace?" I said. "You could've dated someone else—or no one. You could've just had fun."

"I had fun with her, too, just in a different way. Some people are just special for you. They have that magic."

"What do you think happened to her?"

"I have no idea."

"Fuck."

"I know." An appropriate moment of silence passed.

"You don't think you'll do anything to hurt yourself again, will you?" I said.

"Me?" he said. "I'm good now. Thanks for asking, though, buddy."

"No problem."

He smiled philosophically. We finished our beers.

"Should we get more beer?" I said.

"Nah," he said. "I don't really believe in getting seriously drunk. It just isn't really a good idea, generally. It's nice to just have one or two beers, I think. Besides, we have to drive."

"Oh, right."

"You know what we should do? There's a White Castle here in New Brunswick, on Route 27. Have you ever been?"

"No."

"Oh, man, it's great. They have these tiny little burgers. You can eat like fifty of them. I'm already getting hungry again."

I thought of demurring on account of my vegetarianism but didn't want to spoil his fun: maybe they had tofu sliders? Tyler's philosophical smile had broadened into a dumb grin.

"Let's go," I said.

We left the bar, and the walk to the car seemed to sober me adequately enough that, when I got into the driver's seat of my car, I didn't feel that I was breaking the law in any significant way—even though, since I didn't have a license, I was of course a lawbreaker every time I drove, regardless of my sobriety.

Tyler directed me, and together we traveled a few miles, passing on the way a stylishly lit mononymous establishment called *Sunchoke*, instantly identifiable as an expensive restaurant bearing (or attempting to bear, as best it could, within this regional, non-cosmopolitan cultural hub) a cool, contemporary vibe that, in Weybridge, simply didn't exist in any form. I felt impressed as I watched two well-dressed grownups pass beneath the tastefully fonted sign to its glass door, dimly glowing from the tasteful lighting behind it. Was this my future? Would I someday—as a gainfully employed adult who had *earned* his pleasures—be able to process an evening at a fancy restaurant as an experience of pure sensual gratification rather than an anxious signifying ritual of my social station? How in the world was anyone capable of truly caring how something *tasted*? I felt a shiver of horror, subsiding as we approached the rectangular white castellated structure of our destination, between an AutoZone and McDonald's. At the drive-thru, Tyler ordered a mere 25 sliders; I ordered fries and a coke. He paid.

He seemed puzzled by my daintiness but didn't question it; I didn't volunteer an explanation. I just watched him eat, slowly munching on my fries as he did—one by one, barely eating them in fact, letting each linger between my lips like a crinkle-cut cigarette. When he'd finished ten or twelve burgers, my attention began to wander from his relentless animalistic intake: had I learned anything from my evening with the suicidal boy? No, probably not. Nothing made sense or amounted to anything—but I hadn't learned this, I'd already known.

My gaze drifting across the parking lot, I noticed on the right side of my windshield a bright white illumination, spotty between the trees that flanked the backend of the lot. The lights were somewhere above us—as powerful almost, it seemed, as the UFO-style beams that loomed over professional football stadiums. I continued to stare through the raggedy copse—really just a single remaining line of greenery between one developed parcel and another, not quite demolished but pitifully bedraggled— toward the floodlit space, and a picture started to emerge: a park, some people, a soccer ball. Weybridge didn't have a single public recreation space lit up for nighttime activity; this was a surprising novelty to me.

"I think there's a park on the other side of those trees," I said, by this point already certain. "It looks people are playing soccer over there."

"Oh, cool," Tyler said with apparently genuine enthusiasm. "We should go play!"

"Us?"

"I'm not that good at soccer, but I bet you could pick up the slack."

"I don't know. We just had pizza and beer and fast food."

"So what? I feel fine," he said, still gobbling. "Let's check it out."

He put down his half-eaten burger and got out of the car; I had no choice but to follow—and then to follow him further, to the mucky zone of neglect where the trees grew like gangly abused orphans beside a torn metal fence. We made our way through, however, and on the other side, across a residential street and between two apartment buildings, I saw what I'd already seen, the sight now confirmed: two basketball courts, a children's playground, and between them, a fluorescent field of grass where eight Latino men of unidentifiable age passed around a soccer ball, as if warming up before a pickup game—they had two cone-based goals set up already.

"I kind of suck at soccer now," I said to Tyler. "Actually, I'm not sure I ever was good."

"You're way too hard on yourself, bro. I bet you're awesome at it."

Tyler continued onward, surprisingly (for someone from Weybridge) unfearful in the face of a multitude of minorities.

"Hey, can we play?" Tyler said, loudly, as he got close enough for communication. We weren't really dressed for it, but I at least was wearing Sambas.

A few of the players turned their heads to us. The others didn't bother. The one with the ball nodded, passed it to Tyler. I came closer, and Tyler weakly passed it to me, still slightly removed from the group, near the edge of the grass. I passed it to one of the men.

Who did they think we were? Dumb college kids, maybe, here on a dare, braving the dangers of an "ethnic neighborhood" as part of some frat initiation. More than anything else, I didn't want to offend these men—I recognized that for us to create any sense of unnaturalness, through our presence, would also be to create the implication that for us to be there wasn't natural, i.e. that their game was not the sort of game into which well-meaning strangers could join in friendly accordance with the usual rules of park-based pickup sports and therefore was somehow, by virtue only of the race of its participants, disreputable within the context of the larger world—and yet the offense felt inevitable, with my patronizing high school Spanish bubbling up within me, cracked and idiotic, alongside various stuttering, spluttering mannerisms that would surely betray my terror (terror not in fact of the men in the park, who had brought a ball and set up cones with the obviously wholesome intention of playing soccer, but terror of creating offense through some accidental impoliteness, though it might be taken the other way: another reason to be terrified). But if I called Tyler back now, pleaded with him to go home with me, halting his naïve puppyish pursuit of fun for some complicated reason I couldn't say in public, would I only make it worse?

Improbably, even amid these apprehensive thoughts, when the ball touched my feet a second time, I felt, for the first time in a while, the old pleasure of it as it knocked up against the sides of my Adidas flats: the familiarity of an old lover, every curve in its right spot, nuzzling up to my own experienced touch. Or at least it was the closest I would ever know of that imagined sensation—how could I, then, reject it?

There was no Adam Nordmark here, so maybe I *was* good at soccer— and it seemed possible that the beer might make me even better, loosen me up, allow a freer style of athletic self-expression—and I felt myself wanting to *let go*, to keep kicking the ball, to slip into the unselfconscious happiness that well-intentioned white people condescendingly believed themselves capable of achieving by embedding themselves in the poorer races' "simple pleasures" (usually of the bodily variety): sensual dancing, nobly purposeful physical labor in movie-montage format, sports that required less expensive equipment than skiing or sailing.

The guys were beginning to halve themselves, to form teams: I juggled the ball a little before passing it off. If I could forget the clichéd and offensive nature of the narrative I was already beginning to create in my head—helplessly wanting to believe that, among these Latinos, I would recover the purer, stripped-down satisfaction of the game itself, previously lost to the institutionalized version of the sport (not true: lost to the shaming example of a supernatural talent, or else never known in the first place)—I would play well, I knew. They were all probably good players themselves—was that itself a racist assumption?

I might even (the narrative growing still cornier in my brain) play my best soccer ever. This pickup game, rather than my failed high school career, might with some poetic strangeness serve as the secret culmination of all those hours of practice: a truer triumph, somehow, for its unexpectedness, its meaninglessness—all truly sublime moments in life must be hidden. I could feel my recently unused ability welling up inside me like an erection after not jerking off for a week.

I shuffled after Tyler, committing vaguely to one side, as the ball came back to me once more. I kicked it: why not? If I was going to take away something graspable from this evening with the suicidal boy, it would be here: it would be happiness—another cliché to add the pile, an irony so obvious as to be the opposite of irony. But I could disregard, for just a moment, the inherent dishonesty of earnest things, couldn't I? I just had to play. I could play. I knew how.

Chapter Eleven

As it turned out, Emily Grace was only the first. Jillian called me about it in the morning, the panic conspicuous in her voice.

"Do you know Nicole Burdette?" she said, without a greeting, when I picked up.

"No, not really," I said. So many kids in our town—too many: why did we all think we were so important? Waking thoughts. It was a Saturday morning; the phone had roused me from sleep.

"Well, she's gone. She lives next door to Karen, and the police are all at her house."

"At Karen's?"

"No, at Nicole's. She disappeared. The police are talking to her parents."

"She's just—gone? Like Emily Grace?"

"Yeah. I'm starting to get really, really scared. Like, what are we supposed to do? Should we all just run away from this town? Something super fucked up is going on, and we all just keep acting normal, like nothing's happening. School, soccer games, parties, dentist appointments, whatever. Like everything is fine."

Jillian didn't play a sport: was the mention of "soccer games" a shot at my own inactivity, my inability or unwillingness to rise up manfully and protect the helpless female and animal populations of our town? Or was soccer only an incidental symbol of the wholesome normalcy that the autumn's hidden violence had undercut? If the latter, I could understand: I'd pursued it as such a symbol all my life.

"What else are we supposed to do? It's all we know," I said. The latter phrase, meant usually for some faraway benighted group (*coal mining is all they know*, etc.), felt just a little wrong in its self-applied form. But it was true: banality *was* all we knew.

"We can't just pretend," she said. "It'll keep happening."

"We don't know that. I'll come over, OK?" I said. "You're at home?"

"Yeah," she said.

"I'll be right there," I said.

I staggered out of bed, a little annoyed at first in my early-morning depression and then, once I'd brushed my teeth and fully shaken off my sleep, suddenly grateful for the opportunity to soothe a female girl's trepidation: grateful to be needed not on account of any skillful service I could provide but just for the stupid reassurance of my bulkier male presence—I sensed in it the basic pleasure of being a husband, a father, the reason men all walked around looking so self-satisfied.

Fifteen minutes later, I was in Jillian's bedroom, sprawled on her bed in jeans and socks, her strange body pressed against mine, clingingly extracting its tense warmth (cuddling still felt unnatural to me) in some atavistic conflation of heat and safety. We looked at each other, the terrible thought briefly but unmistakably passing between us: what if she was next? Since we still hadn't had sex and yet were still so close to making it happen, her mysterious departure would at this late stage probably strike me most of all, in my crude boyish selfishness, as some bitter taunting fuck-you from the universe, aimed at me. But how would I feel, hypothetically, about her ensuing disappearance if we already had done it? Maybe it wouldn't be so bad. Glumly I considered the prospect that Catherine's victims (this was how I viewed them, even as I had no clue what Catherine was doing to them or why and indeed possessed no proof that she was involved whatsoever) might always be people I'd only vaguely heard of, the meaningfulness of their tragedies distant and unreal to me like all the invisible forces of love and sorrow that animated human life. If so, was I fortunate or deprived—unbereft or bereft through lack of bereavement? Was it true that the preciousness of life became apparent only once some integral chunk of one's own life had (heartbreakingly) vanished?

"Did you know Nicole?" I said. We were already using the past tense: Tyler was right—these girls were gone for good, it felt obvious somehow.

"A little," Jillian said. "She liked to read a lot. I saw her sitting alone at lunch sometimes with a book—with this look of, like, intense but pleasurable concentration. And total confidence—you could tell she was alone by choice, not embarrassed about it."

"What kind of stuff did she read?" I said. The idea of extracting any amount of enjoyment from a book was completely insane to me: who in the world was capable of thinking about something other than himself long enough to follow a 300-page story to its conclusion?

"I think fantasy novels mostly. I'm not totally sure, though. I didn't really look at the titles most of the time. I was just kind of in awe of her self-possession or something. The way she could tune out everything— how immersed she was, right in the middle of the school day."

Maybe that was happiness: to be so empty of personal conflict that the travails of a fictional character were more preoccupying than one's own. Or was that only a sign of idiocy?

"We really need to get far, far away from here," she said. "College applications feel a lot different now, don't they?"

"What do you mean?" I said.

"It feels like a life-or-death issue now. Like, we have to escape. I think about the places more than the schools now—how far they are from here."

"Wasn't that always sort of the case for you?"

"Yeah, I guess. There's just more riding on it now."

"How many applications have you done?"

"Ten so far."

"That's a lot."

"Have you been working on yours?"

We hadn't talked much about college, being in that early fingers-crossed stage of coupledom where neither of us was quite ready to believe that it might matter where the other person was going off to school, hesitant to admit that it might make sense for us to think of our own plans in light of another—yet neither was Jillian able to flaunt callously her big dreams of moving away and sadly but inevitably forgetting about me. College dominated the collective conversation; our private conversation had been a refuge from it.

"Not really," I said. "I'll probably just end up at Rutgers, honestly. My grades aren't strong enough for me to get in anywhere *really* good, so I might as well just go to school for cheap."

As I'd more or less tuned out my guidance counselor at each of our mandatory meetings, I wasn't sure how accurate this assessment really was: my grades *were* pretty good—strong enough that, in my parents' generation, before Asians had been invented, they probably would have put me near the very top of my class, and even now I expected a full scholarship from our State University of New Jersey. Jillian's first choice, at the moment, was U.C. Berkeley—I probably had as good a shot at getting in as she did; I just didn't see the point.

"Don't be so defeatist," she said. "You're too hard on yourself."

"I don't feel defeated. I don't think life begins and ends with college."

"Well, it definitely doesn't *end* there, but I'm hoping it might begin."

"I still have time to fill out some more applications, just in case. Not everyone's on the ball the way you are."

Her body hadn't moved, as far as I could tell, yet it seemed slightly less close—she didn't believe me.

. . . .

There were three more in quick succession the following week: a girl named Lacy Ramos and then two boys, Thomas Mancini and Mark Sokolowski—seniors, all of them, gone without warning. It had never occurred to me that the *boys* of Weybridge were in any danger; I'd assumed that whatever grisly appetite had engulfed Emily Grace Pomeroy and Nicole Burdette required female parts to get its juices flowing.

Even so, with five whole students missing from our 819-person senior class, school continued on in a way that, perhaps as a consequence of Jillian's earlier commentary upon the same issue, seemed very odd and artificial. According to my teacher Mr. Wilkes—who prided himself on his just-one-of-the-guys attitude of openness among his students— there had been some talk of canceling school indefinitely, until one of the administrators brought up the point that, in school, at least, the students appeared to be protected: the victims had all vanished from their homes, during the night—fully removing us from the apparent safe haven that was Weybridge High could only exacerbate the problem. So they kept us cooped up with our textbooks and notebooks and number-two pencils while the newly evil world swirled around us. There was nothing they could tell us to pretend they could keep us secure, no way of spinning the crisis as a preventable situation, so they didn't say much of anything at all.

It became clear, in pseudo-death, how little a teenage life amounted to: I had expected Lacy, Thomas, and Mark, like Nicole and Emily Grace before them, to receive each some degree of the mythological treatment typically applied to youthful victims of mortal bad luck— which, in a spirit less of generosity than of self-preservation (of the need, specifically, to believe that a human life had value, and to construct a reflection of that value in language and emotive display on behalf of the dead in a subconscious effort to give the deceased the affirmative send- off one ultimately wanted for oneself, I assumed), would elevate their smallest talents into awesome gifts, their vaguest dreams into surefire would-have-been destinies, their loosest acquaintanceships into bone- deep ties of love—but already our collective energies in this direction had apparently exhausted themselves. I tried to engage the other guys on my soccer team on the subject of our vanished peers: did anyone know Mark? Had they thought Nicole was hot? But they didn't want to talk about them, their minimal emotional wells already spent—like Civil War mothers who, having lost four sons before, could spare no tears for the fifth. If we allowed these tragedies to compel us to think more deeply about the meaning of human life, then the terrorists had won. We *had* to go on being the worst: fucking around on our phones all the time like the satirically exaggerated teenagers on multi-camera sitcoms, being the last young people in America who hadn't realized that indoor shopping malls had become uncool, taking worthless weekend trips by bus to a circumscribed version of Manhattan whose grandest landmark was the M&Ms superstore in Times Square.

Within this mindset, the amorphousness of the threat that faced us and the obscurity of its consequences—which made them even more difficult to talk about, probably, than life's normal tragedies, whatever those were—worked to our advantage, allowing us to remain, in a sense, people who had never known tragedy, for whom life had been only good. For us to believe otherwise would have required a self-reconceptualization so radical as to require a lot more than five (potential) deaths to get the ball rolling—I'd been naïve to think otherwise. We were going to college in nine months, as Jillian had often pointed out: why should we allow unknown terrible things to derail our clear, certain trajectories at this late stage? Catherine would have to pry our happy stupidity from our cold dead hands.

I felt the coldness (of our hands, our hearts) already, or else—more likely—it was all in my head: the imagined lovelessness that loveless people accusingly attributed to the world around them. But in any case I found no help as I sought to reimagine my classmates' unimportant bodily presences—observed hazily through the school-day crowds and remembered more hazily still—as souls, contributors to the secret narrative of our species, in which everybody counted for something: every tear nourishing the dirt, every smile helping to lift the sun. Of course I couldn't do it, had no imagination whatsoever, no ability to create satisfactory stories for these people in the absence of real information.

And then, on a Thursday night, when I was hanging around the house with Jillian, each of us on our separate laptops, already like an old couple with nothing to say each other (a state of near-bliss), Matt texted me and asked if we wanted to go to Denny's that night. I said yes before asking Jillian—she said yes once I had asked. We got in my car and drove over.

Inside, it was a near-perfect recreation of our previous Denny's gathering—Matt, George, Karen, Annie—but with one addition: a notably ugly boy with small sharp teeth, his mouth like a zip-fly, wedged between the two girls. They were all set up already. Jillian and I took the two vacant seats casually, allowing them to continue their conversation.

"It's very, very obvious," the ugly boy said.

"I don't see it," Karen said.

"Just think about them. Think about who they are," said the ugly boy.

"Jeff," said Matt, pointing to the ugly boy, "do you know Leo?"

"No," I said, turning to Leo. "I'm Jeff Conwell."

"Leo Klattenhoff," Leo said. A ridiculous old man's name: it seemed simultaneously implausible and familiar. Did I know him somehow?

"We're getting a little dark tonight," George said. "Leo's about to explain the one thing that Thomas, Mark, Lacy, Nicole, and Emily Grace all had in common."

"The missing link," Annie said.

"Well, obviously all the disappearances are connected, but no one knows how," Leo said. "And I don't know how either, at least not for sure. But I have a theory."

"Which is what?" Matt said.

Leo cracked his knuckles. "Think about them. What do you know about Emily, Nicole, Lacy?"

"You want us to play detective?" Karen said.

"Well, Lacy didn't talk much," Annie said.

"Emily talked all the time," George said. "Mostly judgmental Christian bullshit."

"I think Lacy was considered, like, the greatest mathlete in the history of our school," Karen said. "But, yeah, primarily nonverbal. Her brain was full of numbers."

"She owned it, though—she was sort of cool in her own way," Annie said.

"So was Nicole," Jillian said. "She kind of existed in her own world. Books, in her case."

"Yeah," Karen said. "Nicole was my neighbor, but I felt like she never really let me into whatever she was up to. And I think her parents actually felt the same way. They were very nice, outgoing people, but she was much more private. A dreamer. I was a little jealous—she seemed so tied up in her made-up stories, totally uninterested in me. I was *always* interested in her."

"She was actually really pretty," Matt said, "but in that way where she didn't really seem to notice or care how she looked."

"Uh huh," Leo said, sounding a little impatient. "What about Thomas and Mark?"

"Thomas was into theater," Matt said.

"Yeah, he seemed kind of gay, I guess? But, like, I don't think he was open about it?" George said.

"He never admitted it," Matt said, "but you're right: I'm sure he was secretly gay—kind of in that old-fashioned, tortured way? He seemed really anxious all the time."

"That's sad," Jillian said. "He was a terrible actor, though. I saw him in *My Favorite Year*, and it was just brutal."

"And Mark—I think he managed the boys' basketball team?" Annie said.

"I thought it was the baseball team?" Karen said.

"It was both," Matt said.

"What kind of guy is the manager for two different sports teams?" George said.

"I'll tell you who: a desperate, pathetic nerd with low self-esteem, who can't play sports himself," Leo said. "No offense to Mark—he was actually a great guy."

"So what are you getting at?" Karen said. "What's the common thread?"

"We have a Jesus freak, a math geek, a bookworm, a repressed homosexual, and a boy so unathletic he probably got cut from the chess team," Leo said. "You don't see it?"

"No," Annie said.

"Not really," Matt said.

"They were all virgins," Leo said.

"Oh, come on!" Karen said. "You don't know that."

"Yeah, I've got to say, I don't think virginity can be stereotyped like that," George said. "Sex is probably as common among social undesirables as it is among the social elite. It's just that no one wants to think about it."

"Ugly people fucking ugly people," Matt said. "It's harrowing but real."

"I'm not relying on stereotypes," Leo said. "I just brought them up because I thought they would help you guys connect the dots. But I *know*. I always know."

That sinister tone of intrusive familiarity: now I remembered—Leo was the semi-infamous archivist of school sexual lore, the one who knew which girls spat and which swallowed, the one who would be the first to whisper the rumor that Debra Lind was fucking her art teacher or that Brad Schneider consistently suffered from impotence.

"What, exactly, do you know?" Jillian said.

"I know that Emily never went past making out with Tyler Hankin," Leo said.

"Everyone knows that," I said, finally speaking up.

"I also know that, since the seventh grade, Lacy Ramos masturbated every day in the girls' bathroom during her lunch period but has never touched another human being."

"Oh, yeah, I think I heard her doing that once, actually," Annie said.

"And that Nicole Burdette blew Barry Hoffman and Allen Wong last year but hasn't been sexually active otherwise."

"*Ew*, those guys are dumb," Jillian said. "I'm kind of disappointed in her."

"She never mentioned either of them to me," Karen said.

"How much did she *ever* mention to you, Karen?" Leo said. "I also know that Thomas Mancini once kissed Ted Lazar, but they were both too scared to follow up, and they just pretended it never happened."

"Sounds plausible," George said.

"And that, in a rare moment of philanthropy, Kristine Burchard once let Mark Sokolowski dry-hump her, strictly out of pity, but she never let him touch her again."

"OK, OK," Matt said. "So they're all virgins. So what? A lot of people are virgins."

"Fewer than you might think, actually. Not everybody talks openly about their sexual activity. Did you know that Gina Pappas lost her virginity in the sixth grade?"

"We don't want to know about that," Karen said.

"Even if you're right," Matt said, "what does virginity have to do with their disappearances? How does it factor in?"

"Let's just be honest and cut to the chase here," Leo said. "I think we all know that Catherine Harding is a witch and is consuming the blood of innocents in order to increase the power of her witchcraft. I mean, we don't need to beat around the bush at this point."

We all looked at one another, unsure whether to giggle or sob or get up and leave.

"She started with puppies and kittens," he said, "and now she's moved on to the delicious virginal flesh of unattractive and unpopular high school kids. It's beyond obvious."

"You're saying she's a cannibal?" Matt said.

"No—I mean, sort of. I'm guessing she just tosses the vital parts into her cauldron or whatever, boils it up with some eye of newt and toe of frog, and then makes the whole thing into a smoothie with strawberries, banana, and kale," Leo said. "And then, afterward, she's able to cast some spells or whatever."

"Why does it matter whether the victims are virgins?" Annie said. "Having sex doesn't *do* anything to a person—I mean, it doesn't make you taste different or change your blood type."

"Don't ask me. I'm no expert on witchcraft. But it seems fairly clear to me that Catherine is in the business of virgin sacrifices. It's a pretty common thing in horror movies."

"Yeah, those are *movies*," Karen said.

"Also, I think you're mixing up mythologies. Witches don't care about virginity. That stuff is for vampires," George said.

"Also, I don't think my dog was a virgin," Matt said.

"Dogs aren't contaminated by sins of the flesh," Leo said. "They're inherently innocent."

"So are people," I said, immediately unsure why I'd said it.

"You guys can believe whatever you want to believe," Leo said. "I'm just sharing a theory. But the truth is that *my* theory is supported by certain facts."

"Maybe we can just change the subject?" Annie said. "It was grim to start out with, but now it's just getting weird."

"Sure, keep living in a world of denial," Leo said. "I have to get going anyway. My parents have been on my case all week—these college applications are a killer, huh?"

"Oh my *god*, tell me about it," said Karen—and indeed a new subject (the same old subject) commenced as Leo slipped off. But didn't we all keep thinking about what he'd said? The college conversation was rote; we could have it without thinking about it. Didn't our anxious minds now lay elsewhere—or was that the case only for those of us who were virgins?

Chapter Twelve

At school, I sensed a certain politically correct fear regarding the term *witch*, with its sordid history of unjust violence against nonconformist women. In conversations relating to Catherine, I could see Matt and George hesitating to employ the word even hypothetically, their reluctance likely due as much to its regressive politics as to its superficial absurdity. I understood why, as the label seemed to attribute Catherine's necromantic abilities specifically to her womanhood, as if witchcraft were an expression or distillation of the essential wrongness of femaleness in general: hence the usual trope of the witch's magic manifesting itself in early adolescence, by implication at the start of menstruation —as though all menstruators were perhaps latent witches, their voodoo thus far undiscovered and therefore unused and yet still present, somehow, in the beguiling and pernicious nature of womankind even at its most upright and proper. Like virtually everything else in human culture, the whole mythology of witches was a product of misogyny, the accumulated bullshit piled up over the centuries by people like me, for whom girls were so very frightening. We would each add our part, Matt and George and I, but not publicly, not in words our peers could hear.

So what happened next was kind of surprising to me.

It happened because Catherine, still green-eyed and beautiful (though no more beautiful than a lot of the beautiful girls at Weybridge High), was still showing up innocently to school as though she hadn't stolen five members of the student body—mostly disposable ones, it was true, but it was the principle that mattered—even as, by now, from what I could tell, most of the senior class subscribed to the notion that she was, if not fully responsible, at least connected to the foul play at hand. According to a few witnesses in the schoolyard, she had openly shown off her paranormal legerdemain during the snow day, after I'd left, by snapping her fingers to halt the snowfall instantaneously once the accumulation on the ground had reached a sufficiently impressive height. The tritely theatrical signification of the trick's end sounded, to me, as unlikely as her yelling *abracadabra* at its beginning: a finger-snap, really? I wasn't sure I bought it, but I didn't know what else might have tipped everyone off about her. Had she appeared in every bedroom window in town, not just mine?

For the first time in my scholastic career, I had begun to perceive the senseless daily gathered mass of child-humans inside the sprawling municipal holding facility that was our high school as a kind of miniaturized society, as advanced as any other, with shared signs, accumulated meanings, interdependent relationships, and its own unique news cycle: a community not so much brought together by tragedy as made visible by it, the connections traceable by the particular route each piece of horrible-exciting news traveled through the school. Of course, I perceived this not through communal immersion but through its opposite: the feeling of exclusion, of catching tidbits here and there, of not fully knowing or understanding, of being one step behind, of trying to talk to people about what was going on and having them cut me off midsentence in order to switch to some superior conversational partner. Yet I was close *enough* that, outside of this community of my peers, every observation or analysis of the strange goings-on felt almost offensively irrelevant: the thoughts of my parents, of newspaper writers, of TV journalists were all forever *three* steps behind, infuriatingly uninformative, often hopelessly clueless. So as I sought to contextualize my school's unreality within the broader, saner perspective of the universe at large, the world of Weybridge High became only more vivid and persuasive by comparison, and gradually I allowed its bubble to close around me even as I remained stuck at its periphery: it was still more absorbing, still more real.

But considering my relative remove, I found it strange, just three days after Mark Sokolowski's disappearance, to experience up close a particular event that would for at least a few hours monopolize our school's all-important rumor mill, where normally I would have to come begging a day or two later for scraps. I was walking through the lunchroom when, first, I saw Catherine—strange enough on its own, since she didn't typically share my lunch period, and I started to wonder whether she had a real schedule with classes and teachers or simply floated ghost-like through the building, doing as she pleased—and then saw Victor Bogdan (that usually affable party boy of great popularity and no consequence) moving toward her with a gleam of menace in his eye. Catherine was carrying her plastic tray—which meant, I supposed, that witches ate shitty cafeteria-made pizza just like the rest of us, not just the raw blood-soaked internal organs of stolen house pets—when Victor approached from the side and, with a swift swing of the arm, knocked the tray loose from her grasp, scattering the food to the floor, a few bits nearly hitting me.

His face, suddenly, was red, frantic, furious. Catherine turned to him with unshaken equanimity. The cafeteria had gone imperfectly silent— a few morons in the back not realizing what was unfolding—but silent enough.

"If you fucking think you're going to get away with all this," he said, stopping there.

"What?" she said, and then clarified, in case we thought she had actually misheard or reacted in surprise: "If I think so, then *what*?"

Victor was wordless for a moment.

"Bitch," he said. "Fucking bitch."

Now she didn't reply. At this point, the silence *was* perfect, or else I could no longer perceive anything else, so focused was I on the scene in front of me.

"We're going to figure out what's going on," he said. "We're not going to let you . . ."

"Let me what?" Catherine said.

"We're going to find out *what.*"

There was no good way to talk about what was going on, no good way even to be angry—the word *what,* standing in for everything, proved it. Catherine shrugged, turned, walked out of the cafeteria. Maybe witches didn't eat pizza after all.

....

Once it had happened, it felt extremely odd that no one had previously confronted this assumed murderer wandering free and unrepentant in our midst. But of course the teachers had had (and still had) no clue about Catherine, and maybe most of the students had been too scared or uncertain to do anything—or else all but Victor Bogdan had actually been won over by the two extra days off from school that Catherine had given us, had thereby forgiven her for everything. I wasn't sure why Victor, of all people, should have been the first to accuse her of those nonspecific crimes—had he confused his trivial brand of popularity (he was well-liked, not admired) with status and thus with an obligation to leadership? In the cafeteria it had looked as though he might hit her, but he wasn't a meathead, was not typically a bully—though, like all teenage boys, he was apparently a misogynist: even as a failed rapist, I knew better than to use the word *bitch,* even if the target was a mass-murderess.

When I got home, I was still thinking about the incident and, in thinking about something other than myself, inevitably fell asleep on my unmade bed. When I woke from the late-afternoon nap, the sky had darkened, and the fire outside my bedroom window was back. *Catherine* was back. I got up, wiped my eyes of the congealing sleep-jizz, went downstairs, slipped outside, ducked into the trees.

I found her, as expected, beside her usual hallucinatory campfire. I waved slightly; she waved back. I came closer. Again, it all felt weirdly casual.

"Why are you back here?" I said. "I thought you didn't like me anymore."

"Jeff, I never liked you in the first place," she said.

"So what's the story?"

"I needed somewhere to go. It isn't safe at my house."

"What happened?"

"Victor Bogdan, Paul Sodano, and Kevin Duan broke in tonight. I'm not sure what they were expecting to find, but they didn't find me. They trashed the place, though."

"You're afraid of them? Couldn't you just kill them all if you wanted to?"

"It isn't about fear. I just don't like being bothered by people."

"So you're going to spend the night here instead?"

"Why not?"

"Well, it's starting to get cold."

"Weather isn't really a big deal for me."

"What about your family?"

"It's my grandmother's house."

"What about her?"

"She died three years ago."

"So you're going to live in my backyard now?"

"It's not your backyard. This is unclaimed territory."

"It belongs to *someone*. Probably a property developer."

"Right now it belongs to me."

She gave up nothing. Even her skin had no pores.

"If you're going to live in my backyard, you need to explain a few things," I said.

"Like what?"

She seemed friendly—not open, but cheerfully willing to indulge me within her strict self-imposed limits. What could I ask? I already knew, basically, what she had done, so what *was* the one big question? If I asked her to explain everything, she would just ask, in turn, what there was to explain.

"How did you get this way?" I said. "How do you do the things you do?"

"It started when I was thirteen," she said.

"When you got your first period?"

"Mind your own business, asshole. It started in the eighth grade, and it's just been steadily getting stronger over the past few years. At first it was just little things, then bigger things. I couldn't control it, and then I could. I'm still learning."

Again, she had said nothing, really.

"But why you? Where did it come from?" I said.

She sighed. "I can tell you the family story, if you really want to know."

"Yes, please."

"In the early nineteenth century, there was a warlock named Paikei who controlled all the land between Farrington Lake and the South River. My great-great-great-great grandmother was a reclusive widow and amateur alchemist who—"

I realized she had already lost me. "Actually, never mind. I'm not really into genre fiction. None of it's going to make any sense anyway, right?"

"It won't make sense if you don't believe in it," she said.

"I do and I don't. I guess I'm all right with it staying that way."

"So I can stay, too?"

"I'm not stupid enough to try to stop you, but I'm not sure what my parents will say when they notice. Or am I the only one who can see you here?"

"I'm real, Jeff."

"I don't think that answers the question."

"There are no good answers to your questions."

"They're pretty simple questions."

"Yeah. Stop asking them."

....

Regarding Victor, Catherine had no true cause for concern. He had vandalized her house, but he hadn't accomplished anything. Even so, at first, the kids at school seemed to regard Victor as a more important figure for what he'd done, as if he were manfully leading a charge against evil. But then, dragging his reputation down with him, he began to shrivel—quite literally, like a rotten fruit. The difference was noticeable. *Don't fuck with Catherine Harding*, kids.

Over the course of a week, his skin turned patchy and sallow, and slicks of black and green slime grew on his teeth. His spine hunched, as if curling into itself through fear or defeat. He seemed to lose a few inches of height, and his hair began to fall out. In a way, his appearance was more disconcerting than any of our class's *disappearances* had been. Every day, he showed up at school looking worse, and I wondered why he didn't just stay home, speculating that maybe he *felt* fine and only *looked* bad—and yet was so accustomed to looking good that he couldn't process his new ugliness. Was Catherine doing this not as an act of revenge but as a gift to me, to assuage the pain of all my homely years of envy? It was a possibility, but of course neither Victor nor anyone else had ever wronged me, so I didn't actually want revenge—I had no idea what I wanted.

By Friday, it seemed clear that Victor did not, in fact, feel fine, and after the final bell, I witnessed him hobbling outside to his car as if he'd been injured in a war—mangled so badly that his feebleness couldn't be traced to any single wound but belonged rather to a body that, on the whole, just wasn't really supposed to be alive anymore. His girlfriend Alice assisted him on the excruciating trudge between building and vehicle, propping him up on one side with her own skinny but clearly healthful frame. I hadn't thought about them in a while: did her current loyalty suggest that, all along, it had been true love between them? Well, only a week had passed—I'd keep an eye on her, see how she acted in a month, with Victor presumably no longer able to recognize faces or control his bowels.

It seemed to take everything the wizened young man had for him to pull his keys from the pocket of his jeans—as if lifting the anchor of a ship—and to click the unlocking button. When the time came for him to open the driver's side door, his hand missed the handle, and he fell backward, tumbling from Alice's grasp. She tried to help him up, but he didn't do his part. He stayed.

I was watching all of this, and I noticed—as Victor rested on the ground, his eyes open, apparently no more hurt than he had been before the fall but probably a little more depressed and in any case beginning to shiver—that it was kind of cold outside, finally. I was wearing a brown leather jacket—trying to look cool, but in a stroke of random luck it had turned out to be temperature-appropriate. Victor was only wearing a T-shirt with especially short sleeves, as if to show off his previously meticulous physique, now so frail.

Alice was still standing beside Victor and crying a little now, covering her mouth with her fist. Other students walked by, ignoring the embarrassing scene. An opportunity to come to the rescue (or at least to demonstrate my willingness to rise to such tests of character—to assist the downtrodden, forgive my enemies, and refuse to pass selfishly by as innocents cowered in pain and fear) seemed to exist here in clear and obvious terms: I wondered why others didn't take advantage. Thanks perhaps to some greater depth of self-hatred and its occasional corresponding need to exploit (through the moral showcase of public charity) someone else's moment of weakness by wringing from it all its capacity to make one feel good about oneself, I knew that *I*, at least, would do *something*.

I walked over to Victor. What, in fact, could I do? Alice seemed to glance at me fearfully.

"Hey, do you need any help?" I said.

"No, I'm fine," he said. Mumbling, pathetic.

"Are you sure?"

"I'm just . . ." He trailed off, then began again: "I'm just cold."

I nodded and, in a moment of inspiration, took off my jacket. "Here, take my jacket."

Reaching out to hand it to him, I assumed he would reject the gesture, which was somewhat homoerotic by *bro* standards, but to my surprise he raised no objection—yet he didn't seem to have the strength, either, to accept my offer, to hold the jacket and put it on. He was sitting on the floor now, leaning forward, his legs splayed. With fatherly tenderness, I put the jacket around him, draping it over his shoulders like a cloak, wondering, as Alice continued to cry, whether I might have to call an ambulance or something—some minor practical measure to back up the truly significant symbolic deed.

Funnily, the jacket looked good on him, even in his decrepit state, and only as I made this observation did I process the irony—or whatever it was—of this situation in which *Victor* was now wearing *my* clothing. And I could tell in that moment that I'd done the right thing, if not from a moral perspective then at least from a fashion standpoint: the jacket had never suited me, of course—I'd picked it out myself.

And then, as I wondered what made the jacket look natural on him and unnatural on me, there was a transformation (of him, not of the jacket)—gradual, at first too subtle to penetrate my preoccupation, then suddenly unmistakable. Victor stood up, his skin abruptly back to its normal hue, his posture straightening before my eyes. Alice, correspondingly, stopped crying. Was I imagining it, or was he really all better, just like that?

"I think I'm fine, actually," Victor said. "I don't really know what that was all about."

Restored to normalcy, he seemed to take it in stride. Why wouldn't he, that dickhead? I already regretted helping him.

"No big deal," I said, as if he had thanked me.

"I guess I was a little underdressed."

"It happens."

He made as if to take off the jacket.

"No," I said. "Keep it. Honestly, I was about to get rid of it anyway."

"How come? It's pretty nice." A compliment: condescension already. A moment ago he'd been near death or something like it, something worse.

"Oh, I don't know," I said. "Even in brown, leather kind of seems too deliberately cool or edgy for me, I think. I'm a very bland-looking person —my wardrobe needs to reflect that, or else my clothes just look wrong on me."

"Wow, uh, OK. Well, I appreciate it, man."

I realized, as he got into the car (successfully this time), that he didn't remember who I was. Surely Alice did? But she'd said nothing.

So I had saved the day—or my jacket had, or Catherine had by casting some kind of regenerative spell upon my jacket. But why that particular garment, and why, if it was magical, hadn't it done anything for *me*? I had my own nebulous wounds that could have used healing. Was it possible that, in fact, the magic was in *me*, and that I'd saved Victor not through the transference of a piece of clothing but through a transference of personal energy, the sharing of a sacred power that, all my life, had dwelt unknown in my covertly divine being, until finding expression through an act of kindness?

To be honest, it didn't seem likely.

I looked around, hoping that someone at least had seen what I had done—had seen that, for whatever reason, I had been for one moment a hero. But predictably, the parking lot was now empty, and *I* was now shivering in the cold, and who would rescue me?

Chapter Thirteen

I was sitting amid the scattered front-seat debris of oily sandwich wrappers and empty coffee cups (if only all the admirers of my car's famous cleanliness could see it now), my semi-nightly stakeout nearly complete, rain lightly falling over Barnwell Street and Adam's recalcitrant little dog, when—*finally!*—Adam glanced in my direction: not just at my car, but at me, specifically. Our eyes met, and at first it felt more like a movie actor looking directly into the camera—observed doing so through the one-way glass of a remote cinema screen—than a live meeting between two sets of living eyeballs, one of which was my own: it took me a moment to understand that he could see me, that we were looking at each other, that I wasn't a ghost.

He came up to my window, dragging the dog along with him. Cordially I rolled the window down, the panic reaching me only when the glass had fully retracted.

"Hey, Adam," I said. *Fuck fuck fuck.*

"Hey, Jeff," he said, and for a second I felt a discordant thrill: *he knew my name!*

"What's up?" I said.

"I was just wondering why I keep seeing you outside my house," he said. "Do you live around here?"

"Oh, no, not really."

"So . . ."

I was a little slow in picking up where he'd trailed off. He and I had seen each other every weekday since the start of tryouts, but we'd never talked—it would have been scary for me to tell him some mundane truth, let alone to invent an outrageous lie.

"Can I be honest with you, Adam?" I said.

"Sure," he said.

I bit my lip, my brain fiercely tunneling into the wall of my own incomprehensible behavior, looking for a way out. At the last moment, it came to me.

"So you've probably heard that there's a witch in the twelfth grade who's murdering all the virgins in our school, right?" I said.

"Yeah, I guess I heard something about that," Adam said.

"Well, no offense, man, but there was a team meeting, and we decided that the most likely guy to be a virgin was you. It's nothing personal— you're just the only freshman on the varsity squad, so it would make sense."

"When was this meeting?"

"It was a while ago. Seniors only. Very hush-hush. Don't worry about it. Anyway, we decided that one of us needed to look out for you during after-school hours. You're too valuable to the team. We can't afford to lose you just because you're probably too young to have fucked anyone. I volunteered."

"That's, um, really nice of you, Jeff."

"Yeah, it's no big deal. We've all got to do what we can for the team. We considered just hiring a prostitute for you, but this seemed more ethical and cheaper. So I've been parked out here, watching out for killers, kidnappers, witches, whatever. Honestly, you should probably get someone else to walk the dog. Someone who's had sex—maybe even someone who's had a child, to be really safe."

"It's my responsibility. I have to walk him."

"Can't you just let him out in the backyard occasionally?"

"*I've* been keeping *him* safe. It's been an even more dangerous autumn for pets than for people. I'm not so worried about myself."

"The rest of us are worried about you."

"Haven't all the victims been seniors? In general, the freshmen aren't that concerned."

"We have a lot riding on you, Adam. We can't take any risks."

"I kind of thought you didn't care whether we won or lost."

"*What?* Of course I care. Why do you think I'm out here? We're not all as talented at soccer as you are. I'm trying to contribute the only way I know how."

"Thanks, but I don't think I really need a bodyguard in my own neighborhood."

"Frankly, you don't have a choice. It's already been decided. Sorry, kid."

"Oh. Well, OK."

What would he do now if I just rolled up the window, refused to keep talking—determined to execute my professional duty, but under no obligation to fraternize? The lie had *worked* yet hadn't resolved the strangeness of the situation.

"If you want," Adam said, "you can walk Maximus with me."

"Who's Maximus?" I said.

"My dog. It seems boring for you to just sit here in the car."

I looked down at the dog's fluffy face, its black eyes of incuriosity. I got out of the car.

"What kind of dog is he?" I said, not remotely caring.

"A cairn terrier," Adam said.

We started walking, my right foot asleep from prolonged stillness.

"Why'd you get such a small dog?" I said, trying to make conversation as I hobbled awkwardly.

"What do you mean?" he said.

"Like, what's the point? It's basically just an oversized hamster, right?" I said, picturing on the other hand some huge sloppy sheepdog, barreling through a house, knocking over the heirloom china, reminding its owners that life was a big, stupid, hilarious adventure—what could this little dog do except complain via high-pitched dog noises and take small shits?

"It was my uncle's dog," Adam said. "He passed away two years ago."

We were heading away from Adam's house. The neighborhood was very quiet—the quietude of boredom, not of menace. It did feel awfully unlikely that a witch would snatch us here.

"Oh, I'm sorry to hear that," I said, barely processing what he was saying. Who had died again—the dog or the uncle? Was it a dead, taxidermied dog that Adam was now dragging along the sidewalk? Did that explain everything?

"Thanks," he said.

"Were you two close?" I said.

"Yeah—he used to live only a block away. A block away from where we used to live, I mean. Even though he was a lot older than me, he was probably my best friend."

"Is that so?" I said, idly wondering whether the older man had been sexually abusive. Why else would an uncle ever want to hang out with his nephew? It seemed suspect.

"Yeah," Adam said. "I guess that's why I'm so glad to have Maximus around. He kind of reminds me of Uncle James. Maximus connects me back to him."

"So you used to live somewhere else? You only moved here recently?" I said.

"Just before the start of eighth grade," he said. "We used to live in New Brunswick, but my parents moved us here because they wanted us to go to better schools."

"Oh, yeah, all the parents here say that," I said. "But I think the schools in Weybridge are probably the same as anywhere else, right? We just average better scores on standardized tests because of all the Asian kids. But our teachers are still morons like any other teachers in the country."

"It's actually pretty different here. At my old school we had to walk through metal detectors every day."

"Really? That's odd. I feel like it's always suburban schools like ours that end up getting shot up by some mass-murdering psycho. I mean, just look at what's happening now."

"Well, this is a whole different kind of thing."

"Yeah, that's for sure. So your parents are still married, huh? You're not from, like, a broken home?" It had been hard to discern much from outside in the dark; I'd actually learned nothing, had seen very little coming and going apart from Adam himself.

"No. What made you think so?"

"I don't think I've seen your parents at any of the games."

"Actually, they've come once or twice. But they both work, and my younger sister has MS, which is a lot for them to deal with, so they don't have as much time as they'd like to watch me play soccer. But it doesn't really bother me that much."

"What's MS?"

"Multiple sclerosis."

"Oh, right."

I knew the term and had heard the abbreviation before as well but had little memory of what this particular disease or condition entailed, although I had some sense that it was a well-known one and that its victims possibly were "retarded" in addition to suffering from various physical disabilities—in any case it registered in my mind as being quite bad. I tried to make my face look sympathetic, but without any suggestion of horror or melodrama, as if to show that I was aware of the problems faced by children with multiple sclerosis but also respected his sister as a human being, rather than viewing her strictly as a tragic case or a burden upon society. Were there kids with a single sclerosis, or did sclerosis come only in packs, like hijinks?

"Hey, I was just wondering," I said. "Have you ever met Catherine Harding?"

"She's the girl everyone thinks is behind all the weird shit going on, right? No, I've never met her. Someone showed me a picture of her in last year's yearbook, but I barely even remember what she looks like."

"Oh, OK. She's pretty attractive."

"Honestly, I'd like to meet her. I don't think I've ever run into her at school. But I don't feel afraid. I'd want to talk to her. Just have a conversation."

"Well, that's really stupid—sorry, kid. Anyway, I have another question: how did you really get so good at soccer?"

"I think just, like, natural ability? Like how some people are good at math or drawing."

Nearly prepared now to accept this answer, I said, "So you really had never played before this year?"

"Oh, no, no, I've been playing soccer my whole life. But last year I was still kind of bummed about my uncle and then about moving, so I didn't go out for the eighth grade team. I actually hadn't played that much *organized* soccer anyway and wasn't sure I'd like it."

"So what kind of soccer had you played?"

"Well, when I lived in New Brunswick, there were always a lot of pickup games at Archibald Park. Even at night. Sometimes I played in the afternoon, went home for dinner, and then snuck out again to play some more. The park had lights, so you could play until midnight if you wanted to. I was there all the time."

"And that's where you learned to play?"

"Mostly, yeah. I played on a few kids' teams, too, but they were all kind of too easy."

"I guess that makes sense."

He continued to pull the leash, Maximus yielding to fate with the resistance only of his complete indifference; I hadn't seen him pee yet, though we were nearing the circular end of the cul-de-sac, about to start on our way back.

"You have a gift, Adam," I said, feeling rushed. "Obviously you must know that. How do you feel about that? Does it make your life better?"

"Um, well, I guess I can't say, since I've always had it, or pretty much as long as I can remember," he said. "I didn't play a lot of soccer last year, and I kind of missed it, but I still knew it was inside me, so I don't know.

I don't see it as that big a deal, though. I assume everyone has *some* kind of talent, right?"

"No, not really."

"I mean, if you look hard enough."

"Well, I don't, for example. I have—I have the opposite of talent."

"In soccer?"

I shrugged. "In everything."

I stopped walking for a moment, unexpectedly paralyzed by my own self-pity. Adam paused, too, puzzled, and I wondered whether he would have to drag me and Maximus both. Why not let him, on the street as on the soccer field?

Chapter Fourteen

Around the time of the disappearance of Doug Burfield—by general consensus the ugliest boy at our school, unfuckable by any standard—I accepted that Leo Klattenhoff had been right and that, therefore, I was actually living inside an inverted teen slasher movie, where the local hedonists had no cause for alarm, while the prudes and untouchables were whisked off one by one by some shadowy villain. The rules were reversed, but the structure was the same—except the structure, too, felt negated, in a way, by own possible apathy about whether I would live or die: I wasn't fully sure whether I *cared* that Catherine might snatch me up to boil me alive in her notional smoky cauldron, and where was the suspense in that?

She had gone off the grid, was living off the land—the land of her choice, as it happened, being right outside my bedroom window, where she camped without supplies, disappearing and reappearing according to her witchy whims. Occasionally I saw a male-shaped figure out there with her, perhaps some additional supernatural entity—vampire, werewolf, or elf—with whom she was carrying out a sub rosa interspecies love affair. I didn't mind her being out there, exactly, but it did compel me to make a choice. I couldn't ignore her: did I *want* to offer her my precious virgin blood, say goodbye to this not especially cruel yet still somehow kind of lame world—or did I want to survive long enough, at least, to experience sexual intercourse, the sensation of my long-snubbed penis finally triumphant inside a lubricated vagina? Sex and survival had become linked: I could choose both or neither. And of course I wanted to have sex—it was the only thing I really wanted, except maybe death.

At the same time I felt that I was handling my role as Jillian's boyfriend almost surreally well—taking pleasure in her company, giving her the reciprocal pleasure of my own, providing emotional support and stability rather than the usual stress and volatility that seemed to define most high school relationships. The only explanation for this was that I had become too good at concealing myself, the nonviolent ickiness of my diseased brain. It would have felt better if our relationship had been a little worse—it would have meant that my actual personality was at least somewhat involved, that I wasn't being fully inauthentic. Instead it all felt like theater: I sensed not that she was deliberately holding anything back but that, within my dishonesty, I couldn't receive her *honesty*, so even as we sat side by side, I could only wonder who she was, what she might be like. I wanted a firmer connection, an enlivening touch of reality; it was a problem not of ethics but of loneliness.

At some point I came up with a plan to take Jillian out on a second *official* date, this time to a fancy restaurant with white tablecloths, candlelight, and polished silverware, a cellar full of pinot and cabernet that we wouldn't be allowed to drink, a laboratory-white kitchen churning out plates of tartare and foie gras that I wouldn't be able to eat. My father's yearly salary was just over $250,000; even so, I'd never visited a restaurant fancier than the Olive Garden, and the idea of traveling beyond the town limits to a genuinely upscale eatery was actually a little frightening, causing me to wonder whether, as obvious teenagers (dressed up, maybe, but if so then inevitably in the wrong way, my tie askew and my fly down) and thus potential hooligans, we might be rejected at the door, the maître-d' turning us away with scoffing Frenchified laughter. Still, the grossness of the central idea—of an exorbitant dinner and the interrelated expectation of next-level status (i.e., sex, our bare overstuffed bellies bumping against one another as consummation of our shared commitment to epicurean luxury and consumer prestige)—seemed too correct for me to turn away from, too complete in the nastiness it created: the transparency of its objective, the bullying heavy-handedness of its attempt to push us over the edge of our barely maintained celibacy, its traditionally disrespectful assumptions about what female humans wanted and what they might be willing to give up in exchange for large sums of money spent upon them. Jillian would receive this passive-aggressive ugliness and, then, ideally, the ugliness of my naked body: all in all, it would be *me*—she wouldn't be able to prevent herself from seeing it. I also hoped she'd have a good time—although, if she ordered the foie gras, I might have to break up with her. (Did I owe myself that much? Probably not: I'd sit there eating salad, unable to muster the energy to pass judgment.)

I suggested the Friday date on Thursday, having already made a reservation at Sunchoke in New Brunswick by calling them up the night before and asking for a table for two and then confirming that it was OK that the two of us were only seventeen; the reservationist ("Oh, how sweet!"), if anything, had seemed surprised that I wasn't younger. Jillian readily agreed to the proposal, apparently touched by the suggestion: to her, it was a declaration—possibly clumsy, but all the more endearing if so—that she was important to me, and that it was important to me that she know it. *Was* that all it was? On Friday, my thoughts became more and more muddled as the hour approached. I put on an Oxford shirt with jeans and dress shoes, staring at myself in the mirror, putting on a tie (like a little boy dressing up for church) and taking it off: was there any version of myself that would ever seem forgivable, that would not deserve a punch in the face? Did *anyone* who had ever worn a button-up shirt basically just deserve to die?

When I picked Jillian up she was wearing a purple dress with black leggings, lipstick, and assorted other makeup. Together we blew past the stalled southbound traffic on Route 18, everyone retreating deeper into suburbia. It was just past five, already dark.

"You look handsome," Jillian said. "I don't think I've ever seen you in a collared shirt."

"With jeans, though. Staying hip," I said, jokily, my face reddening: I was not handsome—did she know that she was lying? Did it break her heart to do so?

With my newly gained savvy from my previous trip to New Brunswick, I parallel-parked a block away from the restaurant—imperfectly, bumping the curb a bit, but well enough to earn a respectful nod from Jillian. Arm-in-arm, we strolled down the quiet condo-lined street to the stylishly small blue building on the corner. I gave my name to the host (a real live urban gay man, by the looks of him), and he led us to our table—right in the middle of the room, so everyone could see how adorable we were: were we on our way to some school dance?

"I've never been to an actual nice restaurant before," I said. "My family never does anything."

"I once went to one in New York," Jillian said. "You'll be fine. Just don't forget to lift your pinky."

Our waitress gave us our menus and told us about the specials, to which I failed to pay attention. On the menu, every entrée but one cost more than thirty dollars, and as the single slightly cheaper dish (the wild nettle spaghetti with pine nuts and chèvre) appeared also to be the only meatless option, I wondered whether, when I ordered it, Jillian would in some subconscious irrational fashion suspect that my vegetarianism was only a ruse to conceal my stinginess. I wanted to reassure her that *she* could order whatever she wanted, regardless of price, but it seemed offensive for me to suggest that she might not already know that she could do as she pleased without my overt paternalistic permission. I hoped she knew it. It wasn't the *money* part of our money-spending that bothered me—I lived within the fathomless infinity of all spoiled children, bounded only by the narrow limits of my imagination—but rather the sense of ridiculousness, if I was bothered at all. Still, was she going to order an appetizer, too?

If so, I needed to have a choice prepared for my own pre-entrée snacking: the baby greens salad with puffed amaranth and hemp seeds or the potato gnocchi with leeks, crème fraiche, and dill. I had no very idea what anything on the menu really was and didn't much care, wanting only to make the best impression with my choices—but then Jillian was probably as confused as I was. She didn't look nervous, though. In fact, she seemed delighted and at ease as, eventually, we placed our orders, sat back, and began to chat while sipping ice water (somehow we had each independently recognized that it would feel more grown-up to order no beverage at all than to order a Coke).

"Do you know what 'ramps' are?" Jillian said when the waitress was gone.

"No," I said. "Maybe they're very small fish, like sardines?"

"What about 'guanciale'?" she said.

"I think maybe a type of cheese?" I said.

The first course was set carefully before us, the waitress (as I now inspected her) looking younger than I had thought she would, almost our age, though infinitely more polished: a 21-year-old girl working her way through college, maybe. I imagined that, though not wealthy herself (if she was struggling with state school tuition), she'd had an extremely rich best friend whose manners she'd learned to ape while growing up, and from her she'd learned what guanciale was and how to laugh elegantly. When our appetizer plates were empty, Jillian smiled at me.

"That was really good," she said.

"Maybe New Brunswick isn't so bad," I said, venturing a veiled plea for forgiveness on my own behalf: I still hadn't applied to any school but Rutgers, and Jillian knew it. She didn't take me up on it, but she was still smiling.

I tried to really taste my spaghetti when it finally arrived, but mostly I failed again. It tasted indistinctly fancier than the plain boiled noodles I might have cooked at home, but why? I couldn't pin it down. For dessert, Jillian and I shared a Kokoleka chocolate mousse with passion fruit, coconut snow, and banana ice cream. The bill, before tip, was $114.49.

I thought of taking her to the Copper Monkey afterward for some illicit drinking but didn't want to press my luck, either with Jillian or the sullen bartender: we'd had fun, would go home and have sex stone-cold sober—in appropriately grim, tense recognition of the momentousness of the task. I would, in my pre-coital terror, find a secluded place to vomit the overpriced goat cheese in my stomach, would then achieve an erection and insert it inside the girl who now sat beside me, if she wanted me to: it was no guarantee, but I'd gotten a good vibe during the meal—light touches, caresses, eye contact, an obvious determination not to talk about Doug, Thomas, Mark, Lacy, Nicole, or Emily Grace: a walling off of this particular night as a time for good things only, a special evening just for us, the happiness of ourselves.

We drove to my house; I asked her in (when we were already there), and she said yes. The house was quiet as we casually dashed upstairs to my bedroom, shutting the door behind us and then making out. Not for the first time I wondered why she hadn't already had sex with someone —it was hard to fathom how anyone else could have wasted high school as thoroughly as I had: I felt actually unsympathetic to it, the inability of people other than myself to accept and navigate life's pleasures and possibilities. But, *well*, we were all flawed (that was the problem—it brought me back to myself), getting lost on fruitless paths, stuck on dumb internal narratives that would take us nowhere, one inch away from happiness and yet unable or unwilling to budge laterally. It sometimes took years to escape, the minor miracle of another person to help us see how obvious and easy it all really was, and I knew all this as I kissed her, touched her breasts, squeezed her butt, pulled off her shirt.

"Do you have a condom?" she said eventually, nervously.

Holy shit: the plan was working. I nodded—then realized that, no, I didn't. So I shook my head.

She laughed. "Yes or no?"

"I want to, yes," I said.

"No, I mean—do you have one?" she said.

I wanted to laugh, too, almost—I had planned the whole thing out, forgotten the key ingredient: a wedding without a ring, a tennis match without a ball. I was literally the stupidest person on earth, or maybe it was only a little funny—I couldn't be sure.

"I'm going to go get one," I said.

"Where?" she said.

"The pharmacy, I guess?" I said. "I'll be back in two minutes. I'll drive very fast."

"Are you serious?"

"Yeah, for real, just stay here, if you don't mind," I said. "Buying condoms is awkward enough. I'll handle it for us. No need for you to endure that particular type of eye contact with the CVS cashier, you know?"

I grinned at her, as if I were an old hand at condom shopping, my supply only recently exhausted. She didn't look fully convinced as I stood up.

"Just think sexy thoughts till I get back," I said.

She laughed again, a little awkwardly this time. "About whom?" she said.

Playfully I threw a pillow at her, then with urgent rapidity put my shirt and shoes back on, and was out the door before she could protest further. As I got in the car, I realized I was probably doomed: the nearest pharmacy was in fact five minutes away even if I drove like a lunatic, which meant that the soonest I could expect to be back was eleven minutes from now, assuming that there was no line at the CVS and that I could, with no real knowledge, select a condom brand in less than a minute: this was too long an interruption in any case—the mood (whatever mood there had been) wouldn't last.

But maybe we could pretend? Maybe she'd be a good sport? Maybe, deep down, she wanted this as impatiently as I did and was willing to endure an imperfect version of it?

I peeled out loudly on Caswell Road, woke up the neighbors: a young man was about to get some pussy for the first time—sound the bugle, they *deserved* to know. But once I'd exited my cul-de-sac, I felt invisible on the empty streets—just a blur of sound, there and gone—and felt comfortable outstripping the speed limit by thirty miles an hour at some points. The 24-hour CVS sat bright and pointlessly open at the end of Englewood Drive; I parked two feet from the door—not in a real spot —and dashed in. I found the Family Planning aisle, snatched a box of Trojans (not caring which variety—or in fact caring somewhat, slightly worried about my choice, but not enough to sacrifice any time for a closer inspection), and paid quickly.

Back in the car, I felt that I'd done well—from the bedroom to the cash register, only *four* minutes had passed, and on the way back I decided that I would play it safe and exceed the speed limit by no more than ten miles an hour. Everything ahead of me was a no-brainer: kiss Jillian again for a while longer, cover my erection in a rubber sheath, and insert it into the vaginal canal of my girlfriend; then I could finally be a happy person for the rest of my life. I just had to avoid doing anything stupid. I was on Weaver Street and made a left onto Lakewood Avenue, beginning to pick up speed when I had this precise thought—that I just had to be normal and not do anything idiotic, and that this lay within my abilities.

And as if the universe were responding to the thought, I kind of sort of crashed my car. I had been the only person on the road, and then, suddenly, I hadn't been. A glimpse of taillight, a metallic smash, a forward jolt—and then I was sitting still. It had all happened very, very quickly—as people always said it did, but really: even as I pulled over and got out of my fucked-up car, it still hadn't completely registered as a real event, the horror still hovering above me.

With both engines now off—mine and that of the vehicle that had gotten in my way—the street was completely silent, and in the dark, the face of the other driver wasn't visible until he was within a few feet of me. He was a pale gray-haired man in a wrinkled brown button-up shirt. He frowned at me.

"I'm really sorry," I said.

"You need to slow down, young man," he said, seemingly no more than annoyed. The damage, after all, was much worse on my car than on his, now that I'd looked: a shattered headlight and a slightly tented hood versus a scratched bumper.

"Yeah, I know. I was in a rush. I'm sorry. I'm an idiot. I'll pay to fix your bumper or whatever. It's not a problem. The whole thing was all my fault."

"What's your name, junior? You old enough to be driving?"

"I'm seventeen, sir," I said. "My name's Jeff Conwell. What's yours?"

The man scratched his temple. "Mine's Paikei Smith, and I'm a lot older than that."

"Your car doesn't look so bad."

"No—it's seen better nights, but I don't think we need to call the police. Still, I should take down your information. Do you have your license, insurance, registration—all that stuff?"

"Oh, yeah," I said. "Let me go grab all that for you."

Couldn't he just take down my phone number? Was he *entitled* to all my documentation? What would he do with it? I wasn't sure, but in any case I went back to my car, pulling whatever unknown papers lurked in my glove box. I still felt that I would escape from this mishap unharmed —that I could wait till the next day to tell Jillian or my parents about it, that it would create some small trouble for me, but that mostly it would just make the story of my virginity loss more memorable when eventually imparted to my male grandkids, long after humans had stopped strapping primitive rubber bags onto their dicks to prevent disease and pregnancy.

It was only as I rummaged through the glove box, somehow, that I remembered the bizarre accident I'd had during my last driver's test, where I'd also rear-ended someone—this wasn't my first car crash, was it? I looked again at the car in front of me, and instantly, now, it clicked: the same green Ford Fiesta. It wasn't so much a *shock* at this point—if anything, it made me feel a little better. I wasn't a bad driver; I was just being fucked with.

I got out of the car again, ready to tell Paikei Smith—what the hell kind of name was that?—to get his phantasmal ass out of my way and allow me to please fuck my girlfriend in peace when, of course, he disappeared: him and the car, both vanished into thin air. And I was left standing there with my certificates of insurance and registration, my fake ID in my pocket, my car still damaged (so it hadn't *all* been a dream—it never seemed to work that way). I just stood there for a moment, erection-less, wondering whether Catherine knew what was going on and would spend the entire rest of the night cock-blocking me or whether I might still get home in a minute or two and proceed as planned.

Now another car was coming down Lakewood Avenue, and when I saw it was a police car, I didn't realize that this was a bad thing until it pulled over in front of me. Its engine stayed on as the officer—wide-chested, short-legged—got out of the vehicle.

"Everything all right?" said the cop.

"Oh yeah, I was just heading on my way," I said.

"How'd this happen?" he said, pointing to the damage at the front of my car.

"That?" I said. "Oh, it's been like that."

"It still runs?"

"Yeah, I mean, I think so." I was doing a bad job.

"You know it's illegal to drive with a busted headlight."

Shit. "Oh yeah. I was just heading home. I only live like a mile from here."

I was panicking, but my normal daily state was something close to full-on panic; I would survive, wouldn't I? Yet I felt my strained courage giving way already and sort of suspected that I might even start crying—it felt almost like the *right* thing to do, as if this paradigmatic authority figure might draw me in, dry my cheeks on his shirt, and absolve me.

"Are you old enough to drive, kid?" the cop said.

"I'm seventeen," I said.

"Can I see your license?"

I reached into my pocket for the fake—would he fall for it? How much more trouble would I get into if he didn't? Not just not having a license, but trying to pass off a forgery—it was an additional crime, maybe the one that would put me over the edge. I crumbled, and my hand stayed in my pocket.

"I'm sorry," I said. "I don't have one."

"You don't have one?" he said.

"No, I never got one. I failed the test."

"And whose car is this?"

"It's mine. I mean, it belongs to my parents, I guess."

"They let you drive it without a license?"

"No, they think I have a license. I lied to them."

"Christ. That isn't good, kid."

"I know."

"What's your name?"

"Jeff Conwell."

I hung my head, hoping he'd recognize my repentance. I was a good kid who'd made a mistake! It happened sometimes! I glanced up again, sheepishly, and he returned a look of sympathy.

"Here's what I'm going to do, Jeff," the cop said. "I'm going to call your parents and tell them what you've been up to. Then I'm going to drive you home in the squad car, and your parents can come and pick up *their* car. You said you only live about a mile from here?"

"Yeah. I mean, maybe two."

"Well, this should be all right parked here for a little while. What's your parents' number, Jeff?"

I realized, as he asked, that this was *the* best-case scenario following my confession: I could be going to *jail* right now, but the surely racist, classist cop could tell by the way I talked and dressed (still in my Oxford shirt) that I had a respectable bourgeois family whom he could trust to handle my discipline at home. There would be no legal consequences. It was the whitest moment of my life, the most demonstrative of my social privilege, and still I wanted to die. I was fucked, my life was over; I would be in a sort of jail anyway—had always been in one, had almost escaped, and now was being sent back.

Chapter Fifteen

Nobody but me really needs to know too much about the scene that followed: with a wobbly upper lip I quietly received the shock and disappointment of my parents, the inevitable dressing-down, proportionately severe. The only strange part was that, unknown to my mom and dad, Jillian was still in my bedroom the entire time: I'd texted her from the police car (with the officer's permission—what a guy!), telling her that I'd been in an accident and that I was unhurt but that she should please stay still until she heard from me again. My parents met me and the cop in the driveway as the patrol car pulled in, and I allowed them to vent their anger for a sufficient period (by my own judgment) before interrupting to tell them that my girlfriend was upstairs and that she probably needed a ride home. They asked me why, if she was in my bedroom, I'd been out on the streets. I couldn't think of a lie, so I told them that I'd gone out to buy condoms.

This wasn't an easy thing to say to my parents, but once I'd said it, I felt that it might actually earn me some points—for exercising responsibility in my sexual life—and even win me back some of their respect: if I wasn't man enough to drive a car, at least I was making the normal strides toward adulthood in other spheres. But the impact was hard to measure—the initial read, of course, being embarrassment on their part, overwhelmingly.

Later that night, Jillian and I had a horrible conversation about the incident, the emergent conflict between us all the worse because the basis of it was never fully clarified—I admitted that I'd never earned a driver's license, trying at first to be lighthearted about it, as if in my jaunty youthful insouciance I'd simply forgotten to collect it from the DMV, but naturally she wasn't buying this, and when we ended the call I could tell that she could see there was something strange and horrible about me that she hadn't fully noticed before but possibly, deep down, had long intuited and denied. The next morning, I pumped up my old bicycle's tires, and on Monday, I caught the school bus for the first time that year.

....

On Monday and Tuesday, Jillian and I managed to avoid each other and thus to avoid any confrontation or elucidation. But I didn't eat anything on either day, immersed as I was in an all-consuming state of humiliation, and on Wednesday I realized I couldn't duck Jillian forever and in fact didn't want to—yet I also knew that I couldn't reappear as my old self, as if nothing had happened, and therefore I needed some new tack: a revision of self-presentation that, without undercutting all the work I'd done, would explain not only the lie about my driver's license but, in a demonstration of *over-the-top* honesty, some other lies that had yet to demand explanation ... all the while showing, somehow, that on some essential level *I* was not a lie. I felt lost without her, and although I recognized that this was not a proof of love, just a proof of desperation and of my fearfully flimsy grip upon personal stability (and thus proof that I really didn't have the emotional tools to be in a relationship at all), it was nevertheless striking how badly I wanted her back— not that she'd officially gone, but she was headed in that direction—and not just for another chance at the impossible glory of sexual intercourse. I was heartsick, stomach-sick, ready to vomit all my inner organs. She was on my mind all the time, in that special way that only bad things could be; I'd never thought about her so often or so intensely while we'd been happy together.

I didn't have a real plan when, without forewarning, I bicycled to Jillian's house late Wednesday afternoon, formulating more or less nothing along the way, and rang the doorbell. Her mom answered, and I asked if Jillian was there, and I could tell from Mrs. Heller's facial expression that she hadn't known anything strange was going on between us but that she knew now (this was not how her daughter and I usually arranged our meetings); still, she said yes and invited me in, and I went upstairs and knocked on Jillian's bedroom door. She said "Hello?"—not *come in*. Still, I opened the door. She was lying on her bed, her eyes on the ceiling.

"Hi," I said.

"Hi," she said, after a moment.

I felt, even in my awareness that I had no speech memorized and no particular narrative in mind, that this meeting-cum-confession ought to go well: who could look at a person wanting love and forgiveness and not grant it to that person? It was humanly impossible. Still, my heart was thumping—I was going to reveal not my true hideous self but at least some part of it, and I really, really wanted it to be received with more warmth and acceptance than I was capable of extending to myself. Why shouldn't she give me that? Other people's flaws were *easy*, compared to one's own. I closed the door behind me, took a deep breath.

"I've failed the driving test five times," I said, not coming closer to her. "I'm not a bad driver, or at least no worse than everyone else our age. The accident wasn't my fault, actually. I just keep fucking up the road test because I'm a nervous, neurotic person, and after I failed the test once, the idea that I would keep failing it forever kind of got stuck in my head, and I've been subconsciously self-sabotaging ever since. At least I think that's what's going on."

"Jeff," she said, "it doesn't matter whether you're a good driver or not. You can't drive if you don't have a license."

I bit a fingernail. Was she really hung up on the driving thing? The issue was so much bigger—I had to broaden the parameters of our conversation.

"Yeah, I understand that," I said. "But, like, I'm not a normal person —I've kind of had to invent my own guidelines for how to operate in the world."

"You're a rebel," she said, probably rolling her eyes.

"No—I wish. Rebels do things *on purpose*. It's hard to explain, but I feel horrible all the time, and I've never enjoyed anything, and everything I say or do is kind of just a byproduct of that constant oppressive misery and isn't really a reflection of anything else. The question for me isn't whether something I might say is true, it's whether saying it carries some tiny chance of making me feel slightly less miserable for half a second, whether it moves me toward what I think for a moment might be the vague direction of some distant happiness that I probably wouldn't recognize even if I came close enough to touch it. None of my actions are really *choices*. I don't know what it's like to make a choice, to feel possibility."

"I'm not sure I understand. Actually, I'm not sure I *want* to."

I decided to continue. "I'm just, like, funneled helplessly in one direction or another by my depression or anxiety disorder or whatever it is. My inner life is like a shitty, horrible waterslide—I'm just out here flailing around on the way down. It's just chaos."

Now she took a breath. Her room was *actually* looking a little messy today: clothes strewn about, bed unmade, backpack dropped in the middle of the floor.

"You should go to therapy," she said. Then, more kindly: "I went to a therapist for like a year when I was twelve and had an eating disorder, and it actually helped a lot. I don't think you're as bad off as you feel right now, but *I* can't be the one to solve your problems."

She'd never told me about her eating disorder before—did this mean we were making progress? But I didn't want to accept her suggestion; she probably meant well, but I was certain that, consciously or not, she was just trying to pawn me off on someone else.

"You're probably right," I said. "Therapy would make sense. But I think I'm kind of too addicted to being *me*. It's weird but true. Becoming sane would be sort of too strange at this point. I've never thought a sane thought, but I've thought *about* those thoughts, and from my own sick perspective they just don't seem right. I don't want them. I just want to be happier while still being insane and miserable, and I think I have to figure that out for myself."

Was I doing well here? It didn't necessarily feel as though I was. My brain *was* a waterslide: it was going too fast. I could see that Jillian was crying now.

"Yeah, I definitely can't help you with that," she said. "It's like you said—you have to figure it out yourself."

"You don't have to *help* me. I want you anyway," I said, barely loud enough to be heard. "You help without trying to. I need to *do* things, to figure it out through experience—I need to be involved in the life of another person, go places, talk about stuff. I can't just sit there alone with the same old thoughts."

"Jeff, I don't know you. I think I just wanted a boyfriend, and you seemed nice. You *are* nice, I think. But obviously there's more to it than that."

I was in the past tense now, like Doug, Thomas, Mark, Lacy, Nicole, Emily Grace. I was disappearing. We didn't *need* Catherine Harding to kidnap *me*.

"What more is there?" I said, frantic, almost indignant. "I can be as good a boyfriend as anyone else. Occasionally some weird shit will probably happen, but that could just make it more interesting, if you look at it a certain way."

"But, um, everything you've said about yourself has been a lie—who you are, what you think and feel," she said, more wounded than accusatory.

"Yeah, but so what? I'm not a *dishonest* person—I'm just not able to sustain any connection to the truth. I don't follow it or betray it. I have no *idea* what it *is*. I just have this weirdness in my brain; it's the only thing—it's hard to explain. But please just take me anyway. I mean, yes, I've done a bad job communicating my personality to you. It's not an easy thing to communicate. I'm trying now. I don't know you either, to be honest."

She turned to me, finally. "You don't think so?"

"Maybe being boyfriend and girlfriend isn't about knowing someone else. It's probably just more of a lifestyle choice for the most part, you know, like living in the city versus living in the country. Or in the suburbs. Being coupled versus being single—dependability versus possibility. Staying in versus going out. It doesn't really matter *who* the other person is."

"But I don't want a relationship like that."

"You just said you did. You said you just wanted a boyfriend."

"I did. I think I've learned my lesson on that one."

I winced a little, but I felt strongly that I wasn't beaten, that I could keep pushing forward—or backward, any direction: it would all lead somewhere in the end. We were looking each other in the eye now. There was a lot inside me, more than she knew (all bad, but even so)—I could go forever.

"Well," I said, "let's keep learning lessons together, then. It turns out you don't want, like, a standard boyfriend whose main job is to stand next to you in photos, who politely takes your virginity on prom night, gets along with your parents, and allows you to amicably break up with him two days before you both leave for college so that you can each find someone new and yet *exactly the same* at each of your new schools? Fine, OK, let's not do that—I mean, I *can* do it, to some degree, if you want me to, and I'm not knocking that strategy. I don't have the answers. But if you want to do something else, I'm up for whatever—any journey you can think of."

She laughed a little, despite herself, and had to make up for it: "Like what? You don't even have a car anymore."

"Who needs a car? That car belonged to the *old* boyfriend. I wouldn't go *near* a gaudy piece of shit like that. I ride a child's bicycle now. I can probably find another one if you're interested."

"Uh-huh. What would we do on our bikes? Where would we go?"

"I don't know. What's in Central Jersey? There's the convenience store where they filmed *Clerks*, I guess. Bruce Springsteen's childhood home. You and me."

"So we'll go—"

"Deeper into each other's souls."

Another laugh. She was standing now. I still hadn't moved an inch.

"We don't always have to be in Central Jersey," she said.

"There's college next fall, from what I can remember, I said. "Or not, if you'd rather not. I could go either way."

"I think I want to go to college."

"It's still Berkeley, right?"

"For now, yeah. That's at the top of the list."

"So I'll apply tomorrow."

She raised her eyebrows skeptically. "And you think you'll get in?"

"Probably. My grades are good, actually. For some reason I pretend that I get mostly B's with the occasional A, but actually I get all A's. I guess I thought I'd be seem more sympathetic with like a 3.2 GPA, but I can't remember the last B I really got—maybe in sophomore year, first semester?"

"Wow. Maybe you'll get into Cal instead of me. You could be stealing my spot."

She had come closer. I was winning.

"Or maybe we'll both get in," I said. "Anyway, you can't expect me to stay *here* forever, can you?"

"I thought you wanted to stay here."

"I don't know what I want. I don't have a single clue."

"No? How's that going to work for us?"

"Better than my pretending that I *do* know, maybe. I told you: I'm a disaster—I can't help it. The only thing I can do better is to stop trying to act like I'm not—stop flailing on the way down."

"And you think that'll help?"

"Being a disaster isn't nothing. It's a mess, but at least it's something. There's material for us to work with here. Some people don't have any-thing at all."

"What makes you believe I'd be interested?"

"I don't know. Don't we all secretly just want an adventure?"

She looked me in the eyes, nodded.

"Maybe," she said. "Yes, I think so."

She had come even closer, and closer, until we were almost touching; then we were hugging, and then kissing, her face still a snotty mess—possibly mine too, the held-back emotional secretions of my sinuses dislodged by the face-to-face contact. I was dizzy, and she must have been too, remaining upright for a little while and then collapsing, with me, onto the bed.

....

Again, I hadn't brought a condom—we did it anyway.

Afterward, I almost couldn't believe that it'd happened this way: not only because, to my mind, we so fully fit the profile for "sexually responsible" teens that it hadn't ever occurred to me that, given the opportunity, I might engage in unprotected intercourse with her like any horny illiterate boy from remote Appalachia—but also, more importantly, because I had in a broader sense done something *spontaneously*, had succeeded in entering a state of pure instinct and action. The whole thing had lasted about forty-five seconds: the best three-quarters of a minute of my life, by far—in fact, the only good three-quarters of a minute of my life, the first time I had understood what it meant for something to feel good.

Following my orgasm, I wondered for a moment whether my parents had actually fucked up by failing to pull me aside at some point in the oversensitive, embarrassed years of my early adolescence in order to give me "the talk," detailing in horrifyingly earnest tones the life-threatening terrors of irresponsible copulation, its certain path toward disease and pregnancy and doom—a seemingly pointless or even regressive ritual that the three of us had for various reasons been happy to skip. But then again, Jillian wasn't on the pill, and maybe a few traumatizing minutes of parent-child interaction some years earlier would have made all the difference in my behavior today. Had my mom and dad just assumed that no girl would ever want to fuck me?

These questions weren't powerful enough to puncture my euphoria; they existed peaceably alongside it. It took only three or four seconds of nude post-coital reflection for me to realize that, whatever the consequences, I had made the right choice in Jillian's bedroom: the preceding moment had been worth more than all the previous moments of my life combined—what counterargument could exist against that? As I imagined myself inhabiting a parallel universe wherein, recalling the necessity of prophylactics just before penetration, I'd responsibly halted our course of action (which, unlike that of Friday night, had issued entirely from heedless impulse and would *not* have survived a tactical trip to the drugstore, no matter how prudently navigated), I could feel only more grateful that I lived in my own dangerous reality, and this gratitude traveled through my body like a sugar-rush even as I recognized the possibility that I had impregnated Jillian—this was before she suggested that we go out a little later and purchase a dose of Plan B. Somehow I had forgotten that emergency contraception existed, but I knew now that we'd be OK: it didn't make me feel *better*—I'd already felt fine.

How did Jillian feel? To ask her would have violated some ideal of wordless intimacy, the notion that through our bodies we'd shared something deep and communicative and thus, for the moment at least, didn't require language: if it wasn't true, we could at least act it out. Still, I was curious—more curious than concerned—as to whether she felt the same happiness that I did now. In my daze of pleasure, I could only stare at her and smile; she stared back, smiled, and then turned to the side, her body still pressed into mine. I threw an arm over her—affectionately, possessively.

After a minute of silence, she laughed softly, apropos of nothing.

"What did we just do?" she said.

"I think that was what sex is?" I said. "I'm not totally sure."

"I don't just mean that. Weren't we about to break up?"

"We did. Our old relationship ended. This is a whole new phase, a new era."

"It's a little scary."

"Yeah."

"Our old relationship really wasn't scary at all."

"I was scared the whole time."

"Why?"

"Scared of being found out, I guess."

"And now?"

"I'm an open book. Ask me anything."

"Do you really know how to change the oil in your car?"

"No, never—I have no clue. I don't even know what an oil change *does*."

She laughed again. "I knew that was a lie the whole time."

"How did you know? I don't look like someone who knows about cars?"

"I saw the Jiffy Lube mileage sticker on your windshield."

"Oh, shit. I can't believe I didn't think of that. I should've covered my tracks."

"Yeah, you did a bad job on that one."

"I can learn how to change oil if it'll make up for it.

"It's all right. I probably haven't been totally honest about everything either."

"Like what?"

"Oh, I don't know. I can't really think of any outright lies right now —but, well, I think honesty isn't just about telling the truth. It's about self-expression, being yourself. I'm not sure I've ever really been *myself*, around you or anyone else. I don't even know what it means, maybe."

"We can figure it out."

"Yeah, well, I guess I'm willing to give it a try if you are."

"It *is* scary."

I squeezed her, then released. Gently she pulled herself free of me.

"I have to use the bathroom," she said, quietly.

She swung her legs to the edge of the bed, stood up, and gathered her clothes. I stayed in her bed, wondering whether I would soon have to stop being naked as well—was the real world returning? If she came back clothed and I hadn't moved, would my unclothed presence suddenly be bizarre and disgusting, as if a stranger had invaded her room in order to rub his bare penis against her bedsheets? In the end, I compromised and put on my boxer shorts and T-shirt but not my jeans, socks, shoes, or jacket. When Jillian returned from the bathroom, I was on top of the covers, and she lay down again beside me.

"I wanted to ask you another thing," she said.

"Go for it."

"Well, Gail Aselton once told me a weird thing about you. I didn't believe it, but it kind of stuck with me and bothered me. I just tried not to think about it."

"What was it?"

She sat up, and I sat up beside her.

"She told me that, at a party at Victor's house, you hooked up with Victor's girlfriend, Alice Brubaker, right in front of him. But, well, that wasn't the bad part—Gail told me that you actually *grabbed* Alice when you were both drunk and kind of forced her to make out with you, and Alice had to push you off of her. It didn't sound like you at all, but after Friday night, I realized I couldn't be sure—I wasn't sure who you really were. That was bothering me more than anything else—more than the driver's license thing."

I had begun to sweat at the first mention of Victor's name, and by the end of Jillian's story, it was as though our sexual encounter had never happened. I was back in hell, at first sick and terrified, then almost relieved by the recollection that—*oh, right*—this was where I belonged. I would never get out. I wanted to flee from the room, but I had to talk.

"Yeah," I said. "I think that's basically what happened. I was really drunk. I don't know why I did it—I wasn't, like, in love with Alice or even feeling, um, aroused at the time. I was just sad and weird and drunk, and it happened. I think it only lasted a second—I tried to kiss her, and she shoved me away or whatever."

Jillian covered her face with her hands as I spoke, made a small indecipherable noise, and shook her head. I felt the same way she did, didn't need words to know.

"That's really, really bad," she said.

"I know," I said.

"What did you do afterward? Did you apologize?"

"No, I just ran away and haven't talked to her since. I think she's probably afraid of me or something—she hasn't come near me since it happened."

"I would be afraid, too. I *am*, I think."

"Yeah, I guess that's understandable."

She was crying again. We were back at square one, but this time I had no energy to fight my way forward—it was impossible.

"Jeff, what are we doing?" she said. "This is not the kind of insanity I want in my life."

"Yeah, that's understandable, too," I said.

She wiped her tears, pulled herself together. "I wish you the best. I really do. I know you're trying. But I can't be with someone who does the things you do. Thinking about what you did to Alice, and then thinking about what we did together—it makes me kind of sick."

I stood up, already collecting my things.

"I think you need to leave," she said.

Chapter Sixteen

After a couple days, depression gave way to a particular elation that was itself probably a subcategory of depression. No one would ever have sex with me again, but so what? I'd done it once. Had anyone *else* in the world ever actually had sex? I was beginning to suspect that I was the only man in the history of the planet who had truly ejaculated inside a woman's vagina: now that I'd done it, it somehow seemed *more* implausible that this sort of thing happened all the time on earth—it had felt so much like something I myself had discovered, a one-time-only miracle.

In the days following our argument, I didn't talk to Jillian, and she didn't talk to me. Already our relationship felt like something from a past life, a barely retained memory not much worth thinking about. In fact, I'd more or less stopped thinking at all: my typically frantic need to figure things out incorrectly—to break them down into larger chunks than they'd originally constituted, to mystify them through failed demystification—had more or less disappeared, along with any belief that I might have once harbored normal human romantic feelings for Jillian. I didn't feel lonely—aloneness seemed like my natural and correct state. By natural inclination I spent more idle time outdoors and considered taking up smoking cigarettes to justify the habit. In reality, the reason was Catherine, who, by popping up daily and then disappearing again amid the shrubs and trees of my neighborhood, had rendered my subdivision infinitely more intriguing while also existing comfortably outside the parameters of my feeble brain and its capacity to be intrigued by *specific* ideas: instead, it was like being a child—submitting, with intense curiosity but no aim toward understanding, to the superior and unintelligible surrounding world. More and more, Catherine occupied my brain, not as a thought but first as an image and then, eventually, as a weird nonsexual erotic presence whose oblique sensual pull took me a while to grasp, as I'd recently (and quite abruptly) lost the urge to masturbate. On one particular sunny afternoon, following a rain, I saw her performing what looked to me like levitation, her feet hovering a few inches above the ground for a moment before dropping suddenly to the wet, shining grass.

As a possible consequence of the peculiar mindset of awed and indifferent incomprehension that I'd lately embraced, life became increasingly cinematic to me during this period, more strikingly visual, the world simultaneously gauzier and more precise, its broader atmospheres registering more dramatically and its smaller nuisances and distractions—the pin-pricks of reality—fading away. I did no homework, never exceeded a light jog on the soccer field, had not only written off all long-term goals and short-term endeavors (scholastic, athletic, interpersonal, and romantic) but had nearly forgotten that they'd ever existed; at the same time, I began to notice the bird's nests in the powerlines, the shapes of clouds, a leaf at the very moment at which it loosed itself and fell from its branch. FBI agents were perhaps prowling within earshot, skeletons sticking up from the dirt—I saw only the beautiful things. In the grips of this persuasive material pleasure, I realized instinctually that the capacity to process one's life as a movie was in fact a universal prerequisite to happiness, as central as any other, almost certainly predating the actual invention of cinema, and throughout my defective life (until just now) I'd simply never possessed this ability for any sustained period. Now everything had changed, and I wondered why the full force of my personal lyricism had been so long in coming, whether the delay owed to some disability in myself or was simply an effect of where I lived: in the past, I'd tried and failed (via boredom) to watch *real* movies about suburbia and had sensed above all else the implicitly judgmental reserve of their cinematography even at its crispest and most beautiful. Even for imaginative artists, it was evidently impossible to view these identical overlarge houses with pleasure: no filmmaker, it seemed from my somewhat limited experience, had been able to achieve any degree of poetic immersion here—for them, the lawns were always dyed an upsettingly insistent shade of green, the fences were too white, the kitchens odorless, the neat bedrooms disturbingly undisturbed by the messy maneuvers of love. The entire way of life of my family and friends was deeply repellent on an aesthetic level, its setting overly suggestive of human deliberateness, absent the mad creative brilliance of nature.

And yet, by all appearances, each of my classmates *had* successfully embedded himself within his own existence (if not as a lyrical experience, then as another kind of full-body enterprise) by way of some possibly inartistic but nevertheless effective iteration of the aforementioned capability to receive his moment-by-moment life as a series of vivid and engrossing scenes of human narrative. For whatever reason, I'd been the exception. I knew that this town was objectively horrible and that everyone raised here would in some way be deficient forever—that by occupying a fully corporatized landscape of artless subdivisions, hostile roadside architecture, and mechanistic selling, devoid of local enterprise and public spaces, they'd inevitably learn within their sealed-off nuclear families to regard money-making as a business disconnected from communal responsibility and thus to see the stories of their own money-making lives as unnecessarily thin and simplistic and possibly a little dissatisfying or something (oh well)—yet I'd never *disliked* my town, at least from what I could tell of my own preferences. Still, no one here had ever felt the way I'd felt, taking it all in not as some banal yet nonetheless harmonious version of the grand symphonic passage of earthly life but rather as a sort of maddening unsolvable brainteaser that I'd somehow been forced to *inhabit*, unnaturally, forever. I was sure glad *that* was over.

Needless to say, I did not, after all, submit my high-school transcript for consideration by the University of California, Berkeley, or by any other school apart from Rutgers, to which I'd already sent my cursory application. Why did anyone want to do anything? In my pseudo-stoned tranquility, I could look inside my classmates' heads, see the unadventurous adventures they were cooking up for the next four years and beyond: the fraternities and sororities they'd join, or the temporary assortment of determinedly idiosyncratic hobbies and interests they'd accumulate instead to shore up their post-high-school identities; the supposedly vibrant cityscapes they'd briefly inhabit as clear cultural deficits in their twenties, their tastes and habits helping to covertly suburbanize the already half-sterilized condo-loaded boulevards of their gentrified metropolises, where they would imagine that they were hip and happening young people undergoing a necessary rite of passage—that of active, edgy urban living—which would provide them with colorful, worldly anecdotes for decades to come, all the while knowing that this was not where they'd make true homes for themselves (the idea was ridiculous, the public schools were unacceptable). I shrugged at them, cheerfully rather than angrily: you probably shouldn't bother, but *whatever*, man. I had no interest at this point in determining what specifically was bad about their plans, but I also felt no jealousy. I knew only that I didn't really need to do any of the stuff that they wanted to do, could stare at the blue November sky instead and be fine. It was like being on drugs, only better because I didn't have to talk to anyone to procure them.

The world—my own world—was beautiful, and at the center of it was Catherine. I thought about her even when I wasn't thinking about her: it was she, I knew, who infused the sights and sounds of my life with their newly filmic, aestheticized quality, drawing out the invisible manifestations of whichever nature deities—Gaea and Pan—still dwelled within our developed world. I didn't dare talk to her much, but I didn't need to, anyway.

Was she still murdering my classmates? I had no idea, didn't care. I sort of almost wondered whether that made me a sociopath—especially as, almost without meaning to, I had without instruction wandered over to the Timberland Meadow subdivision to retrieve for her, with my own hands, an unsupervised porch-dwelling brown dog, offered up to her like a cat's dead mouse to its owner—but I doubted it: I'd never be anything as cool as that. But I was also done worrying about my own coolness—done worrying, period.

....

During the state semifinal, Matt and I switched jerseys just for the hell of it (or not so much for the hell of it as in a last-ditch effort, conceived by him, to prove that we still held the comic ability to amuse ourselves together on the bench, long after the novelty of our mutual demotion had worn off—our pranks were getting tired, I'd stopped trying, we had nothing else) and then had forgotten to return them to each other at the end of the game, which our team had won. I realized later that day but didn't care; however, Matt called in the evening and asked if he could pick up his green number-17 shirt, and I said yes, assuming he just wanted a reason to hang out, a concept about which I felt neutral.

I met him at the front door, and we went upstairs to retrieve the jersey as he handed me mine. I'd left the screened windows open in my bedroom.

"Jesus, it's cold in here," Matt said. "Why are the windows open?"

"Feels fine to me," I said.

Matt grabbed the windows' handles, one in each hand, winding them till the glass pulled rheumatically back into its slot. I shrugged.

"I felt like your jersey was larger than mine," he said, "even though supposedly they're the same size. It felt off."

"They seemed the same to me."

"No, it was definitely throwing me off. I couldn't get into the *zone* out there. My intensity was compromised. It's a miracle we managed to pull off the win in spite of it."

"It was a closer game than the score suggested."

"Yeah, it felt more like a three-one game than a four-zero game. I thought so too."

"We got into dangerous territory at a few points. In the second quarter, Morrisville almost came close to almost coming close to scoring once."

"You think we can beat Brearley in the finals?"

"Not if we play the way we did today."

"Brearley is no joke."

"You can't make mistakes against a team like that."

"They don't suffer fools kindly."

It was an old routine—Brearley was the team we'd have to face in the state championship, but we knew nothing about them and of course didn't care. Matt fingered the unstained polyester of his jersey in feigned contemplation, as if dreaming up strategies.

"*You* seem a little off," he said.

"My game wasn't on point?" I said.

"No, no, your play was exquisite as always. It's something else."

He looked out the window, his pose of contemplation gradually becoming real, possibly. Did he want something from me? What was I supposed to do with other people?

"What's that?" he said, pointing at the glass.

I switched positions—perhaps not needing to. I looked out the window, then back at Matt, and decided to play dumb, just in case.

"What's what?" I said.

"That fire behind your backyard," he said. "There's a person standing next to it."

"You can see her?"

"Why wouldn't I be able to see her?"

"I don't know. Other people don't seem to see her. Or the fire."

"They must not be very observant. How long has that fire been going?"

"Off and on for, like, two weeks, I think."

"What? That doesn't make any sense."

"No one in this neighborhood notices anything."

"Who's the girl?"

I hesitated to answer. "Catherine Harding," I said.

"Oh, shit," he said.

"Yeah."

"She's just, like, haunting your family? You think you're her next victim?"

"I don't think so. I don't think that's how she operates."

"It seems ominous. Like a warning."

"Really? I've actually never seen it that way."

"Then what do you think she's doing out there?"

"I've never asked."

"You've talked to her?"

"A few times, but it's hard to get anything out of her. She's pretty mysterious."

Matt's expression was now drained of irony. He looked curious, confused, and excited all at once. I understood but somehow didn't feel the same way.

"Can I go out there?" he said.

"Free country," I said.

"Seriously. Is it a good idea? Is she going to kidnap me?"

"You? No, I don't think so."

"Then I'll do it."

"Do what?"

"Go talk to her. I've never talked to her. Hardly anyone at school has. We're all cowards."

"I think people just have more important stuff on their minds."

"More important stuff? Like what?"

"College applications, I guess?"

"She's a potential sorceress, Jeff. And a potential murderer."

"Well, you can try to talk to her."

"I *said* I will. I'm not a virgin, so it should be OK. Do you want to come?"

"No thanks. I've tried before. It doesn't do anything."

"But it's safe?"

"I think so."

"OK. Will you be my lookout?"

"Your lookout?"

"Yeah, just glance out the window every now and then to make sure I'm still alive."

"Sure, fine. Good luck out there."

"Thanks, Jeff. Wish me luck."

"I just did."

In the way he picked up his shoulders and marched with wide, deliberate steps out of the room, I could *see* Matt gathering his courage, and I followed him with my eyes as he made his way down the stairs and then disappeared, only to reappear moments later (once my gaze had shifted) through the window, in my backyard and then in the woodsy patch beyond it. I watched for a minute or so: his approach, Catherine noticing him, their still bodies as they talked. And then my attention rapidly faded—I was a bad friend, but it was boring, so I grabbed my iPad and put on an episode of *The Andy Griffith Show* on Hulu. Watching, I more or less forgot about Matt. But he came back near the twenty-minute mark, reappearing at the bottom of the stairs (I hadn't closed the door) and then climbing up to reach me. I put down the iPad when I spotted him, as if to hide that I'd been watching a quaint 1960s sitcom during his moment of danger.

"Hey," I said.

He didn't respond. As he came closer, shutting the door behind him, I noticed that he had changed between departure and return: he was paler, somehow shaken-looking, possibly still slightly shaking. Had I missed some preventable horror, failing significantly—rather than trivially—in my duties as a lookout?

"What happened?" I said.

"Were you watching?" he said.

"No," I said, looking down. "Sorry. I was at first, but—I don't know. It felt like spying."

"That's OK," he said. "Actually it's a good thing. I'm glad you weren't watching."

"Oh. So what happened?"

"I came up to her, and she asked who I was. So I told her my name, and then she grabbed me."

"She grabbed you?"

"Yeah. I thought I was going to die."

"But you didn't."

"No, I'm alive."

He sat down on my bed next to me and looked at his own skin as if amazed by it. I waited for him to say more.

"She kissed me," he said.

I stood up involuntarily, as if a bullet had whizzed past me. "She *kissed* you?"

"Yeah."

"Why the fuck would she do that?"

"I don't know. I guess people kiss people sometimes."

"But why *you?*"

"I have no idea."

"So what happened after she kissed you?"

"Well, one thing led to another."

"*One* thing led to *another?*"

"Yeah. It was really weird. It was like I didn't have a choice—I mean, it just happened."

"*What* did?"

We stared at each other—incipient anger on my side, some mixture of terror and pride on his.

"We had sex," he said.

I sat down again, mostly baffled but also very clearheaded in the knowledge that whatever gorgeous inexplicable reverie I'd occupied since my breakup with Jillian had instantaneously ended. Catherine, the magical abstract entity hovering above my life, dictating its shadows and sun, sprinkling drops of equanimity onto me, had returned to earth and fucked Matt Spruell. OK, fine, that was her prerogative—but my precious sexless serenity, inspired by the example of *her* numinous superior apathy, had apparently been predicated on an equal dispassionate sexlessness on her part, and now it just wouldn't work, obviously.

If she'd wanted to fuck some random average-looking dude, why not *me*? Already I could feel life—multi-pronged and intolerable—speeding back up or slowing back down to its normal pace, its patina of beauty fully removed. I wanted to tell Matt to get out of my room or at least for him to tell me that he was kidding, though I could tell he wasn't— instead I urged him on, once I'd sufficiently recovered.

"What was it like?" I said.

"It was like something from another universe," he said. "I can't even describe it."

"That just sounds like normal sex. Isn't it always like that?"

"No. No, it wasn't normal."

No shit it wasn't. I could only silently ask again, and again: why not me? Why not me? *Why not me why not me why not me why not me why not me why not me.*

Chapter Seventeen

I dreamt that I was at IHOP again, at the same table, this time with Catherine sitting across from me instead of Jillian. The server was no longer the middle-aged lady with the nametag; the discreetly sexy waitress from Sunchoke had replaced her, and she was, at intervals, laying down before us a multi-course set menu of elegantly prepared dishes, all of them composed of the body parts of my lost classmates.

Catherine wore a dress, looking polished and beautiful, and while gazing meaningfully at each other, we munched on the grilled ears of Lacy, served with preserved Meyer lemon, garden mint, and wild arugula; the sautéed kidneys of Doug with fava beans and Périgord truffle; the braised leg of Mark with potato pavé and braised kale; and the smoked heart of Emily Grace with parsley root and wild onion.

Still, I could see the grim Red Lobster through the window behind Catherine's dazzling face, and as the meal wound down, she began asking me annoying first-date questions. What was my favorite movie? What was my favorite book? Who was my greatest role model? Somehow, to all three, I could only dumbly respond "Harry Potter" even though I had never read or seen any of the *Harry Potter* books or movies. Each time Catherine rolled her eyes with obvious scorn and exasperation.

"What's *your* favorite movie?" I finally said.

"This one," she said. "The one we're in right now. It's the only good movie ever made."

At some point I must have woken up—but not in my bed, not the following morning, not with mussed hair and the realization that I'd been dreaming but, instead, sometime on the drive from the restaurant back to my house, where, ultimately, I spent the rest of the evening watching TV, understanding only gradually that what had happened in the preceding hours couldn't have happened. The barriers were dissolving, the activities of my dreams leading without shift or interruption into the activities of my daily life.

I checked my credit card bill a few days later; there was a seven hundred dollar charge at the International House of Pancakes. *Hmm.* What could I do? I decided to eat the cost rather than try to claim fraud.

....

The second time I rode my undersized bicycle to Jillian's house, my back started to ache, the pain setting in alongside a belated realization of the long-term impracticability of my new mode of transport. I knew even on my way over that I wouldn't knock on her door, wouldn't attempt to talk to her. What could I say to her if I did? That she should take me back? I honestly didn't feel that she should.

I was too sad to talk to anyone—heartbroken by Catherine, who, until Matt's intrusion, I had never realized was in any way accessible as a romantic object for humans. Could she have been the Edward to my Bella, rescuing me from the horrible tedium of my life instead of simply lurking on its fringes to confuse me? Instead her (brief) love had gone to Matt, who didn't even *need* it. Oddly, it was this unexpected, additional heartbreak that allowed the initial heartbreak of my loss of Jillian to register, finally. The grace period of spellbound brainlessness following my breakup with Jillian had evidently expired, and as I became more aware of her lasting imprint upon me, I became more and more embarrassed by the thought of existing within some college-aged Jillian's memory as an occasional dark intrusion: a doubt-causing strangeness, an unmentionable error of judgment, one of those unclassifiable experiences of male weirdness (slightly beyond the usual realm of romantic disappointments) that nice girls had to endure on their way to happy romantic stability, the sort of misguided emotional involvement that one basically just had to pretend never happened. This was her first sexual experience—probably quite typical, relative to some horrifying international average of female first-time trauma. Even so, as I considered it, I wanted nothing more to be than to be able (as I'd been able two months earlier) to say that, in my high school, I'd made no impact on anyone, had meant nothing to any girl or boy. Why had I ever thought it was a *curse* to be overlooked, unknown, forgotten?

Of course I *knew* why, as I approached her house, pedaling down Branchwood Avenue. I wanted it—her, and not just her—so badly. Yet even at their peak of longing, my feelings were undeniably mixed and sat flat and heavy in my stomach instead of spurring me into action: it was still in some a sense a relief, given the absorbing nature of my own problems, not to be someone's boyfriend. Why couldn't I be more like all the other teenagers in the world, blissfully unaware of their common incapacity to sustain a healthy and mutually enjoyable relationship yet fucking nevertheless like acne-covered rabbits with no regard for tomorrow, completely unconcerned by the ways in which they might hurt one another or themselves? One sexual encounter was not enough for a lifetime, in fact; it wouldn't sustain me forever.

I was watching the afternoon light drop on Jillian's house as I wondered how many more times before graduation I would stand silently and purposelessly outside someone else's home without their knowing it. I was ready for this part of my life to be over. When the vinyl siding had turned from orange to gray, I turned but couldn't leave, and that was when I spotted another familiar house, the one I'd come to before I'd ever entered Jillian's. I'd almost forgotten how I'd gotten *in* in the first place —it had been another boy in love.

It had been Aaron Grasso—a pang of nostalgia at the reawakened memory of his name—who had taken out the obstacle of Melanie Heller so that I might access her older sister. In the countless hours I'd spent at Jillian's house, I'd seen little of Melanie and even less of Aaron after their mutual virginity-loss, a moment where (as I now saw it) I'd been present like a proud uncle introducing his nephew to the local brothel and thus to the ways of the world. For them, Branchwood Avenue was still a happy place—genuine happiness, joy even.

I felt myself drawn again to the Grasso house, not for any purpose or scheme this time except to give, retroactively, a purpose to my own journey—or maybe that wasn't it: to continue to be a witness to his happiness if I couldn't have it myself? My thinking wasn't fully clear when I rang the doorbell and the same balding lame-dad answered and I asked for Aaron.

"He's studying," Mr. Grasso said.

"Well, tell him to come out here," I said, less bashful this time. "It's important."

The little man gave in, and I waited as he retrieved his son.

"Hey Aaron," I said, when the small-framed boy appeared, the father gone. "Want to hang out?"

"Hey, uh—"

"Jeff."

"Hey, Jeff. What's up?"

"Not much. I was just in the neighborhood. You feel like going for a walk?"

He eyed me cautiously. "Uh, sure," he said.

He stepped out to meet me on the stoop, closing the door behind him. He was wearing sweatpants. I felt better just looking at him. We started walking—literally, we were taking a walk. Why not?

"So, uh, you need my help again?" he said.

"Nah, not really," I said. "I mean, only in a very loose sense."

"I don't get it."

"Just talk to me, Aaron. You're still young and full of hope—the world looks like a beautiful place to you. And maybe it *is*. Maybe you're *right*."

"Right, um—it's fine. My mom's picking up Chinese food tonight."

"You like Chinese food, Aaron?"

"Yeah, it's my favorite."

"That's beautiful, man."

We were heading in the opposite direction of Jillian's house. We climbed a small hill; I didn't turn to admire the twilit view behind us. I noticed that Aaron was wearing flip-flops, his cold white toes exposed to the evening air.

"How's Melanie?" I said.

"Why do you ask?" he said.

"I enjoy hearing about the happiness of young couples. It's not something *I'll* ever experience, but it's reassuring to know that it exists."

"Melanie and I broke up."

"*What?*"

"Yeah, it didn't work out. She's into Simon Woodrow now."

"She broke up with you?"

"No, I could tell she liked Simon, but instead of breaking up with me, she just talked to me about Simon all the time, and it got so annoying that I had to break up with her."

"Wow, that's a bummer. It must be weird being neighbors with her now."

"Well, not for long. It looks like I'm going to move. My parents are getting divorced."

"Jesus, Aaron."

"It's fine, honestly. It'll be nice to have a fresh start. I fucking hate this town."

"Really?"

"Yeah, for sure. It's boring as hell, full of assholes. What, you like it here?"

"I don't know—I thought everyone liked it here."

"I don't think so. People here are sad and confused."

"Huh. Well, how bad can your life here really be? You're fifteen and you've already had sex."

"Yeah, I guess that is a relief, especially with all that's going on right now."

"So you still have something to thank Melanie for, at least."

"Melanie? No, I lost my virginity in freshman year to Naomi Yuan."

"Seriously? Damn, fuck you, Aaron."

"How old were you when it happened?"

"The same age I am now, minus a few days."

"Well, at least you're safe now. You could have been number eight."

"Eight?" I counted in my head: Doug, Thomas, Mark, Lacy, Nicole, Emily Grace. The next one would be seven.

"You didn't hear?" he said. "There was another one today."

"Who?"

"Another senior. Some guy named Tyler Hankin."

I turned around—I believed I was done with Aaron. He followed me back to his own house, and we said goodbye. The only good thing I'd ever done in my life—bringing Melanie and Aaron together, to spend their adolescences in safety and certitude instead of loneliness and confusion —had actually amounted to nothing, and as I biked home, I tried to figure out how I felt about that. My conclusion was: bad. Also, Tyler was dead or whatever—the world didn't seem like such a beautiful place.

When I got home, I dropped my bike in the front yard and went directly to Catherine's hiding spot in back, not knowing whether she'd be there. As it turned out, she was, the eternal fire burning. It felt very hot as I came closer—it seemed to vary in temperature though not in size. I stared at Catherine for a moment before speaking, but she didn't look at me despite the noise I'd made on my approach, the kicking of leaves and twigs.

"What are you really doing with all of these people?" I said, finally.

"What does it matter?" she said.

"They're people," I said. "They have families and friends."

"That's the best explanation you can come up with—for why they *matter*?"

"Tyler was a friend of *mine*."

"He was not. You guys hung out *once*."

"That doesn't qualify as friendship?"

"Not to most people."

"Well, I have lower standards. I still want to know what happened to him."

"That's my business."

"How is it your business? It's his parents' business. His girlfriend's business. The police's business."

"Bring them on, Jeff."

"You know that's not what I'm talking about. I'm not making threats, Catherine. Can you at least tell me why you're doing it? What does it do for you?"

"I'm doing it to become more powerful, obviously. I thought everyone knew that?"

"More powerful for what? To do what?"

"Jeff—if you could have one superpower, what would it be?"

"I've never thought about it. I don't think about that kind of thing."

"So think about it. You never read a comic book? Everyone wants the same one."

I didn't want anything except to *escape*—from my life, my thoughts, myself. I looked up at the sky. It was a clear night, full of moons and stars.

"I'd want to be able to fly," I said.

"Exactly," she said.

"You can't fly already?"

"I'm working on it."

"It seems like it'd be kind of easy, compared to the other stuff you've done. Changing the weather and all that. Making cars appear out of nowhere."

"What do you know about what's easy and what's not? You've tried this stuff before?"

"It just seems simpler."

"None of it is simple."

"So what do you need to make it happen?"

"Something more. Something special."

I realized I was crying. Catherine didn't seem to care.

"Why not me? You could take me," I said, realizing I was begging.

"You? No, that wouldn't work."

"Because I had sex *once*? That rule doesn't even make any sense."

"You don't understand."

"I only lasted forty-five seconds! That barely counts! Tyler got like a hundred handjobs! Who cares if he never put his dick inside a vagina?"

"You wouldn't have been any good for my purposes anyway."

"How come? I think, um—I think I am special. Like you."

"You really don't get it? Jeff, why do you think I've been so interested in you this whole time?"

"I have no idea. Actually, you don't seem *that* interested."

"You're different, Jeff. I knew it from the first time I saw you."

"That's what *I'm* saying."

"Different in the *wrong* way. How can I put it? This town has no magic in it except me. I've known that since before *I* was magical. I *know* when something is off here."

"You mean that I'm magical, too."

"You're the *opposite* of magic. Everything I do comes from the earth —children and animals, the sun and the moon. You're a *drain*. You're a *sinkhole*. Everywhere you go, there's less energy to work with, less potential for magic."

Interestingly, this didn't hurt my feelings. I wasn't sure I fully understood—but it sort of made sense, didn't it? We were getting somewhere.

"So why hang around me?" I said.

"To test myself," she said. "You're a natural antidote to everything I do. A cosmic buzzkill. Like you were put here on earth for the purpose of dragging down anything sublime or beautiful in the universe. You melt my snow. You turn my whiskey back into iced tea. You're a cock-block of the *spirit*, Jeff. I don't know what it is in you, but it's something very, very bad."

I shrugged. "I guess I can't argue with that."

"I've been playing with you. Good spells and bad ones—just to see what sticks. I've been testing myself against you. You're stubborn, but I'm getting too strong for you."

"Are you? I touched Victor *once*, and the curse you put on him ended, didn't it?"

"That wasn't my best work. But wait and see."

"Why do you want to fly anyway? Where are you going to go?"

"I'm not telling *you*. But it'll be some place very different from here."

"All places are like here."

"You *would* think that, but it's not true."

"How much longer will you be here?"

"I'm not sure yet. I told you—I'm still looking for the final ingredient. Something special."

"Something especially tasty for you to boil in your cauldron? Do you *literally* have a cauldron?"

"Don't be ridiculous. 'Ingredient' was just a figure of speech."

"If I find it, I'm going to jump in. Ruin the whole broth."

"Shut up, Jeff."

"Am I really *so* ... unmagical?"

"In a way, it's better, isn't it? Better to be the *worst* person than somewhere in the middle?"

"You're a murderer, Catherine. How am *I* the worst?"

"You know how, Jeff."

She was right: I knew. I felt it in my bones—and I wanted to throw them in the soup, right next to Tyler's. But was it ultimately a relief to know for sure how rotten my bones really were?

Chapter Eighteen

The NJSIAA Group 1 Championship was played on neutral ground, on the campus of Kean University in Union, New Jersey. It was a larger and faintly more glamorous venue, a gift intended to make us players feel important, but because the stadium's prickly artificial turf—somehow less kind than regular grass—overlay a football field with all the distracting white marks pertaining thereto, the playing surface was in a practical sense worse than any of the standard high school soccer pitches where we'd played to crowds sometimes not exceeding fifty, with home and away fans both confined to a single set of bleachers.

But as we warmed up on the enormous (yet same-sized) field, running our usual drills, the metal stands surrounding us somewhat distantly on both sides, beyond the rubber red oval of the stadium's track, began to fill. With *whom* I wasn't sure, but before long the seats were respectably occupied if not quite packed, as though an actual event of public interest were set to occur—as if we'd attained a level of athletic mastery sufficient to attract general admiration rather than that, only, of those adults and peers invested in our general development as humans. Were we, in fact, good enough to serve as entertainment—that highest (and somehow not demeaning) purpose of athletics?

I could see my teammates becoming inattentive during their pregame exercises, letting passes skid past them as they stopped to gape at the crowd—and, then, to shrink amid the bigness around them, to realize that they were nothing, that they didn't belong here, that the only talented one was Adam, and that, given that soccer was a team game in which (according to conventional wisdom) one spectacular player could never on his own bring an entire squad of sad sacks to victory against any formidable opponent, we were doomed. In their palpable terror I registered for the first time all year how much my team's success meant to them—to everyone except me and possibly Matt—even as it said nothing about *them* specifically except that they were average, competent high-school athletes who happened to have found themselves in the right place at the right time. Any other arbitrary set of ten players could have stepped in for them without altering the results, but for my teammates, arbitrariness wasn't the same thing as meaninglessness. They valued their luck and could see how, at some future distance, it would amount to the same thing as merit: a story of high school glory that they would earnestly value as one of the "great moments" of their lives, along with their business school graduations, their expensive weddings, and the instantaneously Facebook-shared births of their white children. The credulous simplicity of other people's storytelling—not the *real* stories of their lives, which presumably were complicated and problematic and obscure, but the stories they invented in order to give their lives the upward-building structure of what they believed to be meaning—was enough to make me want to die; they would never see how degrading it all was. But, then again, of course the problem was my own: an inability to take part in the real everyday magic of this dehumanizing, reductive version of human life—Catherine had been right about me. At least they *had* a narrative—I had no more complex and satisfying narrative of my own, only a crueler set of reductions. My teammates wanted to *win*. Winning was better than losing. *Duh*.

I glanced over at Adam, gracefully nonchalant as usual during the drills, not trying too hard but not making mistakes, either. Predicting that my other teammates would yield not a single useful maneuver for the duration of the game, I sensed that Adam might really have to play the best soccer of his life—his own version of the enchanted pickup game that I'd more or less dominated in New Brunswick despite my beer-sloshing belly and some considerable competition for a friendly match—in order to allow us to win, and for a moment I doubted him: was it really possible that he was perfect, already, at age fourteen, or was I seeing him through the paradoxically rose-colored glasses of my depression, a manifestation of my covert desperation to see something special in the world when I saw no such specialness in myself? If he *was* perfect, it meant that over the next three years (and the ensuing four years of college), he wouldn't improve, *could* not by the very definition of the word *perfect*—he'd already peaked. In this sense, his perfection was an imperfection, as it implied a forthcoming failure to follow the necessary path of growth and refinement that led to higher-level success. I felt a little confused: Adam was either a flawed, still-developing soccer talent (in which case we surely had no chance in the state championship game) or else, with otherworldly precocity, had already reached the sport's zenith (in which case, at age fourteen, there was no place for him to go but down, and this sadly was the summit of his existence)—was that it?

I considered for a moment if I cared whether I might someday catch a glimpse of Adam Nordmark in some World Cup game on my television. The answer, I believed, was no: I did not care. I preferred to win today. Adam was a nice kid, but fuck his future and the future in general: if his soccer never became an entertainment product for the masses, all the better—in fact that *was* degrading, fuck whatever I'd thought before. The game was set to start in a few minutes—I kicked my own ball away, ran up to Adam, threw my arms around him, gripped him tight like a child I was about to give up for adoption because I couldn't shake my drug habit. He just stood there and accepted my embrace without reciprocating, but I wasn't embarrassed. I knew that all of my teammates wanted to do the same thing.

....

The game started, and almost instantly we were losing—if not according to the scoreboard then in some equally recognizable style: they were stronger, faster, and sharper than we were. From the kickoff, Brearley High controlled the ball with all the strategic expertise that made Americans hate soccer—we rubbed up against them like puppies at their feet.

In the first quarter, Adam barely touched the ball, and Brearley scored on a header off one of their four corner kicks. In the second quarter, Matt Spruell—inserted into the game on account of Jimmy Severino's twisted ankle—scored a freakish lucky long goal off an unexpected (and therefore mostly unguarded) shot from the distant right sideline. Brearley, however, scored twice more, and by halftime I could tell that we would never beat them.

Adam hadn't played well in the first half. It wasn't just that his passes were less creative and his shots off the mark—it wasn't just that he'd turned the ball over twice. More importantly, the ball wasn't coming to him the way it normally did; it wasn't appearing inexplicably at his feet the way it was supposed to, and as a result he had faded into the background. Still, it had taken me until the game's midway point to wonder whether I was to blame. Had it required only a touch from me to neutralize his athletic wizardry? Had I somehow never touched him before, in all our shared time on the field? Had we never once made contact? And if my own opposite-of-magic was this powerful, could I do the same to Catherine by hugging *her* (if she let me—I wasn't about to force myself on another girl even if it would save lives)?

I wasn't sure. It was possible that Adam just wasn't playing well—even during our endless stretch of victories he had varied somewhat, albeit never straying below the spectacular. Still, he hadn't faced competition as fierce as this—or maybe they only looked fierce because Adam was finally playing poorly enough to allow other players' merits to shine through. It was hard to tell.

Either way, I really didn't want to see the rest. As I watched him walk off the field for the halftime break, I, too, got up for a walk, and no one seemed to notice or care as I left the pitch and then the stadium. I speculated that removing myself from the premises might cure whatever curse I'd inflicted upon Adam—without the weight of my negative presence, his talent might regenerate. But really, I had no idea; I just didn't want to watch him suck. Still clad in my jersey and cleats and shin guards, I passed the smaller baseball stadium and strode through a parking lot onto

the central campus. It looked like a bigger version of my high school—
it was not the college of anyone's ivy-wrapped dreams. Still, I found a
nice sturdy tree near the library and sat down beside it in the grass. It
was cold, but I pretended that it wasn't. In my stiff reverie, I tried not to
think about the game, and in its place I found myself composing mental
notes of belated apology to Alice Brubaker for what I'd done to her in
August—three months had passed.

Why *hadn't* I ever said sorry? I'd labored partly under the ridiculous
delusion that, if no one ever acknowledged the incident, then maybe it
hadn't happened—but I'd also (predictably) processed the event primarily
as something that had happened to *me*. I'd barely thought of her. Still,
what could one say? I felt that any man who touched a woman against her
will should probably just die, but I wasn't dead: I had to keep living, I had
no choice. An attempt to initiate communication with her of any sort
might have been taken, fearfully, as an attempt to initiate an interaction
in which I might commit further abuses. Had I been right to back off,
leave her in peace? No, I had been wrong—I'd done wrong and would
continue to do wrong to her no matter what I did. That was the nature
of doing something very wrong; there was no way to right it—instead
the deed would only continue to issue forth more wrongs, whichever
direction you chose thereafter. It was hopeless.

Well, then again, everybody made mistakes. Maybe it was better for
me to think about soccer after all—not in terms of Adam, but in terms
of myself.

Sitting alone in the grass, I was experiencing the final game of my
soccer career—I knew I'd never play the sport again. I would miss it not
because I'd liked it but because it would be gone. In general, I'd miss high
school intensely, not for what I'd done but for what I hadn't: the girls I
hadn't talked to—all the ones who'd secretly had an even worse time than
I'd had (they existed, I was sure, silent victims of parental abuse or peer
bullying or mental illness more severe than whatever afflicted me)—and
all the opportunities for affection, exploration, creativity, and physical
pleasure that had evaded me. I hadn't known them as presences—I had

forever backed away in terror—but I would know them more and more as absences; the details would come in long after the opportunities had passed. With absence I was and would be *intimate.*

When a half hour seemed to have passed, I wandered back to the stadium, getting lost slightly along the way, and when I finally reentered, I looked up at the scoreboard and saw that Weybridge was winning, nine to three, with a minute left: a blowout—a football score, not a soccer score, really. I found my teammate Jimmy Severino on the sidelines, simultaneously nursing his ankle and looking on in amazed glee.

"Adam scored eight goals?" I said.

"No—haven't you been paying attention?" he said.

"I had to leave for a minute. My grandfather just died or something, whatever. I'm back now."

"Oh. Uh, well, Adam scored four. Matt scored *five.*"

"Wow."

"It's really weird, isn't it? He hadn't scored all year."

"Yeah. I wonder what happened to him."

"I guess it just shows you that true champions rise to the occasion."

"Well said."

He turned to me and grinned. "We did it, bro. State champs."

I smiled back. "It's a memory we'll cherish forever."

"Yeah, for sure. Sorry about your grandfather."

. . . .

On the bus back to Weybridge, it seemed possible that my ecstatic teammates might be planning a celebration, some massive post-game bash with strippers and cocaine in which we might finally cut loose from the socially acceptable dorkiness of student athletics, but I wasn't listening to anything they said, and when I got home it was as though nothing had happened, the only clue that I'd taken part in some event that day being a vague sense that something had *ended.* In the evening, I ate dinner with my parents and then went back to my bedroom and stared out the window: Catherine was reading a book by the firelight, shifting positions on the ground and flipping the pages slowly—she looked bored, too. When I heard my parents go upstairs to their own bedroom, I tiptoed back down, stole the keys to my dad's car from the hook by the door, and drove off. The Lexus's engine was quieter than the BMW's.

On Barnwell Street, I parked at my customary spot on the street and strolled up to Adam's door, ringing the bell. Adam himself answered a moment later: *did* he actually have parents, or was he another weird self-sufficient orphan like Catherine, somehow overlooked by Child Protective Services?

"Hey, Jeff. What's going on?"

"Hey Adam. We're having a championship celebration. You have to come."

He shrugged. "OK."

I wanted to say more, to bolster my lie; his agreement had come too soon. All I could do was lead him back to the car. We got in.

"You got a new car."

"Yeah. A gift for winning the New Jersey high school soccer championship."

"Congratulations."

"Thank you."

I started driving. I felt nervous but also somehow at ease, confused by my own actions but also possessed of a remarkable clarity. I noticed that Adam wasn't talking.

"There's no actual celebration," I said. "There's no party."

"I know," he said.

"So why'd you come with me?"

"I figured you were lonely or something."

"Do I come across as a lonely person, Adam?"

"Yes."

"Well, I am, but it's also more complicated than that."

As we pulled into my driveway, I felt embarrassed of my house, even though it looked more or less the same as every other house in town, including the one where Adam lived. I told him to be quiet as we left the car and, together, snuck into the backyard and then past the property line, into Catherine's undefined abode.

She wasn't facing us, and I cleared my throat to her dark head of hair, but she didn't turn. Did she need to? Could she see us anyway? Maybe, but then again maybe not—she couldn't even fly.

"Adam, this is Catherine," I said. "You said you wanted to meet her."

At this, Catherine turned. She didn't look at me, looked directly at him.

"Catherine, do you know about Adam?" I said. "He's a soccer player."

"I don't pay a lot of attention to sports," she said.

"Adam is something special," I said. "Isn't that so, Adam?"

To my surprise, Adam nodded.

"*How* special?" Catherine said.

"I guess you'll have to be the judge of that," I said.

"I guess I will," she said.

They stood eying each other in an apparent state of perfect calm, and in their presence, it was impossible for me to feel any different. I was strangely at peace with what I'd done—whatever I'd done—as I left the two together, turning back and heading into the house.

But once I'd crept up to my bedroom and shut the door, I found myself both wanting to look out the window and wanting not to. For this reason I also wanted to be somewhere else entirely, but still I needed to be in my own private space, amid whatever comfort it offered: it was complicated. In an effort to solve the problem, I opened the window, slipped through it and, courageous in the dark and too quick to hear anything by accident, hopped onto the garage roof. From there, I climbed onto the house roof, facing the street—although if I had crossed the roof's spine to the other side, the tops of the trees would have blocked my view of Catherine's outdoor lair anyway: I was safe.

I lay down on the sandpapery shingles, looked up at the sky: uninterrupted black this time, no stars, no moons. Had I just killed Adam, led him to a gruesome demise at the hands of a demonic eater of children? Possibly, but I also sensed that I probably needed to stop looking at things so literally. Did it still make sense, given everything I'd witnessed, to regard life and death as simple biological binaries, with no other options between or beyond? Was Catherine not something more than alive, and I something less—but neither of us dead?

If I *had* brought Adam to destruction, why had he gone along with it? He had known who Catherine was; he had known that he himself was a delectable innocent: an angel on and off the soccer field. He had *known* what would happen. He had wanted it. Why? Some part of me had wanted the same thing for him—why?

I hoped it wasn't spite or envy. In some broader, vaguer way, it had made sense to bring these two superhuman energies together, whatever the subsequent means of fusion or absorption might be: a deeper kind of sense that, as I stared into the endless blackness, I felt empowered finally to accept as a reality of life on earth—a mysterious and extraordinary place after all. I would never fully know how its parts, physical and numinous, fit together, but I could know, at least, that I didn't know. Dead or alive, Adam would exist if he ever had existed.

Or maybe I was misunderstanding how this whole murderous witchy business worked. Did I comprehend anything about Catherine, really? Why, for instance, did she even go to high school? It made no sense. She was a witch. Then again, why did *I* go to high school?

I was on the verge of smiling at my own confusion—which possibly had just caused the violent death of the most magnificent boy in my town—when I noticed Catherine hovering twenty feet above me in the sky: not hovering in the performatively wobbly manner of cinema, as if emphasizing the challenge of the feat, but appearing to stand, stockstill, as if upon some firm invisible platform nailed into the firmament. Stupidly, I waved. She gently dropped a few feet. Closer to her, I could see that *she* was smiling.

"I owe you one, Jeff," she said. "You're not so bad after all."

"Are you leaving?" I said.

"I'm sure not staying here."

"What about me? You can't just leave me here."

A surge of panic flooded me. *Kill as many of us as you want! Just don't let the real world set in again.*

"It's not like I can take you with you," she said.

"You said you owed me one," I said, desperately.

"I do. It'll be a surprise. It won't be long coming. I can do a lot of things now."

"It better be good. I really need something good."

"What do you want more than anything?"

I paused. "I have no idea."

"Exactly. So let me figure it out for you."

"OK. I trust you."

"You shouldn't. Bye, Jeff."

"Bye, Catherine."

She rose again, higher and higher until she slipped into the blackness of the night. I stood up—it was all over, I might as well go to bed. I climbed down to the garage roof, and from there it would have made more sense to swing back around to my bedroom window, but instead I jumped, half-believing as I did that my body might rise into flight as Catherine's had. Of course I fell, wondering midair whether life after Catherine might not be so bad. Being the opposite of magic, of talent, of pleasure, of love—that, too, as she'd said, was something, not a void: a quality with which one could navigate the world in some particular way, building some form of inverted meaning. It was the way in which I was special—I *was* special. Conceivably I could have a richly and interestingly horrible life, creating a viable identity and personal philosophy around what was probably, within consensus-reality, just a treatable mental illness but was also *possibly* something more (I wanted it to be more).

Or, then again, I might not have any such life at all. For some unidentifiable reason, I still had to go to school tomorrow, to finish high school, to go to college. Already I felt trapped and wanted to give up. It seemed unlikely that I'd be able to *use* my altered self-perception within my current life, where everything about me already meant whatever it meant.

....

I hit the ground, got up, and went into the house. I opened the door very softly. As I did, light spilled out, and instantly I knew that something was wrong.

My parents were in the living room, watching TV, with all the lights on, as if it were still early evening—as if they hadn't already gone to bed. I caught them off-guard for a fraction of a second, still gazing at the screen, not waiting for me. Then they noticed me in the doorway, their eyeballs shifting, their heads tilting in what looked like alarm. I felt a thrilling dread as they sized me up, and I them: my mom in her bathrobe, my dad in his old pajamas—clothing so familiar, and suddenly foreign to me.

"Excuse me," said my father. "Who are you?"

I looked up as if I could still see Catherine above me, as if my home had no ceiling, as if Catherine might be looking down at me, smiling with some kindly helpful form of malevolence.

www.ingramcontent.com/pod-product-compliance
Lightning Source LLC
Chambersburg PA
CBHW050509190726
48284CB00003B/750